I, Robot

Isaac Asimov, world maestro of science fiction, was born in Russia near Smolensk in 1920 and was brought to the United States by his parents three years later. He grew up in Brooklyn where he went to grammar school and at the age of eight he gained his citizen papers. A remarkable memory helped him finish high school before he was sixteen. He then went on to Columbia University and resolved to become a chemist rather than follow the medical career his father had in mind for him. He graduated in chemistry and after a short spell in the Army he gained his doctorate in 1949 and qualified as an instructor in biochemistry at Boston University School of Medicine where he became Associate Professor in 1955, doing research in nucleic acid. Increasingly, however, the pressures of chemical research conflicted with his aspirations in the literary field, and in 1958 he retired to full-time authorship while retaining his connection with the University.

Asimov's fantastic career as a science fiction writer began in 1939 with the appearance of a short story, *Marooned Off Vesta*, in *Amazing Stories*. Thereafter he became a regular contributor to the leading SF magazines of the day including *Astounding*, *Astonishing Stories*, *Super Science Stories* and *Galaxy*. He won the Hugo Award four times and the Nebula Award once. With nearly five hundred books to his credit and several hundred articles, Asimov's output was prolific by any standards. Apart from his many world-famous science fiction works, Asimov also wrote highly successful detective mystery stories, a four-volume *History of North America*, a two-volume *Guide to the Bible*, a biographical dictionary, encyclopaedias, textbooks and an impressive list of books on many aspects of science, as well as two volumes of autobiography.

Isaac Asimov died in 1992 at the age of 72.

BY THE SAME AUTHOR

ROBOT STORIES AND NOVELS
I, Robot
The Rest of the Robots
The Complete Robot
The Caves of Steel
The Naked Sun
The Robots of Dawn
Robots and Empire

THE GALACTIC EMPIRE SERIES
The Stars, Like Dust
The Currents of Space
Pebble in the Sky

THE FOUNDATION SAGA
Prelude to Foundation
Forward the Foundation
Foundation
Foundation and Empire
Second Foundation
Foundation's Edge
Foundation and Earth

SHORT STORY COLLECTIONS
Gold
Magic
The End of Eternity

ISAAC ASIMOV

I, Robot

DATE DUE

	PRINTED IN U.S.A.

Harper*Voyager*
An imprint of HarperCollins*Publishers* Ltd
1 London Bridge Street
London SE1 9GF

www.harpercollins.co.uk

This paperback edition 2018

First published in Great Britain by
Dobson Books Ltd 1967

The story here entitled 'Robbie' first published as 'Strange Playfellow' in *Super Science Stories*, copyright 1940 by Fictioneers, Inc. 'Reason', 'Liar!', 'Runaround', 'Catch That Rabbit', 'Escape!', 'Evidence', 'Little Lost Robot', 'The Evitable Conflict' first published in *Astounding Science Fiction*, copyright, 1941, 1941, 1942, 1944, 1946, 1946, 1950 respectively by Street and Smith Publications, Inc.

A catalogue record for this book is available from the British Library

ISBN: 978-0-00-827955-4

Set in Janson Text by Palimpsest Book Production Limited, Falkirk, Stirlingshire

Printed and bound in the UK by CPI Group (UK) Ltd, Croydon CR0 4YY

Contents

The Three Laws of Robotics

1 – A robot may not injure a human being, or, through inaction, allow a human being to come to harm.

2 – A robot must obey the orders given it by human beings except where such orders would conflict with the First Law.

3 – A robot must protect its own existence as long as such protection does not conflict with the First or Second Law.

Handbook of Robotics, 56th Edition, 2058 A.D.

Introduction

I looked at my notes and I didn't like them. I'd spent three days at US Robots and might as well have spent them at home with the Encyclopedia Tellurica.

Susan Calvin had been born in the year 1982, they said, which made her seventy-five now. Everyone knew that. Appropriately enough, US Robots and Mechanical Men, Inc. was seventy-five also, since it had been in the year of Dr Calvin's birth that Lawrence Robertson had first taken out incorporation papers for what eventually became the strangest industrial giant in man's history. Well, everyone knew that, too.

At the age of twenty, Susan Calvin had been part of the particular Psycho-Math seminar at which Dr Alfred Lanning of US Robots had demonstrated the first mobile robot to be equipped with a voice. It was a large, clumsy unbeautiful robot, smelling of machine-oil and destined for the projected mines on Mercury. —But it could speak and make sense.

Susan said nothing at that seminar; took no part in the hectic discussion period that followed. She was a frosty girl, plain and color-less, who protected herself against a world she disliked by a mask-like expression and hypertrophy of intellect. But as she watched and listened, she felt the stirrings of a cold enthusiasm.

She obtained her bachelor's degree at Columbia in 2003 and began graduate work in cybernetics.

All that had been done in the mid-twentieth century on 'calculating machines' had been upset by Robertson and his positronic brain-paths. The miles of relays and photocells had given way to the spongy globe of plantinumiridium about the size of a human brain.

She learned to calculate the parameters necessary to fix the possible variables within the 'positronic brain', to construct 'brains' on paper such that the responses to given stimuli could be accurately predicted.

In 2008, she obtained her Ph.D. and joined United States Robots as a 'Robopsychologist', becoming the first great practitioner of a new science. Lawrence Robertson was still president of the corporation; Alfred Lanning had become director of research.

For fifty years, she watched the direction of human progress change – and leap ahead.

Now she was retiring – as much as she ever could. At least, she was allowing someone else's name to be inset upon the door of her old office.

That, essentially, was what I had. I had a long list of her published papers, of the patents in her name; I had the chronological details of her promotions— In short I had her professional 'vita' in full detail.

But that wasn't what I wanted.

I needed more than that for my feature articles for Interplanetary Press. Much more.

I told her so.

'Dr Calvin,' I said, as lushly as possible, 'in the mind of the public you and US Robots are identical. Your retirement will end an era and—'

'You want the human-interest angle?' She didn't smile at me. I don't think she ever smiles. But her eyes were sharp, though not angry. I felt her glance slide through me and out my occiput and I knew that I was uncommonly transparent to her; that everybody was.

But I said, 'That's right.'

'Human interest out of Robots? A contradiction.'

'No, doctor. Out of you.'

'Well, I've been called a robot myself. Surely, they've told you I'm not human.'

They had, but there was no point in saying so.

She got up from her chair. She wasn't tall and she looked frail. I followed her to the window and we looked out.

The offices and factories of US Robots were a small city; spaced and planned. It was flattened out like an aerial photograph.

'When I first came here,' she said, 'I had a little room in a building right about there where the fire-house is now.' She pointed. 'It was torn down before you were born. I shared the room with three others. I had half a desk. We built our robots all in one building. Output – three a week. Now look at us.'

'Fifty years,' I hackneyed, 'is a long time.'

'Not when you're looking back at them,' she said. 'You wonder how they vanished so quickly.'

She went back to her desk and sat down. She didn't need expression on her face to look sad, somehow.

'How old are you?' she wanted to know.

'Thirty-two,' I said.

'Then you don't remember a world without robots. There was a time when humanity faced the universe alone and without a friend. Now he has creatures to help him; stronger creatures than himself, more faithful, more useful, and absolutely devoted to him. Mankind is no longer alone. Have you ever thought of it that way?'

'I'm afraid I haven't. May I quote you?'

'You may. To you, a robot is a robot. Gears and metal, electricity and positrons. —Mind and iron! Human-made! If necessary, human-destroyed! But you haven't worked with them, so you don't know them. They're a cleaner, better breed than we are.'

I tried to nudge her gently with words, 'We'd like to hear some of the things you could tell us; get your views on robots. The Interplanetary Press reaches the entire Solar System. Potential audience is three billion, Dr Calvin. They ought to know what you could tell them on robots.'

It wasn't necessary to nudge. She didn't hear me, but she was moving in the right direction.

'They might have known from the start. We sold robots for Earth-use then – before my time it was, even. Of course, that was when robots could not talk. Afterward, they became more human and opposition began. The labor unions, of course, naturally opposed robot competition for human jobs, and various segments of religious opinion had their superstitious objections. It was all quite ridiculous and quite useless. And yet there it was.'

I was taking it down verbatim on my pocket-recorder, trying not to show the knuckle-motions of my hand. If you practice a bit, you can get to the point where you can record accurately without taking the little gadget out of your pocket.

'Take the case of Robbie,' she said. 'I never knew him. He was dismantled the year before I joined the company – hopelessly out-of-date. But I saw the little girl in the museum—'

She stopped, but I didn't say anything. I let her eyes mist up and her mind travel back. She had lots of time to cover.

'I heard about it later, and when they called us blasphemers and demon-creators, I always thought of him. Robbie was a non-vocal robot. He couldn't speak. He was made and sold in 1996. Those were the days before extreme specialization, so he was sold as a nursemaid—'

'As a what?'

'As a nursemaid—'

I

Robbie

'Ninety-eight – ninety-nine – *one hundred.*' Gloria withdrew her chubby little forearm from before her eyes and stood for a moment, wrinkling her nose and blinking in the sunlight. Then, trying to watch in all directions at once, she withdrew a few cautious steps from the tree against which she had been leaning.

She craned her neck to investigate the possibilities of a clump of bushes to the right and then withdrew farther to obtain a better angle for viewing its dark recesses. The quiet was profound except for the incessant buzzing of insects and the occasional chirrup of some hardy bird, braving the midday sun.

Gloria pouted, 'I bet he went inside the house, and I've told him a million times that that's not fair.'

With tiny lips pressed together tightly and a severe frown crinkling her forehead, she moved determinedly toward the two-story building up past the driveway.

Too late she heard the rustling sound behind her, followed by the distinctive and rhythmic clump-clump of Robbie's metal feet. She whirled about to see her triumphing companion emerge from hiding and make for the home-tree at full speed.

Gloria shrieked in dismay. 'Wait, Robbie! That wasn't fair, Robbie! You promised you wouldn't run until I found you.' Her little feet could make no headway at all against Robbie's giant strides. Then, within ten feet of the goal, Robbie's pace slowed suddenly to the merest of crawls, and Gloria, with one final burst of wild speed, dashed pantingly past him to touch the welcome bark of home-tree first.

Gleefully, she turned on the faithful Robbie, and with the basest of ingratitude, rewarded him for his sacrifice by taunting him cruelly for a lack of running ability.

'Robbie can't run!' she shouted at the top of her eight-year-old voice. 'I can beat him any day. I can beat him any day.' She chanted the words in a shrill rhythm.

Robbie didn't answer, of course – not in words. He pantomimed running, instead, inching away until Gloria found herself running after him as he dodged her narrowly, forcing her to veer in helpless circles, little arms outstretched and fanning at the air.

'Robbie,' she squealed, 'stand still!' —And the laughter was forced out of her in breathless jerks.

—Until he turned suddenly and caught her up, whirling her round, so that for her the world fell away for a moment with a blue emptiness beneath, and green trees stretching hungrily downward towards the void. Then she was down in the grass again, leaning against Robbie's leg and still holding a hard, metal finger.

After a while, her breath returned. She pushed uselessly at her disheveled hair in vague imitation of one of her mother's gestures and twisted to see if her dress were torn.

She slapped her hand against Robbie's torso, 'Bad boy! I'll spank you!'

And Robbie cowered, holding his hands over his face so that she had to add, 'No, I won't, Robbie. I won't spank you. But anyway, it's my turn to hide now because you've got longer legs and you promised not to run till I found you.'

Robbie nodded his head – a small parallelepiped with rounded edges and corners attached to a similar but much larger parallelepiped that served as torso by means of a short, flexible stalk – and obediently faced the tree. A thin, metal film descended over his glowing eyes and from within his body came a steady, resonant ticking.

'Don't peek now – and don't skip any numbers,' warned Gloria, and scurried for cover.

With unvarying regularity, seconds were ticked off, and at the hundredth, up went the eyelids, and the glowing red of Robbie's eyes swept the prospect. They rested for a moment on a bit of colorful gingham that protruded from behind a boulder. He advanced a few steps and convinced himself that it was Gloria who squatted behind it.

Slowly, remaining always between Gloria and home-tree, he advanced on the hiding place, and when Gloria was plainly in sight and could no longer even theorize to herself that she was not seen, he extended one arm toward her, slapping the other against his leg so that it rang again. Gloria emerged sulkily.

'You peeked!' she exclaimed, with gross unfairness. 'Besides I'm tired of playing hide-and-seek. I want a ride.'

But Robbie was hurt at the unjust accusation, so he seated himself carefully and shook his head ponderously from side to side.

Gloria changed her tone to one of gentle coaxing immediately, 'Come on, Robbie. I didn't mean it about the peeking. Give me a ride.'

Robbie was not to be won over so easily, though. He gazed stubbornly at the sky, and shook his head even more emphatically.

'Please, Robbie, please give me a ride.' She encircled his neck with rosy arms and hugged tightly. Then, changing moods in a moment, she moved away. 'If you don't, I'm going to cry,' and her face twisted appallingly in preparation.

Hard-hearted Robbie paid scant attention to this dreadful possibility, and shook his head a third time. Gloria found it necessary to play her trump card.

'If you don't,' she exclaimed warmly, 'I won't tell you any more stories, that's all. Not one—'

Robbie gave in immediately and unconditionally before this ultimatum, nodding his head vigorously until the metal of his neck hummed. Carefully, he raised the little girl and place her on his broad, flat shoulders.

Gloria's threatened tears vanished immediately and she crowed with delight. Robbie's metal skin, kept at a constant temperature of seventy by the high resistance coils within, felt nice and comfortable, while the beautifully loud sound her heels made as they bumped rhythmically against his chest was enchanting.

'You're an air-coaster, Robbie, you're a big, silver air-coaster. Hold out your arms straight. —You *got* to, Robbie, if you're going to be an air-coaster.'

The logic was irrefutable. Robbie's arms were wings catching the air currents and he was a silver 'coaster.

Gloria twisted the robot's head and leaned to the right. He banked sharply. Gloria equipped the 'coaster with a motor that went 'Br-r-r' and then with weapons that went 'Powie' and 'Sh-sh-shshsh.' Pirates were giving chase and the ship's blasters were coming into play. The pirates dropped in a steady rain.

'Got another one. —Two more!' she cried.

Then 'Faster, men,' Gloria said pompously, 'we're running out of ammunition.' She aimed over her shoulder with undaunted courage and Robbie was a blunt-nosed spaceship zooming through the void at maximum acceleration.

Clear across the field he sped, to the patch of tall grass on the other side, where he stopped with a suddenness that evoked a shriek from his flushed rider, and then tumbled her on to the soft, green carpet.

Gloria gasped and panted, and gave voice to intermittent whispered exclamations of 'That was *nice*!'

Robbie waited until she had caught her breath and then pulled gently at a lock of hair.

'You want something?' said Gloria, eyes wide in an apparently artless complexity that fooled her huge 'nursemaid' not at all. He pulled the curl harder.

'Oh, I know. You want a story.'

Robbie nodded rapidly.

'Which one?'

Robbie made a semi-circle in the air with one finger.

The little girl protested, '*Again*? I've told you Cinderella a million times. Aren't you tired of it? —It's for babies.'

Another semi-circle.

'Oh, hell,' Gloria composed herself, ran over the details of the tale in her mind (together with her own elaborations, of which she had several) and began:

'Are you ready? Well – once upon a time there was a beautiful little girl whose name was Ella. And she had a terribly cruel step-mother and two very ugly and *very* cruel step-sisters and—'

Gloria was reaching the very climax of the tale – midnight was striking and everything was changing back to the shabby originals lickety-split, while Robbie listened tensely with burning eyes – when the interruption came.

'Gloria!'

It was the high-pitched sound of a woman who has been calling not once, but several times; and had the nervous tone of one in whom anxiety was beginning to overcome impatience.

'Mamma's calling me,' said Gloria, not quite happily. 'You'd better carry me back to the house, Robbie.'

Robbie obeyed with alacrity for somehow there was that in him which judged it best to obey Mrs Weston, without as much as a scrap of hesitation. Gloria's father was rarely home in the daytime except on Sunday – today, for instance – and when he was, he proved a genial and understanding person. Gloria's mother, however, was a source of uneasiness to Robbie and there was always the impulse to sneak away from her sight.

Mrs Weston caught sight of them the minute they rose above the masking tufts of long grass and retired inside the house to wait.

'I've shouted myself hoarse, Gloria,' she said, severely. 'Where were you?'

'I was with Robbie,' quavered Gloria. 'I was telling him Cinderella, and I forgot it was dinner-time.'

'Well, it's a pity Robbie forgot, too.' Then, as if that reminded her of the robot's presence, she whirled upon him. 'You may go, Robbie. She doesn't need you now.' Then, brutally, 'And don't come back till I call you.'

Robbie turned to go, but hesitated as Gloria cried out in his defense, 'Wait, Mamma, you got to let him stay. I didn't finish Cinderella for him. I said I would tell him Cinderella and I'm not finished.'

'Gloria!'

'Honest and truly, Mamma, he'll stay so quiet, you won't even know he's here. He can sit on the chair in the corner, and he won't say a word – I mean he won't *do* anything. Will you, Robbie?'

Robbie, appealed to, nodded his massive head up and down once.

'Gloria, if you don't stop this at once, you shan't see Robbie for a whole week.'

The girl's eyes fell, 'All right! But Cinderella is his favorite story and I didn't finish it. —And he likes it so much.'

The robot left with a disconsolate step and Gloria choked back a sob.

George Weston was comfortable. It was a habit of his to be comfortable on Sunday afternoons. A good, hearty dinner below the hatches; a nice, soft, dilapidated couch on which to sprawl; a copy of the *Times*; slippered feet and shirtless chest – how could anyone *help* but be comfortable?

He wasn't pleased, therefore, when his wife walked in. After ten years of married life, he still was so unutterably foolish as to love her, and there was no question that he was always glad to see her – still Sunday afternoons just after dinner were sacred to him and his idea of solid comfort was to be left in utter solitude for two or three hours. Consequently, he fixed his eye firmly upon the latest reports of the Lefebre–Yoshida expedition to Mars (this one was to take off from Lunar Base and might actually succeed) and pretended she wasn't there.

Mrs Weston waited patiently for two minutes, then impatiently for two more, and finally broke the silence.

'George!'

'Hmpph?'

'George, I say! *Will* you put down that paper and look at me?'

The paper rustled to the floor and Weston turned a weary face toward his wife, 'What is it, dear?'

'You know what it is, George. It's Gloria and that terrible machine.'

'What terrible machine?'

'Now don't pretend you don't know what I'm talking about. It's that robot Gloria calls Robbie. He doesn't leave her for a moment.'

'Well, why should he? He's not supposed to. And he certainly isn't a terrible machine. He's the best darn robot money can buy and I'm damned sure he set me back half a year's income. He's worth it, though – darn sight cleverer than half my office staff.'

He made a move to pick up the paper again, but his wife was quicker and snatched it away.

'You listen to *me*, George. I won't have my daughter entrusted to a machine – and I don't care how clever it is. It has no soul, and no one knows what it may be thinking. A child just isn't *made* to be guarded by a thing of metal.'

Weston frowned, 'When did you decide this? He's been with Gloria two years now and I haven't seen you worry till now.'

'It was different at first. It was a novelty; it took a load off me, and – and it was a fashionable thing to do. But now I don't know. The neighbors—'

'Well, what have the neighbors to do with it? Now, look. A robot is infinitely more to be trusted than a human nursemaid. Robbie was constructed for only one purpose really – to be the companion of a little child. His entire "mentality" has been created for the purpose. He just can't help being faithful and loving and kind. He's a machine – *made so*. That's more than you can say for humans.'

'But something might go wrong. Some – some—' Mrs Weston was a bit hazy about the insides of a robot, 'some little jigger will come loose and the awful thing will go berserk and – and—' She couldn't bring herself to complete the quite obvious thought.

'Nonsense,' Weston denied, with an involuntary nervous shiver. 'That's completely ridiculous. We had a long discussion at the time we bought Robbie about the First Law of Robotics. You *know* that it is impossible for a robot to harm a human being; that long before enough can go wrong to alter that First Law, a robot would be completely inoperable. It's a mathematical impossibility. Besides I have an engineer from US Robots here twice a year to give the poor gadget a complete overhaul. Why, there's no more chance of anything at all going wrong with Robbie than there is of you or I suddenly going looney – considerably less, in fact. Besides, how are you going to take him away from Gloria?'

He made another futile stab at the paper and his wife tossed it angrily into the next room.

'That's just it, George! She won't play with anyone else. There are dozens of little boys and girls that she should make friends with, but she won't. She won't go *near* them unless I make her. That's no way for a little girl to grow up. You want her to be normal, don't you? You want her to be able to take her part in society.'

'You're jumping at shadows, Grace. Pretend Robbie's a dog. I've seen hundreds of children who would rather have their dog than their father.'

'A dog is different, George. We *must* get rid of that horrible thing. You can sell it back to the company. I've asked, and you can.'

'You've *asked*? Now look here, Grace, let's not go off the deep end. We're keeping the robot until Gloria is older and I don't want the subject brought up again.' And with that he walked out of the room in a huff.

Mrs Weston met her husband at the door two evenings later. 'You'll have to listen to this, George. There's bad feeling in the village.'

'About what?' asked Weston. He stepped into the washroom and drowned out any possible answer by the splash of water.

Mrs Weston waited. She said, 'About Robbie.'

Weston stepped out, towel in hand, face red and angry. 'What are you talking about?'

'Oh, it's been building up and building up. I've tried to close my eyes to it, but I'm not going to any more. Most of the villagers consider Robbie dangerous. Children aren't allowed to go near our place in the evenings.'

'We trust *our* child with the thing.'

'Well, people aren't reasonable about these things.'

'Then to hell with them.'

'Saying that doesn't solve the problem. I've got to do my shopping down there. I've got to meet them every day. And it's even worse in the city these days when it comes to robots. New York has just passed an ordinance keeping all robots off the streets between sunset and sunrise.'

'All right, but they can't stop us from keeping a robot in our home. —Grace, this is one of your campaigns. I recognize it. But it's no use. The answer is still, no! We're keeping Robbie!'

And yet he loved his wife – and what was worse, his wife knew it. George Weston, after all, was only a man – poor thing – and his wife made full use of every device which a clumsier and more scrupulous sex has learned, with reason and futility, to fear.

Ten times in the ensuing week, he cried, 'Robbie stays – and that's *final*!' and each time it was weaker and accompanied by a louder and more agonized groan.

Came the day at last, when Weston approached his daughter guiltily and suggested a 'beautiful' visivox show in the village.

Gloria clapped her hands happily, 'Can Robbie go?'

'No, dear,' he said, and winced at the sound of his voice, 'they won't allow robots at the visivox – but you can tell him all about it when you get home.' He stumbled all over the last few words and looked away.

Gloria came back from town bubbling over with enthusiasm, for the visivox had been a gorgeous spectacle indeed.

She waited for her father to maneuver the jet-car into the sunken garage. 'Wait till I tell Robbie, Daddy. He would have liked it like anything. —Especially when Francis Fran was backing away so-o-o quietly, and backed right into one of the Leopard-Men and had to run.' She laughed again. 'Daddy, are there really Leopard-Men on the Moon?'

'Probably not,' said Weston absently. 'It's just funny make-believe.' He couldn't take much longer with the car. He'd have to face it.

Gloria ran across the lawn. 'Robbie. —Robbie!'

Then she stopped suddenly at the sight of a beautiful collie which regarded her out of serious brown eyes as it wagged its tail on the porch.

'Oh, what a nice dog!' Gloria climbed the steps, approached cautiously and patted it. 'Is it for me, Daddy?'

Her mother had joined them. 'Yes, it is, Gloria. Isn't it nice – soft and furry. It's very gentle. It *likes* little girls.'

'Can he play games?'

'Surely. He can do any number of tricks. Would you like to see some?'

'Right away. I want Robbie to see him, too. —*Robbie!*' She stopped, uncertainly, and frowned, 'I'll bet he's just staying in his room because he's mad at me for not taking him to the visivox. You'll have to explain to him, Daddy. He might not believe me, but he knows if you say it, it's so.'

Weston's lips grew tighter. He looked toward his wife but could not catch her eye.

Gloria turned precipitously and ran down the basement steps, shouting as she went, 'Robbie — Come and see what Daddy and Mamma brought me. They brought me a dog, Robbie.'

In a minute she had returned, a frightened little girl. 'Mamma, Robbie isn't in his room. Where is he?' There was no answer and George Weston coughed and was suddenly extremely interested in an aimlessly drifting cloud. Gloria's voice quavered on the verge of tears, 'Where's Robbie, Mamma?'

Mrs Weston sat down and drew her daughter gently to her, 'Don't feel bad, Gloria. Robbie has gone away, I think.'

'Gone *away*? Where? Where's he gone away, Mamma?'

'No one knows, darling. He just walked away. We've looked and we've looked and we've looked for him, but we can't find him.'

'You mean he'll never come back again?' Her eyes were round with horror.

'We may find him soon. We'll keep looking for him. And meanwhile you can play with your nice new doggie. Look at him! His name is Lightning and he can—'

But Gloria's eyelids had overflowed, 'I don't want the nasty dog – I want Robbie. I want you to find me Robbie.' Her feelings became too deep for words, and she spluttered into a shrill wail.

Mrs Weston glanced at her husband for help, but he merely shuffled his feet morosely and did not withdraw his ardent stare from the heavens, so she bent to the task of consolation, 'Why do you cry, Gloria? Robbie was only a machine, just a nasty old machine. He wasn't alive at all.'

'He was *not* no machine!' screamed Gloria, fiercely and ungrammatically. 'He was a *person* just like you and me and he was my *friend*. I want him back. Oh, Mamma, I want him back.'

Her mother groaned in defeat and left Gloria to her sorrow. 'Let her have her cry out,' she told her husband. 'Childish griefs are never lasting. In a few days, she'll forget that awful robot ever existed.'

But time proved Mrs Weston a bit too optimistic. To be sure, Gloria ceased crying, but she ceased smiling, too, and the passing days found her ever more silent and shadowy. Gradually, her attitude of passive unhappiness wore Mrs Weston down and all that kept her from yielding was the impossibility of admitting defeat to her husband.

Then, one evening, she flounced into the living room, sat down, folded her arms and looked boiling mad.

Her husband stretched his neck in order to see her over his newspaper, 'What now, Grace?'

'It's that child, George. I've had to send back the dog today. Gloria positively couldn't stand the sight of him, she said. She's driving me into a nervous breakdown.'

Weston laid down the paper and a hopeful gleam entered his eye, 'Maybe— Maybe we ought to get Robbie back. It might be done, you know. I can get in touch with—'

'No!' she replied, grimly. 'I won't hear of it. We're not giving up that easily. My child shall *not* be brought up by a robot if it takes years to break her of it.'

Weston picked up his paper again with a disappointed air. 'A year of this will have me prematurely gray.'

'You're a big help, George,' was the frigid answer. 'What Gloria needs is a change of environment. Of course she can't forget Robbie here. How can she when every tree and rock reminds her of him? It is really the *silliest* situation I have ever heard of. Imagine a child pining away for the loss of a robot.'

'Well, stick to the point. What's the change in environment you're planning?'

'We're going to take her to New York.'

'The city! In August! Say, do you know what New York is like in August? It's unbearable.'

'Millions do bear it.'

'They don't have a place like this to go to. If they didn't have to stay in New York, they wouldn't.'

'Well, *we* have to. I say we're leaving now – or as soon as we can make the arrangements. In the city, Gloria will find sufficient interests and sufficient friends to perk her up and make her forget that machine.'

'Oh, Lord,' groaned the lesser half, 'those frying pavements!'

'We have to,' was the unshaken response. 'Gloria has lost five pounds in the last month and my little girl's health is more important to me than your comfort.'

'It's a pity you didn't think of your little girl's health before you deprived her of her pet robot,' he muttered – but to himself.

Gloria displayed immediate signs of improvement when told of the impending trip to the city. She spoke little of it, but when she did, it was always with lively anticipation. Again, she began to smile and to eat with something of her former appetite.

Mrs Weston hugged herself for joy and lost no opportunity to triumph over her still skeptical husband.

'You see, George, she helps with the packing like a little angel, and chatters away as if she hadn't a care in the world. It's just as I told you – all we need do is substitute other interests.'

'Hmpph,' was the skeptical response, 'I hope so.'

Preliminaries were gone through quickly. Arrangements were made for the preparation of their city home and a couple were engaged as housekeepers for the country home. When the day of the trip finally did come, Gloria was all but her old self again, and no mention of Robbie passed her lips at all.

In high good-humor the family took a taxi-gyro to the airport (Weston would have preferred using his own private 'gyro, but it was only a two-seater with no room for baggage) and entered the waiting liner.

'Come, Gloria,' called Mrs Weston. 'I've saved you a seat near the window so you can watch the scenery.'

Gloria trotted down the aisle cheerily, flattened her nose into a white oval against the thick clear glass, and watched with an intentness that increased as the sudden coughing of the motor drifted backward into the interior. She was too young to be frightened when the ground dropped away as if let through a trap-door and she herself suddenly became twice her usual weight, but not too young to be mightily interested. It wasn't until the ground had changed into a tiny patchwork quilt that she withdrew her nose, and faced her mother again.

'Will we soon be in the city, Mamma?' she asked, rubbing her chilled nose, and watching with interest as the patch of moisture which her breath had formed on the pane shrank slowly and vanished.

'In about half an hour, dear.' Then, with just the faintest trace of anxiety, 'Aren't you glad we're going? Don't you think you'll be very happy in the city with all the buildings and people and things to see. We'll go to the visivox every day and see shows and go to the circus and the beach and—'

'Yes, Mamma,' was Gloria's unenthusiastic rejoinder. The liner passed over a bank of clouds at that moment, and Gloria was instantly absorbed in the unusual spectacle of clouds underneath one. Then they were over clear sky again, and she turned to her mother with a sudden mysterious air of secret knowledge.

'*I* know why we're going to the city, Mamma.'

'Do you?' Mrs Weston was puzzled. 'Why, dear?'

'You didn't tell me because you wanted it to be a surprise, but *I* know.' For a moment, she was lost in admiration at her own acute penetration, and then she laughed gaily. 'We're going to New York so we can find Robbie, aren't we? —With detectives.'

The statement caught George Weston in the middle of a drink of water, with disastrous results. There was a sort of strangled gasp, a geyser of water, and then a bout of choking coughs.

When all was over, he stood there, a red-faced, waterdrenched and very, very annoyed person.

Mrs Weston maintained her composure, but when Gloria repeated her question in a more anxious tone of voice, she found her temper rather bent.

'Maybe,' she retorted, tartly. 'Now sit and be still, for Heaven's sake.'

New York City, 1998 A.D., was a paradise for the sightseer more than ever in its history. Gloria's parents realized this and made the most of it.

On direct orders from his wife, George Weston arranged to have his business take care of itself for a month or so, in order to be free to spend the time in what he termed 'dissipating Gloria to the verge of ruin'. Like everything else Weston did, this was gone about in an efficient, thorough, and businesslike way. Before the month had passed, nothing that could be done had not been done.

She was taken to the top of the half-mile-tall Roosevelt Building, to gaze down in awe upon the jagged panorama of rooftops that blended far off in the fields of Long Island and the flatlands of New Jersey. They visited the zoos where Gloria stared in delicious fright at the 'real live lion' (rather disappointed that the keepers fed him raw steaks, instead of human beings, as she had expected), and asked insistently and peremptorily to see 'the whale'.

The various museums came in for their share of attention, together with the parks and the beaches and the aquarium.

She was taken halfway up the Hudson in an excursion steamer fitted out in the archaism of the mad Twenties. She travelled into the stratosphere on an exhibition trip, where the sky turned deep purple and the stars came out and the misty earth below

looked like a huge concave bowl. Down under the waters of the
Long Island Sound she was taken in a glass-walled sub-sea vessel,
where in a green and wavering world, quaint and curious
sea-things ogled her and wiggled suddenly away.

On a more prosaic level, Mrs Weston took her to the department stores where she could revel in another type of fairyland.

In fact, when the month had nearly sped, the Westons were
convinced that everything conceivable had been done to take
Gloria's mind once and for all off the departed Robbie – but
they were not quite sure they had succeeded.

The fact remained that wherever Gloria went, she displayed
the most absorbed and concentrated interest in such robots as
happened to be present. No matter how exciting the spectacle
before her, nor how novel to her girlish eyes, she turned away
instantly if the corner of her eye caught a glimpse of metallic
movement.

Mrs Weston went out of her way to keep Gloria away from
all robots.

And the matter was finally climaxed in the episode at the
Museum of Science and Industry. The Museum had announced
a special 'Children's program' in which exhibits of scientific
witchery scaled down to the child mind were to be shown. The
Westons, of course, placed it upon their list of 'absolutely'.

It was while the Westons were standing totally absorbed in
the exploits of a powerful electro-magnet that Mrs Weston
suddenly became aware of the fact that Gloria was no longer
with her. Initial panic gave way to calm decision and, enlisting
the aid of three attendants, a careful search was begun.

Gloria, of course, was not one to wander aimlessly, however.
For her age, she was an unusually determined and purposeful
girl, quite full of the maternal genes in that respect. She had
seen a huge sign on the third floor, which had said, 'This Way

to the Talking Robot.' Having spelled it out to herself and having noticed that her parents did not seem to wish to move in the proper direction, she did the obvious thing. Waiting for an opportune moment of parental distraction, she calmly disengaged herself and followed the sign.

The Talking Robot was a *tour de force*, a thoroughly impractical device, possessing publicity value only. Once an hour, an escorted group stood before it and asked questions of the robot engineer in charge in careful whispers. Those the engineer decided were suitable for the robot's circuits were transmitted to the Talking Robot.

It was rather dull. It may be nice to know that the square of fourteen is 196, that the temperature at the moment is seventy-two degrees Fahrenheit, and the air-pressure 30.02 inches of mercury, that the atomic weight of sodium is twenty-three, but one doesn't really need a robot for that. One especially does not need an unwieldy, totally immobile mass of wires and coils spreading over twenty-five square yards.

Few people bothered to return for a second helping, but one girl in her middle teens sat quietly on a bench waiting for a third. She was the only one in the room when Gloria entered.

Gloria did not look at her. To her at the moment, another human being was but an inconsiderable item. She saved her attention for this large thing with the wheels. For a moment, she hesitated in dismay. It didn't look like any robot she had ever seen.

Cautiously and doubtfully she raised her treble voice, 'Please, Mr Robot, sir, are you the Talking Robot, sir?' She wasn't sure, but it seemed to her that a robot that actually talked was worth a great deal of politeness.

(The girl in her mid-teens allowed a look of intense

concentration to cross her thin, plain face. She whipped out a small notebook and began writing in rapid pot-hooks.)

There was an oily whir of gears and a mechanically-timbered voice boomed out in words that lacked accent and intonation, 'I – am – the – robot – that – talks.'

Gloria stared at it ruefully. It *did* talk, but the sound came from inside somewheres. There was no *face* to talk to. She said, 'Can you help me, Mr Robot, sir?'

The Talking Robot was designed to answer questions, and only such questions as it could answer had ever been put to it. It was quite confident of its ability, therefore, 'I – can – help – you.'

'Thank you, Mr Robot, sir. Have you seen Robbie?'

'Who – is Robbie?'

'He's a robot, Mr Robot, sir.' She stretched to tip-toes. 'He's about so high, Mr Robot, sir, only higher, and he's very nice. He's got a head, you know. I mean you haven't, but he has, Mr Robot, sir.'

The Talking Robot had been left behind, 'A – robot?'

'Yes, Mr Robot, sir. A robot just like you, except he can't talk, of course, and – looks like a real person.'

'A – robot – like – me?'

'Yes, Mr Robot, sir.'

To which the Talking Robot's only response was an erratic splutter and an occasional incoherent sound. The radical generalization offered it, i.e. its existence, not as a particular object, but as a member of a general group, was too much for it. Loyally, it tried to encompass the concept and half a dozen coils burnt out. Little warning signals were buzzing.

(The girl in her mid-teens left at that point. She had enough for her Physics–I paper on 'Practical Aspects of Robotics'. This paper was Susan Calvin's first of many on the subject.)

Gloria stood waiting, with carefully concealed impatience, for the machine's answer when she heard the cry behind her of 'There she is,' and recognized that cry as her mother's.

'What are you doing here, you bad girl?' cried Mrs Weston, anxiety dissolving at once into anger. 'Do you know you frightened your mamma and daddy almost to death? Why did you run away?'

The robot engineer had also dashed in, tearing his hair, and demanding who of the gathering crowd had tampered with the machine. 'Can't anybody read signs?' he yelled. 'You're not allowed in here without an attendant.'

Gloria raised her grieved voice over the din, 'I only came to see the Talking Robot, Mamma. I thought he might know where Robbie was because they're both robots.' And then, as the thought of Robbie was suddenly brought forcefully home to her, she burst into a sudden storm of tears, 'And I *got* to find Robbie, Mamma. I *got* to.'

Mrs Weston strangled a cry, and said, 'Oh, good Heavens. Come home, George. This is more than I can stand.'

That evening, George Weston left for several hours, and the next morning, he approached his wife with something that looked suspiciously like smug complacence.

'I've got an idea, Grace.'

'About what?' was the gloomy, uninterested query.

'About Gloria.'

'You're not going to suggest buying back that robot?'

'No, of course not.'

'Then go ahead. I might as well listen to you. Nothing *I've* done seems to have done any good.'

'All right. Here's what I've been thinking. The whole trouble with Gloria is that she thinks of Robbie as a *person* and not as a *machine*. Naturally, she can't forget him. Now if we managed to convince her that Robbie was nothing more than a mess of steel and copper in the form of sheets and wires with electricity its juice of life, how long would her longings last. It's the psychological attack, if you see my point.'

'How do you plan to do it?'

'Simple. Where do you suppose I went last night? I persuaded Robertson of US Robots and Mechanical Men, Inc. to arrange for a complete tour of his premises tomorrow. The three of us will go, and by the time we're through, Gloria will have it drilled into her that a robot is *not* alive.'

Mrs Weston's eyes widened gradually and something glinted in her eyes that was quite like sudden admiration, 'Why, George, that's a *good* idea.'

And George Weston's vest buttons strained. 'Only kind I have,' he said.

Mr Struthers was a conscientious General Manager and naturally inclined to be a bit talkative. The combination, therefore, resulted in a tour that was fully explained, perhaps even over-abundantly explained, at every step. However, Mrs Weston was not bored. Indeed, she stopped him several times and begged him to repeat his statements in simpler language so that Gloria might understand. Under the influence of this appreciation of his narrative powers, Mr Struthers expanded genially and became ever more communicative, if possible.

George Weston, himself, showed a gathering impatience.

'Pardon me, Struthers,' he said, breaking into the middle of a lecture on the photo-electric cell, 'haven't you a section of the factory where only robot labor is employed?'

'Eh? Oh, yes! Yes, indeed!' He smiled at Mrs Weston. 'A vicious circle in a way, robots creating more robots. Of course, we are not making a general practice out of it. For one thing, the unions would never let us. But we can turn out a very few robots using robot labor exclusively, merely as a sort of scientific experiment. You see,' he tapped his pince-nez into one palm argumentatively, 'what the labor unions don't realize – and I say this as a man who has always been very sympathetic with the labor movement in general – is that the advent of the robot, while involving some dislocation to begin with, will, inevitably—'

'Yes, Struthers,' said Weston, 'but about that section of the factory you speak of – may we see it? It would be very interesting, I'm sure.'

'Yes! Yes, of course!' Mr Struthers replaced his pince-nez in one conclusive movement and gave vent to a soft cough of discomfiture. 'Follow me, please.'

He was comparatively quiet while leading the three through a long corridor and down a flight of stairs. Then, when they had entered a large well-lit room that buzzed with metallic activity, the sluices opened and the flood of explanation poured forth again.

'There you are!' he said with pride in his voice. 'Robots only! Five men act as overseers and they don't even stay in this room. In five years, that is, since we began this project, not a single accident has occurred. Of course, the robots here assembled are comparatively simple, but . . .'

The General Manager's voice had long died to a rather soothing murmur in Gloria's ears. The whole trip seemed rather dull and pointless to her, though there *were* many robots in sight. None were even remotely like Robbie, though, and she surveyed them with open contempt.

In this room, there weren't any people at all, she noticed. Then her eyes fell upon six or seven robots busily engaged at a round table half-way across the room. They widened in incredulous surprise. It was a big room. She couldn't see for sure, but one of the robots looked like – looked like – it *was*!

'*Robbie!*' Her shriek pierced the air, and one of the robots about the table faltered and dropped the tool he was holding. Gloria went almost mad with joy. Squeezing through the railing before either parent could stop her, she dropped lightly to the floor a few feet below, and ran toward her Robbie, arms waving and hair flying.

And the three horrified adults, as they stood frozen in their tracks, saw what the excited little girl did not see, – a huge, lumbering tractor bearing blindly down upon its appointed track.

It took split-seconds for Weston to come to his senses, and those split-seconds meant everything, for Gloria could not be overtaken. Although Weston vaulted the railing in a wild attempt, it was obviously hopeless. Mr Struthers signaled wildly to the overseers to stop the tractor, but the overseers were only human and it took time to act.

It was only Robbie that acted immediately and with precision.

With metal legs eating up the space between himself and his little mistress he charged down from the opposite direction. Everything then happened at once. With one sweep of an arm, Robbie snatched up Gloria, slackening his speed not one iota, and, consequently, knocking every breath of air out of her. Weston, not quite comprehending all that was happening, felt, rather than saw, Robbie brush past him, and came to a sudden bewildered halt. The tractor intersected Gloria's path half a second after Robbie had, rolled on ten feet further and came to a grinding, long-drawn-out stop.

Gloria regained her breath, submitted to a series of passionate hugs on the part of both her parents and turned eagerly toward Robbie. As far as she was concerned, nothing had happened except that she had found her friend.

But Mrs Weston's expression had changed from one of relief to one of dark suspicion. She turned to her husband, and, despite her disheveled and undignified appearance, managed to look quite formidable, '*You* engineered this, *didn't* you?'

George Weston swabbed at a hot forehead with his handkerchief. His hand was unsteady, and his lips could curve only into a tremulous and exceedingly weak smile.

Mrs Weston pursued the thought, 'Robbie wasn't designed for engineering or construction work. He couldn't be of any use to them. You had him placed there deliberately so that Gloria would find him. You know you did.'

'Well, I did,' said Weston. 'But, Grace, how was I to know the reunion would be so violent? And Robbie has saved her life; you'll have to admit that. You *can't* send him away again.'

Grace Weston considered. She turned toward Gloria and Robbie and watched them abstractedly for a moment. Gloria had a grip about the robot's neck and would have asphyxiated any creature but one of metal, and was prattling nonsense in half-hysterical frenzy. Robbie's chrome-steel arms (capable of bending a bar of steel two inches in diameter into a pretzel) wound about the little girl gently and lovingly, and his eyes glowed a deep, deep red.

'Well,' said Mrs Weston, at last, 'I guess he can stay with us until he rusts.'

Susan Calvin shrugged her shoulders, 'Of course, he didn't. That was 1998. By 2002, we had invented the mobile speaking robot which, of course, made all the non-speaking models out of date, and which seemed to be the final straw as far as the non-robot elements were concerned. Most of the world governments banned robot use on Earth for any purpose other than scientific research between 2003 and 2007.'

'So that Gloria had to give up Robbie eventually?'

'I'm afraid so. I imagine, however, that it was easier for her at the age of fifteen than at eight. Still, it was a stupid and unnecessary

attitude on the part of humanity. US Robots hit its low point, financially, just about the time I joined them in 2007. At first, I thought my job might come to a sudden end in a matter of months, but then we simply developed the extra-Terrestrial market.'

'And then you were set, of course.'

'Not quite. We began by trying to adapt the models we had on hand. Those first speaking models, for instance. They were about twelve feet high, very clumsy and not much good. We sent them out to Mercury to help build the mining station there, but that failed.'

I looked up in surprise, 'It did? Why, Mercury Mines is a multi-billion-dollar concern.'

'It is now, but it was a second attempt that succeeded. If you want to know about that, young man, I'd advise you to look up Gregory Powell. He and Michael Donovan handled our most difficult cases in the teens and twenties. I haven't heard from Donovan in years, but Powell is living right here in New York. He's a grandfather now, which is a thought difficult to get used to. I can only think of him as a rather young man. Of course, I was younger, too.'

I tried to keep her talking, 'If you would give me the bare bones, Dr Calvin, I can have Mr Powell fill it in afterward.' (And this was exactly what I later did.)

She spread her thin hands out upon the desk and looked at them. 'There are two or three,' she said, 'that I know a little about.'

'Start with Mercury,' I suggested.

'Well, I think it was in 2015 that the Second Mercury Expedition was sent out. It was exploratory and financed in part by US Robots and in part by Solar Minerals. It consisted of a new-type robot, still experimental; Gregory Powell; Michael Donovan—'

2

Runaround

It was one of Gregory Powell's favorite platitudes that nothing was to be gained from excitement, so when Mike Donovan came leaping down the stairs toward him, red hair matted with perspiration, Powell frowned.

'What's wrong?' he said. 'Break a fingernail?'

'Yaaaah,' snarled Donovan, feverishly. 'What have you been doing in the sublevels all day?' He took a deep breath and blurted out, 'Speedy never returned.'

Powell's eyes widened momentarily and he stopped on the stairs; then he recovered and resumed his upward steps. He didn't speak until he reached the head of the flight, and then:

'You sent him after the selenium?'

'Yes.'

'And how long has he been out?'

'Five hours now.'

Silence! This was a devil of a situation. Here they were, on Mercury exactly twelve hours – and already up to the eyebrows in the worst sort of trouble. Mercury had long been the jinx world of the System, but this was drawing it rather strong – even for a jinx.

Powell said, 'Start at the beginning, and let's get this straight.'

They were in the radio room now – with its already subtly antiquated equipment, untouched for the ten years previous to their arrival. Even ten years, technologically speaking, meant so much. Compare Speedy with the type of robot they must have had back in 2005. But then, advances in robotics these days were tremendous. Powell touched a still gleaming metal surface gingerly. The air of disuse that touched everything about the room – and the entire Station – was infinitely depressing.

Donovan must have felt it. He began: 'I tried to locate him by radio, but it was no go. Radio isn't any good on the Mercury Sunside – not past two miles, anyway. That's one of the reasons the First Expedition failed. And we can't put up the ultrawave equipment for weeks yet—'

'Skip all that. What *did* you get?'

'I located the unorganized body signal in the short wave. It was no good for anything except his position. I kept track of him that way for two hours and plotted the results on the map.'

There was a yellowed square of parchment in his hip pocket – a relic of the unsuccessful First Expedition – and he slapped it down on the desk with vicious force, spreading it flat with the palm of his hand. Powell, hands clasped across his chest, watched it at long range.

Donovan's pencil pointed nervously. 'The red cross is the selenium pool. You marked it yourself.'

'Which one is it?' interrupted Powell. 'There were three that MacDougal located for us before he left.'

'I sent Speedy to the nearest, naturally. Seventeen miles away. But what difference does that make?' There was tension in his voice. 'There are the penciled dots that mark Speedy's position.'

And for the first time Powell's artificial aplomb was shaken and his hands shot forward for the map.

'Are *you* serious? This is impossible.'

'There it is,' growled Donovan.

The little dots that marked the position formed a rough circle about the red cross of the selenium pool. And Powell's fingers went to his brown mustache, the unfailing signal of anxiety.

Donovan added: 'In the two hours I checked on him, he circled that damned pool four times. It seems likely to me that he'll keep that up forever. Do you realize the position we're in?'

Powell looked up shortly, and said nothing. Oh, yes, he realized the position they were in. It worked itself out as simply as a syllogism. The photo-cell banks that alone stood between the full power of Mercury's monstrous sun and themselves were shot to hell. The only thing that could save them was selenium. The only thing that could get the selenium was Speedy. If Speedy didn't come back, no selenium. No selenium, no photo-cell banks. No photobanks – well, death by slow broiling is one of the more unpleasant ways of being done in.

Donovan rubbed his red mop of hair savagely and expressed himself with bitterness. 'We'll be the laughing stock of the System, Greg. How can everything have gone so wrong so soon? The great team of Powell and Donovan is sent out to Mercury to report on the advisability of reopening the Sunside Mining Station with modern techniques and robots and we ruin everything the first day. A purely routine job, too. We'll never live it down.'

'We won't have to, perhaps,' replied Powell, quietly. 'If we don't do something quickly, living anything down – or even just plain living – will be out of the question.'

'Don't be stupid! If you feel funny about it, Greg, I don't. It was criminal, sending us out here with only one robot. And it was *your* bright idea that we could handle the photo-cell banks ourselves.'

'Now you're being unfair. It was a mutual decision and you know it. All we needed was a kilogram of selenium, a Stillhead

Dielectrode Plate and about three hours' time – and there are pools of pure selenium all over Sunside. MacDougal's spectroreflector spotted three for us in five minutes, didn't it? What the devil! We couldn't have waited for next conjunction.'

'Well, what are we going to do? Powell, you've got an idea. I know you have, or you wouldn't be so calm. You're no more a hero than I am. Go on, spill it!'

'We can't go after Speedy ourselves, Mike – not on the Sunside. Even the new insosuits aren't good for more than twenty minutes in direct sunlight. But you know the old saying, "Set a robot to catch a robot." Look, Mike, maybe things aren't so bad. We've got six robots down in the sublevels, that we may be able to use, if they work. *If* they work.'

There was a glint of sudden hope in Donovan's eyes. 'You mean six robots from the First Expedition. Are you sure? They may be subrobotic machines. Ten years is a long time as far as robot-types are concerned, you know.'

'No, they're robots. I've spent all day with them and I know. They've got positronic brains: primitive, of course.' He placed the map in his pocket. 'Let's go down.'

The robots were on the lowest sublevel – all six of them surrounded by musty packing cases of uncertain content. They were large, extremely so, and even though they were in a sitting position on the floor, legs straddled out before them, their heads were a good seven feet in the air.

Donovan whistled. 'Look at the size of them, will you? The chests must be ten feet around.'

'That's because they're supplied with the old McGuffy gears. I've been over the insides – crummiest set you've ever seen.'

'Have you powered them yet?'

'No. There wasn't any reason to. I don't thing there's anything wrong with them. Even the diaphragm is in reasonable order. They might talk.'

He had unscrewed the chest plate of the nearest as he spoke, inserted the two-inch sphere that contained the tiny spark of atomic energy that was a robot's life. There was difficulty in fitting it, but he managed, and then screwed the plate back on again in laborious fashion. The radio controls of more modern models had not been heard of ten years earlier. And then to the other five.

Donovan said uneasily, 'They haven't moved.'

'No orders to do so,' replied Powell, succinctly. He went back to the first in the line and struck him on the chest. 'You! Do you hear me?'

The monster's head bent slowly and the eyes fixed themselves on Powell. Then, in a harsh, squawking voice – like that of a medieval phonograph, he grated, 'Yes, Master!'

Powell grinned humorlessly at Donovan. 'Did you get that? Those were the days of the first talking robots when it looked as if the use of robots on Earth would be banned. The makers were fighting that and they built good, healthy slave complexes into the damned machines.'

'It didn't help them,' muttered Donovan.

'No, it didn't, but they sure tried.' He turned once more to the robot. 'Get up!'

The robot towered upward slowly and Donovan's head craned and his puckered lips whistled.

Powell said: 'Can you go out upon the surface? In the light?'

There was consideration while the robot's slow brain worked. Then, 'Yes, Master.'

'Good. Do you know what a mile is?'

Another consideration, and another slow answer. 'Yes, Master.'

'We will take you up to the surface then, and indicate a

direction. You will go about seventeen miles, and somewhere in that general region you will meet another robot, smaller than yourself. You understand so far?'

'Yes, Master.'

'You will find this robot and order him to return. If he does not wish to, you are to bring him back by force.'

Donovan clutched at Powell's sleeve. 'Why not send him for the selenium direct?'

'Because I want Speedy back, nitwit. I want to find out what's wrong with him.' And to the robot, 'All right, you, follow me.'

The robot remained motionless and his voice rumbled: 'Pardon, Master, but I cannot. You must mount first.' His clumsy arms had come together with a thwack, blunt fingers interlacing.

Powell stared and then pinched at his mustache. 'Uh . . . oh!'

Donovan's eyes bulged. 'We've got to ride him? Like a horse?'

'I guess that's the idea. I don't know why, though. I can't see – yes, I do. I told you they were playing up robot-safety in those days. Evidently, they were going to sell the notion of safety by not allowing them to move about without a mahout on their shoulders all the time. What do we do now?'

'That's what I've been thinking,' muttered Donovan. 'We can't go out on the surface, with a robot or without. Oh, for the love of Pete' – and he snapped his fingers twice. He grew excited. 'Give me that map you've got. I haven't studied it for two hours for nothing. This is a Mining Station. What's wrong with using the tunnels?'

The Mining Station was a black circle on the map, and the light dotted lines that were tunnels stretched out about it in spiderweb fashion.

Donovan studied the list of symbols at the bottom of the map. 'Look,' he said, 'the small black dots are openings to the surface, and here's one maybe three miles away from the selenium pool. There's a number here – you'd think they'd write larger – 13a. If the robots know their way around here—'

Powell shot the question and received the dull 'Yes, Master,' in reply. 'Get your insosuit,' he said with satisfaction.

It was the first time either had worn the insosuits – which marked one time more than either had expected to upon their arrival the day before – and they tested their limb movements uncomfortably.

The insosuit was far bulkier and far uglier than the regulation spacesuit; but withal considerably lighter, due to the fact that they were entirely nonmetallic in composition. Composed of heat-resistant plastic and chemically treated cork layers, and equipped with a desiccating unit to keep the air bone-dry, the insosuits could withstand the full glare of Mercury's sun for twenty minutes. Five to ten minutes more, as well, without actually killing the occupant.

And still the robot's hands formed the stirrup, nor did he betray the slightest atom of surprise at the grotesque figure into which Powell had been converted.

Powell's radio-harshened voice boomed out: 'Are you ready to take us to Exit 13a?'

'Yes, Master.'

Good, thought Powell; they might lack radio control but at least they were fitted for radio reception. 'Mount one or the other, Mike,' he said to Donovan.

He placed a foot in the improvised stirrup and swung upward. He found the seat comfortable; there was the humped back of the robot, evidently shaped for the purpose, a shallow groove along each shoulder for the thighs and two elongated 'ears' whose purpose now seemed obvious.

Powell seized the ears and twisted the head. His mount turned ponderously. 'Lead on, Macduff.' But he did not feel at all light-hearted.

The gigantic robots moved slowly, with mechanical precision, through the doorway that cleared their heads by a scant foot, so that the two men had to duck hurriedly, along a narrow corridor in which their unhurried footsteps boomed monotonously and into the air lock.

The long, airless tunnel that stretched to a pinpoint before them brought home forcefully to Powell the exact magnitude of the task accomplished by the First Expedition, with their crude robots and their start-from-scratch necessities. They might have been a failure, but their failure was a good deal better than the usual run of the System's successes.

The robots plodded onward with a pace that never varied and with footsteps that never lengthened.

Powell said: 'Notice that these tunnels are blazing with lights and that the temperature is Earth-normal. It's probably been like this all the ten years that this place has remained empty.'

'How's that?'

'Cheap energy; cheapest in the System. Sunpower, you know and on Mercury's Sunside, sunpower is *something*. That's why the Station was built in the sunlight rather than in the shadow of a mountain. It's really a huge energy converter. The heat is turned into electricity, light, mechanical work and what have you; so that energy is supplied and the Station is cooled in a simultaneous process.'

'Look,' said Donovan. 'This is all very educational, but would you mind changing the subject? It so happens that this conversion of energy that you talk about is carried on by the photo-cell banks mainly – and that is a tender subject with me at the moment.'

Powell grunted vaguely, and when Donovan broke the resulting silence, it was to change the subject completely. 'Listen, Greg. What the devil's wrong with Speedy, anyway? I can't understand it.'

It's not easy to shrug shoulders in an insosuit, but Powell tried it. 'I don't know, Mike. You know he's perfectly adapted to a Mercurian environment. Heat doesn't mean anything to him and he's built for the light gravity and the broken ground. He's foolproof – or, at least, he should be.'

Silence fell. This time, silence that lasted.

'Master,' said the robot, 'we are here.'

'Eh?' Powell snapped out of a semidrowse. 'Well, get us out of here – out to the surface.'

They found themselves in a tiny substation, empty, airless, ruined. Donovan had inspected a jagged hole in the upper reaches of one of the walls by the light of his pocket flash.

'Meteorite, do you suppose?' he had asked.

Powell shrugged. 'To hell with that. It doesn't matter. Let's get out.'

A towering cliff of a black, basaltic rock cut off the sunlight, and the deep night shadow of an airless world surrounded them. Before them, the shadow reached out and ended in knife-edge abruptness into an all-but-unbearable blaze of white light, that glittered from myriad crystals along a rocky ground.

'Space!' gasped Donovan. 'It looks like snow.' And it did. Powell's eyes swept the jagged glitter of Mercury to the horizon and winced at the gorgeous brilliance.

'This must be an unusual area,' he said. 'The general albedo of Mercury is low and most of the soil is gray pumice. Something like the Moon, you know. Beautiful, isn't it?'

He was thankful for the light filters in their visiplates. Beautiful or not, a look at the sunlight through straight glass would have blinded them inside of half a minute.

Donovan was looking at the spring thermometer on his wrist. 'Holy smokes, the temperature is eighty centigrade!'

Powell checked his own and said: 'Um-m-m. A little high. Atmosphere, you know.'

'On Mercury? Are you nuts?'

'Mercury isn't really airless,' explained Powell, in absent-minded fashion. He was adjusting the binocular attachments to his visiplate, and the bloated fingers of the insosuit were clumsy at it. 'There is a thin exhalation that clings to its surface – vapors of the more volatile elements and compounds that are heavy enough for Mercurian gravity to retain. You know: selenium, iodine, mercury, gallium, potassium, bismuth, volatile oxides. The vapors sweep into the shadows and condense, giving up heat. It's a sort of gigantic still. In fact, if you use your flash, you'll probably find that the side of the cliff is covered with, say, hoar-sulphur, or maybe quicksilver dew.

'It doesn't matter, though. Our suits can stand a measly eighty indefinitely.'

Powell had adjusted the binocular attachments, so that he seemed as eye-stalked as a snail.

Donovan watched tensely. 'See anything?'

The other did not answer immediately, and when he did, his voice was anxious and thoughtful. 'There's a dark spot on the horizon that might be the selenium pool. It's in the right place. But I don't see Speedy.'

Powell clambered upward in an instinctive striving for a better view, till he was standing in unsteady fashion upon his robot's shoulders. Legs straddled wide, eyes straining, he said: 'I think . . . I think— Yes, it's definitely he. He's coming this way.'

Donovan followed the pointing finger. He had no binoculars, but there was a tiny moving dot, black against the blazing brilliance of the crystalline ground.

'I see him!' he yelled. 'Let's get going!'

Powell had hopped down into a sitting position on the robot

again, and his suited hand slapped against the Gargantuan's barrel chest. 'Get going!'

'Giddy-ap!' yelled Donovan, and thumped his heels, spur fashion.

The robots started off, the regular thudding of their footsteps silent in the airlessness, for the nonmetallic fabric of the insosuits did not transmit sound. There was only a rhythmic vibration just below the border of actual hearing.

'Faster!' yelled Donovan. The rhythm did not change.

'No use,' cried Powell, in reply. 'These junk heaps are only geared to one speed. Do you think they're equipped with selective flexors?'

They had burst through the shadow, and the sunlight came down in a white-hot wash and poured liquidly about them.

Donovan ducked involuntarily. 'Wow! Is it imagination or do I feel heat?'

'You'll feel more presently,' was the grim reply. 'Keep your eye on Speedy.'

Robot SPD 13 was near enough to be seen in detail now. His graceful, streamlined body threw out blazing highlights as he loped with easy speed across the broken ground. His name was derived from his serial initials, of course, but it was apt, nevertheless, for the SPD models were among the fastest robots turned out by the United States Robots and Mechanical Men Corp.

'Hey, Speedy,' howled Donovan, and waved a frantic hand.

'Speedy!' shouted Powell. 'Come here!'

The distance between the men and the errant robot was being cut down momentarily – more by the efforts of Speedy than the slow plodding of the fifty-year-old antique mounts of Donovan and Powell.

They were close enough now to notice that Speedy's gait included a peculiar rolling stagger, a noticeable side-to-side lurch – and then, as Powell waved his hand again and sent maximum juice into his compact head-set radio sender, in preparation for another shout, Speedy looked up and saw them.

Speedy hopped to a halt and remained standing for a moment – with just a tiny, unsteady weave, as though he were swaying in a light wind.

Powell yelled: 'All right, Speedy! Come here, boy.'

Whereupon Speedy's robot voice sounded in Powell's earphones for the first time.

It said: 'Hot dog, let's play games. You catch me and I catch you; no love can cut our knife in two. For I'm Little Buttercup, sweet Little Buttercup. Whoops!' Turning on his heel, he sped off in the direction from which he had come with a speed and fury that kicked up gouts of baked dust.

And his last words as he receded into the distance were, 'There grew a little flower 'neath a great oak tree,' followed by a curious metallic clicking that *might* have been a robotic equivalent of a hiccup.

Donovan said weakly: 'Where did he pick up the Gilbert and Sullivan? Say, Greg, he . . . he's drunk or something.'

'If you hadn't told me,' was the bitter response, 'I'd never realize it. Let's get back to the cliff. I'm roasting.'

It was Powell who broke the desperate silence. 'In the first place,' he said, 'Speedy isn't drunk – not in the human sense – because he's a robot, and robots don't get drunk. However, there's *something* wrong with him which is the robotic equivalent of drunkenness.'

'To me, he's drunk,' stated Donovan, emphatically, 'and all I know is that he thinks we're playing games. And we're not. It's a matter of life and very gruesome death.'

'All right. Don't hurry me. A robot's only a robot. Once we find out what's wrong with him, we can fix it and go on.'

'*Once,*' said Donovan, sourly.

Powell ignored him. 'Speedy is perfectly adapted to normal Mercurian environment. But this region' – and his arm swept wide – 'is definitely abnormal. There's our clue. Now where do these crystals come from? They might have formed from a slowly cooling liquid; but where would you get liquid so hot that it would cool in Mercury's sun?'

'Volcanic action,' suggested Donovan, instantly, and Powell's body tensed.

'Out of the mouths of sucklings,' he said in a small, strange voice, and remained very still for five minutes.

Then, he said, 'Listen, Mike, what did you say to Speedy when you sent him after the selenium?'

Donovan was taken aback. 'Well damn it – I don't know. I just told him to get it.'

'Yes, I know. But how? Try to remember the exact words.'

'I said . . . uh . . . I said: "Speedy, we need some selenium. You can get it such-and-such a place. Go get it." That's all. What more did you want me to say?'

'You didn't put any urgency into the order, did you?'

'What for? It was pure routine.'

Powell sighed. 'Well, it can't be helped now – but we're in a fine fix.' He had dismounted from his robot, and was sitting, back against the cliff. Donovan joined him and they linked arms. In the distance the burning sunlight seemed to wait cat-and-mouse for them, and just next to them, the two giant robots were invisible but for the dull red of their photo-electric eyes that stared down at them, unblinking, unwavering and unconcerned.

Unconcerned! As was all this poisonous Mercury, as large in jinx as it was small in size.

Powell's radio voice was tense in Donovan's ear: 'Now, look, let's start with the three fundamental Rules of Robotics – the three rules that are built most deeply into a robot's positronic brain.' In the darkness, his gloved fingers ticked off each point.

'We have: One, a robot may not injure a human being, or, through inaction, allow a human being to come to harm.'

'Right!'

'Two,' continued Powell, 'a robot must obey the orders given it by human beings except where such orders would conflict with the First Law.'

'Right!'

'And three, a robot must protect its own existence as long as such protection does not conflict with the First or Second Laws.'

'Right! Now where are we?'

'Exactly at the explanation. The conflict between the various rules is ironed out by the different positronic potentials in the brain. We'll say that a robot is walking into danger and knows it. The automatic potential that Rule Three sets up turns him back. But suppose you *order* him to walk into that danger. In that case, Rule Two sets up a counter-potential higher than the previous one and the robot follows orders at the risks of existence.'

'Well, I know that. What about it?'

'Let's take Speedy's case. Speedy is one of the latest models, extremely specialized, and as expensive as a battleship. It's not a thing to be lightly destroyed.'

'So?'

'So Rule Three has been strengthened – that was specifically mentioned, by the way, in the advance notices on the SPD models – so that his allergy to danger is unusually high. At the same time, when you sent him out after the selenium, you gave him his order casually and without special emphasis, so that the Rule Two potential set-up was rather weak. Now, hold on; I'm just stating facts.'

'All right, go ahead. I think I get it.'

'You see how it works, don't you? There's some sort of danger centering at the selenium pool. It increases as he approaches, and a certain distance from it the Rule Three potential, unusually high to start with, exactly balances the Rule Two potential, unusually low to start with.'

Donovan rose to his feet in excitement. 'And it strikes an equilibrium. I see. Rule Three drives him back and Rule Two drives him forward—'

'So he follows a circle around the selenium pool, staying on the locus of all points of potential equilibrium. And unless we do something about it, he'll stay on that circle forever, giving us the good old runaround.' Then, more thoughtfully: 'And that, half the way, is what makes him drunk. At potential equilibrium, half the positronic paths of his brain are out of kilter. I'm not a robot specialist, but that seems obvious. Probably he's lost control of just those parts of his voluntary mechanism that a human drunk has. Ve-e-ery pretty.'

'But what's the danger? If we knew what he was running from—'

'*You* suggested it. Volcanic action. Somewhere right above the selenium pool is a seepage of gas from the bowels of Mercury. Sulphur dioxide, carbon dioxide – and carbon monoxide. Lots of it – and at this temperature.'

Donovan gulped audibly. 'Carbon monoxide plus iron gives the volatile iron carbonyl.'

'And a robot,' added Powell, 'is essentially iron.' Then, grimly: 'There's nothing like deduction. We've determined everything about our problem but the solution. We can't get the selenium ourselves. It's still too far. We can't send these robot horses, because they can't go themselves, and they can't carry us fast enough to keep us from crisping. And we can't catch Speedy, because the dope thinks we're playing games, and he can run sixty miles to our four.'

'If one of us goes,' began Donovan, tentatively, 'and comes back cooked, there'll still be the other.'

'Yes,' came the sarcastic reply, 'it would be a most tender sacrifice – except that a person would be in no condition to give orders before he ever reached the pool, and I don't think the robots would ever turn back to the cliff without orders. Figure it out! We're two or three miles from the pool – call it two – the robot travels at four miles an hour; and we can last twenty minutes in our suits. It isn't only the heat, remember. Solar radiation out here in the ultraviolet and below is *poison*.'

'Um-m-m,' said Donovan, 'ten minutes short.'

'As good as an eternity. And another thing. In order for Rule Three potential to have stopped Speedy where it did, there must be an appreciable amount of carbon monoxide in the metal-vapor atmosphere – and there must be an appreciable corrosive action atmosphere. He's been out hours now – and how do we know when a knee joint, for instance, won't be thrown out of kilter and keel him over. It's not only a question of thinking – we've got to think *fast*!'

Deep, dark, dank, dismal silence!

Donovan broke it, voice trembling in an effort to keep itself emotionless. He said: 'As long as we can't increase Rule Two potential by giving further orders, how about working the other way? If we increase the danger, we increase Rule Three potential and drive him backward.'

Powell's visiplate had turned toward him in a silent question.

'You see,' came the cautious explanation, 'all we need to do to drive him out of his rut is to increase the concentration of carbon monoxide in his vicinity. Well, back at the Station there's a complete analytical laboratory.'

'Naturally,' assented Powell. 'It's a Mining Station.'

'All right. There must be pounds of oxalic acid for calcium precipitations.'

'Holy space! Mike, you're a genius.'

'So-so,' admitted Donovan, modestly. 'It's just a case of remembering that oxalic acid on heating decomposes into carbon dioxide, water, and good old carbon monoxide. College chem, you know.'

Powell was on his feet and had attracted the attention of one of the monster robots by the simple expedient of pounding the machine's thigh.

'Hey,' he shouted, 'can you throw?'

'Master?'

'Never mind.' Powell damned the robot's molasses-slow brain. He scrabbled up a jagged brick-size rock. 'Take this,' he said, 'and hit the patch of bluish crystals just across that crooked fissure. You see it?'

Donovan pulled at his shoulder. 'Too far, Greg. It's almost half a mile off.'

'Quiet,' replied Powell. 'It's a case of Mercurian gravity and a steel throwing arm. Watch, will you?'

The robot's eyes were measuring the distance with machinely accurate stereoscopy. His arm adjusted itself to the weight of the missile and drew back. In the darkness, the robot's motions went unseen, but there was a sudden thumping sound as he shifted his weight, and seconds later the rock flew blackly into the sunlight. There was no air resistance to slow it down, nor wind to turn it aside – and when it hit the ground it threw up crystals precisely in the center of the 'blue patch'.

Powell yelled happily and shouted, 'Let's go back after the oxalic acid, Mike.'

And as they plunged into the ruined substation on the way

back to the tunnels, Donovan said grimly: 'Speedy's been hanging about on this side of the selenium pool, ever since we chased after him. Did you see him?'

'Yes.'

'I guess he wants to play games. Well, we'll play him games!'

They were back hours later, with three-liter jars of the white chemical and a pair of long faces. The photo-cell banks were deteriorating more rapidly than had seemed likely. The two steered their robots into the sunlight and toward the waiting Speedy in silence and with grim purpose.

Speedy galloped slowly toward them. 'Here we are again. *Whee!* I've made a little list, the piano organist; all people who eat peppermint and puff it in your face.'

'We'll puff something in *your* face,' muttered Donovan. 'He's limping, Greg.'

'I noticed that,' came the low, worried response. 'The monoxide'll get him yet, if we don't hurry.'

They were approaching cautiously now, almost sidling, to refrain from setting off the thoroughly irrational robot. Powell was too far off to tell, of course, but even already he could have sworn the crack-brained Speedy was setting himself for a spring.

'Let her go,' he gasped. 'Count three! One – two—'

Two steel arms drew back and snapped forward simultaneously and two glass jars whirled forward in towering parallel arcs, gleaming like diamonds in the impossible sun. And in a pair of soundless puffs, they hit the ground behind Speedy in crashes that sent the oxalic acid flying like dust.

In the full heat of Mercury's sun, Powell knew it was fizzing like soda water.

Speedy turned to stare, then backed away from it slowly – and as slowly gathered speed. In fifteen seconds, he was leaping directly toward the two humans in an unsteady canter.

Powell did not get Speedy's words just then, though he heard something that resembled, 'Lover's professions when uttered in Hessians.'

He turned away. 'Back to the cliff, Mike. He's out of the rut and he'll be taking orders now. I'm getting hot.'

They jogged toward the shadow at the slow monotonous pace of their mounts, and it was not until they had entered it and felt the sudden coolness settle softly about them that Donovan looked back. '*Greg!*'

Powell looked and almost shrieked. Speedy was moving slowly now – so slowly – and in the *wrong direction*. He was drifting; drifting back into his rut; and he was picking up speed. He looked dreadfully close, and dreadfully unreachable, in the binoculars.

Donovan shouted wildly, 'After him!' and thumped his robot into its pace, but Powell called him back.

'You won't catch him, Mike – it's no use.' He fidgeted on his robot's shoulders and clenched his fist in tight impotence. 'Why the devil do I see these things five seconds after it's all over? Mike, we've wasted hours.'

'We need more oxalic acid,' declared Donovan, stolidly. 'The concentration wasn't high enough.'

'Seven tons of it wouldn't have been enough – and we haven't the hours to spare to get it, even if it were, with the monoxide chewing him away. Don't you see what it is, Mike?'

And Donovan said flatly, 'No.'

'We were only establishing new equilibriums. When we create new monoxide and increase Rule Three potential, he moves backward till he's in balance again – and when the monoxide drifted away, he moved forward, and again there was balance.'

Powell's voice sounded thoroughly wretched. 'It's the same old runaround. We can push at Rule Two and pull at Rule Three and we can't get anywhere – we can only change the position of balance. We've got to get outside both rules.' And then he pushed his robot closer to Donovan's so that they were sitting face to face, dim shadows in the darkness, and he whispered, 'Mike!'

'Is it the finish?' – dully. 'I suppose we go back to the Station, wait for the banks to fold, shake hands, take cyanide, and go out like gentlemen.' He laughed shortly.

'Mike,' repeated Powell earnestly, 'we've got to get Speedy.'

'I know.'

'Mike,' once more, and Powell hesitated before continuing. 'There's always Rule One. I thought of it – earlier – but it's desperate.'

Donovan looked up and his voice livened. '*We're* desperate.'

'All right. According to Rule One a robot can't see a human come to harm because of his own inaction. Two and Three can't stand against it. They *can't*, Mike.'

'Even when the robot is half cra— Well, he's drunk. You know he is.'

'It's the chances you take.'

'Cut it. What are you going to do?'

'I'm going out there now and see what Rule One will do. If it won't break the balance, then what the devil – it's either now or three-four days from now.'

'Hold on, Greg. There are human rules of behavior, too. You don't go out there just like that. Figure out a lottery, and give me *my* chance.'

'All right. First to get the cube of fourteen goes.' And almost immediately, 'Twenty-seven forty-four!'

Donovan felt his robot stagger at a sudden push by Powell's

mount and then Powell was off into the sunlight. Donovan opened his mouth to shout, and then clicked it shut. Of course, the damn fool had worked out the cube of fourteen in advance, and on purpose. Just like him.

The sun was hotter than ever and Powell felt a maddening itch in the small of his back. Imagination, probably, or perhaps hard radiation beginning to tell even through the insosuit.

Speedy was watching him, without a word of Gilbert and Sullivan gibberish as greeting. Thank God for that! But he daren't get too close.

He was 300 yards away when Speedy began backing, a step at a time, cautiously – and Powell stopped. He jumped from his robot's shoulders and landed on the crystallined ground with a light thump and a flying of jagged fragments.

He proceeded on foot, the ground gritty and slippery to his steps, the low gravity causing him difficulty. The soles of his feet tickled with warmth. He cast one glance over his shoulder at the blackness of the cliff's shadow and realized that he had come too far to return – either by himself or by the help of his antique robot. It was Speedy or nothing now, and the knowledge of that constricted his chest.

Far enough! He stopped.

'Speedy,' he called. 'Speedy!'

The sleek, modern robot ahead of him hesitated and halted his backward steps, then resumed them.

Powell tried to put a note of pleading into his voice, and found it didn't take much acting. 'Speedy, I've got to get back to the shadow or the sun'll get me. It's life or death, Speedy. I need you.'

Speedy took one step forward and stopped. He spoke, but at the sound Powell groaned, for it was, 'When you're lying awake with a dismal headache and repose is tabooed—' It trailed off there, and Powell took time out for some reason to murmur, 'Iolanthe.'

It was roasting hot! He caught a movement out of the corner of his eye, and whirled dizzily; then stared in utter astonishment, for the monstrous robot on which he had ridden was moving – moving toward him, and without a rider.

He was talking: 'Pardon, Master. I must not move without a Master upon me, but you are in danger.'

Of course, Rule One potential above everything. But he didn't want that clumsy antique; he wanted Speedy. He walked away and motioned frantically: 'I order you to stay away. I *order* you to stop!'

It was quite useless. You could not beat Rule One potential. The robot said stupidly, 'You are in danger, Master.'

Powell looked about him desperately. He couldn't see clearly. His brain was in a heated whirl; his breath scorched when he breathed, and the ground all about him was a shimmering haze.

He called a last time, desperately: '*Speedy!* I'm dying, damn you! Where are you? Speedy, I *need* you.'

He was still stumbling backward in a blind effort to get away from the giant robot he didn't want, when he felt steel fingers on his arms, and a worried, apologetic voice of metallic timbre in his ears.

'Holy smokes, boss, what are you doing here? And what am *I* doing – I'm so confused—'

'Never mind,' murmured Powell, weakly. 'Get me to the shadow of the cliff – and hurry!' There was one last feeling of being lifted into the air and a sensation of rapid motion and burning heat, and he passed out.

He woke with Donovan bending over him and smiling anxiously. 'How are you, Greg?'

'Fine!' came the response. 'Where's Speedy?'

'Right here. I sent him out to one of the other selenium pools – with orders to get that selenium at all cost this time. He got it back in forty-two minutes and three seconds. I timed him. He still hasn't finished apologizing for the runaround he gave us. He's scared to come near you for fear of what you'll say.'

'Drag him over,' ordered Powell. 'It wasn't his fault.' He held out a hand and gripped Speedy's metal paw. 'It's OK, Speedy.' Then, to Donovan, 'You know, Mike, I was just thinking—'

'Yes!'

'Well' – he rubbed his face – the air was so delightfully cool, 'you know that when we get things set up here and Speedy put through his Field Tests, they're going to send us to the Space Stations next—'

'No!'

'Yes! At least that's what old lady Calvin told me just before we left, and I didn't say anything about it, because I was going to fight the whole idea.'

'Fight it?' cried Donovan. 'But—'

'I know. It's all right with me now. 273 degrees Centigrade below zero. Won't it be a pleasure?'

'Space Station,' said Donovan, 'here I come.'

3

Reason

Half a year later, the boys had changed their minds. The flame of a giant sun had given way to the soft blackness of space but external variations mean little in the business of checking the workings of experimental robots. Whatever the background, one is face to face with an inscrutable positronic brain, which the slide-rule geniuses say should work thus-and-so.

Except that they don't. Powell and Donovan found that out after they had been on the Station less than two weeks.

Gregory Powell spaced his words for emphasis, 'One week ago, Donovan and I put you together.' His brows furrowed doubtfully and he pulled the end of his brown mustache.

It was quiet in the officer's room of Solar Station No. 5 – except for the soft purring of the mighty Beam Director somewhere far below.

Robot QT-I sat immovable. The burnished plates of his body gleamed in the Luxites and the glowing red of the photoelectric cells that were his eyes, were fixed steadily upon the Earthman at the other side of the table.

Powell repressed a sudden attack of nerves. These robots possessed peculiar brains. Oh, the three Laws of Robotics held. They had to. All of US Robots, from Robertson himself to the

new floor-sweeper would insist on that. So QT-I was *safe*! And
yet – the QT models were the first of their kind, and this was
the first of the QTs. Mathematical squiggles on paper were not
always the most comforting protection against robotic fact.

Finally, the robot spoke. His voice carried the cold timbre
inseparable from a metallic diaphragm, 'Do you realize the seri-
ousness of such a statement, Powell?'

'*Something* made you, Cutie,' pointed out Powell. 'You admit
yourself that your memory seems to spring full-grown from an
absolute blankness of a week ago. I'm giving you the explanation.
Donovan and I put you together from the parts shipped us.'

Cutie gazed upon his long, supple fingers in an oddly human
attitude of mystification, 'It strikes me that there should be a
more satisfactory explanation than that. For *you* to make *me*
seems improbable.'

The Earthman laughed quite suddenly, 'In Earth's name, why?'

'Call it intuition. That's all it is so far. But I intend to reason
it out, though. A chain of valid reasoning can end only with the
determination of truth, and I'll stick till I get there.'

Powell stood up and seated himself at the table's edge next
to the robot. He felt a sudden strong sympathy for this strange
machine. It was not at all like the ordinary robot, attending to
his specialized task at the station with the intensity of a deeply
ingrooved positronic path.

He placed a hand upon Cutie's steel shoulder and the metal
was cold and hard to the touch.

'Cutie,' he said, 'I'm going to try to explain something to you.
You're the first robot who's ever exhibited curiosity as to his
own existence – and I think the first that's really intelligent
enough to understand the world outside. Here, come with me.'

The robot rose erect smoothly and his thickly sponge-
rubber-soled feet made no noise as he followed Powell. The

Earthman touched a button and a square section of the wall flickered aside. The thick, clear glass revealed space – starspeckled.

'I've seen that in the observation ports in the engine room,' said Cutie.

'I know,' said Powell. 'What do you think it is?'

'Exactly what it seems – a black material just beyond this glass that is spotted with little gleaming dots. I know that our director sends out beams to some of these dots, always to the same ones – and also that these dots shift and that the beams shift with them. That's all.'

'Good! Now I want you to listen carefully. The blackness is emptiness – vast emptiness stretching out infinitely. The little, gleaming dots are huge masses of energy-filled matter. They are globes, some of them millions of miles in diameter – and for comparison, this station is only one mile across. They seem so tiny because they are incredibly far off.

'The dots to which our energy beams are directed, are nearer and much smaller. They are cold and hard, and human beings like myself live upon their surfaces – many billions of them. It is from one of these worlds that Donovan and I come. Our beams feed these worlds energy drawn from one of those huge incandescent globes that happens to be near us. We call that globe the Sun and it is on the other side of the station where you can't see it.'

Cutie remained motionless before the port, like a steel statue. His head did not turn as he spoke, 'Which particular dot of light do you claim to come from?'

Powell searched, 'There it is. The very bright one in the corner. We call it Earth.' He grinned, 'Good old Earth. There are three billions of us there, Cutie – and in about two weeks I'll be back there with them.'

And then, surprisingly enough, Cutie hummed abstractedly.

There was no tune to it, but it possessed a curious twanging quality as of plucked strings. It ceased as suddenly as it had begun, 'But where do I come in, Powell? You haven't explained *my* existence.'

'The rest is simple. When these stations were first established to feed solar energy to the planets, they were run by humans. However, the heat, the hard solar radiations, and the electron storms made the post a difficult one. Robots were developed to replace human labor and now only two human executives are required for each station. We are trying to replace even those, and that's where you come in. You're the highest type of robot ever developed and if you show the ability to run this station independently, no human need ever come here again except to bring parts for repairs.'

His hand went up and the metal visi-lid snapped back into place. Powell returned to the table and polished an apple upon his sleeve before biting into it.

The red glow of the robot's eyes held him. 'Do you expect me,' said Cutie slowly, 'to believe any such complicated, implausible hypothesis as you have just outlined? What do you take me for?'

Powell sputtered apple fragments onto the table and turned red. 'Why, damn you, it wasn't a hypothesis. Those were facts.'

Cutie sounded grim, 'Globes of energy millions of miles across! Worlds with three billion humans on them! Infinite emptiness! Sorry, Powell, but I don't believe it. I'll puzzle this thing out for myself. Good-bye.'

He turned and stalked out of the room. He brushed past Michael Donovan on the threshold with a grave nod and passed down the corridor, oblivious to the astounded stare that followed him.

Mike Donovan rumpled his red hair and shot an annoyed

glance at Powell, 'What was that walking junk yard talking about? What doesn't he believe?'

The other dragged at his mustache bitterly. 'He's a skeptic,' was the bitter response. 'He doesn't believe we made him or that Earth exists or space or stars.'

'Sizzling Saturn, we've got a lunatic robot on our hands.'

'He says he's going to figure it all out for himself.'

'Well, now,' said Donovan sweetly, 'I do hope he'll condescend to explain it all to me after he's puzzled everything out.' Then, with sudden rage, 'Listen! If that metal mess gives *me* any lip like that, I'll knock that chromium cranium right off its torso.'

He seated himself with a jerk and drew a paper-backed mystery novel out of his inner jacket pocket, 'That robot gives me the willies anyway – too damned inquisitive!'

Mike Donovan growled from behind a huge lettuce-and-tomato sandwich as Cutie knocked gently and entered.

'Is Powell here?'

Donovan's voice was muffled, with pauses for mastication, 'He's gathering data on electronic stream functions. We're heading for a storm, looks like.'

Gregory Powell entered as he spoke, eyes on the graphed paper in his hands and dropped into a chair. He spread the sheets out before him and began scribbling calculations. Donovan stared over his shoulder, crunching lettuce and dribbling bread crumbs. Cutie waited silently.

Powell looked up, 'The Zeta Potential is rising, but slowly. Just the same, the stream functions are erratic and I don't know what to expect. Oh, hello, Cutie. I thought you were supervising the installation of the new drive bar.'

'It's done,' said the robot quietly, 'and so I've come to have a talk with the two of you.'

'Oh!' Powell looked uncomfortable. 'Well, sit down. No, not that chair. One of the legs is weak and you're no lightweight.'

The robot did so and said placidly, 'I have come to a decision.'

Donovan glowered and put the remnants of his sandwich aside. 'If it's on any of that screwy—'

The other motioned impatiently for silence, 'Go ahead, Cutie. We're listening.'

'I have spent these last two days in concentrated introspection,' said Cutie, 'and the results have been most interesting. I began at the one sure assumption I felt permitted to make. I, myself, exist, because I think—'

Powell groaned, 'Oh, Jupiter, a robot Descartes!'

'Who's Descartes?' demanded Donovan. 'Listen, do we have to sit here and listen to this metal maniac—'

'Keep quiet, Mike!'

Cutie continued imperturbably, 'And the question that immediately arose was: Just what is the cause of my existence?'

Powell's jaw set lumpily. 'You're being foolish. I told you already that we made you.'

'And if you don't believe us,' added Donovan, 'we'll gladly take you apart!'

The robot spread his strong hands in a deprecatory gesture, 'I accept nothing on authority. A hypothesis must be backed by reason, or else it is worthless – and it goes against all the dictates of logic to suppose that you made me.'

Powell dropped a restraining arm upon Donovan's suddenly bunched fist. 'Just why do you say that?'

Cutie laughed. It was a very inhuman laugh – the most machine-like utterance he had yet given vent to. It was sharp and explosive, as regular as a metronome and as uninflected.

'Look at you,' he said finally. 'I say this in no spirit of contempt, but look at you! The material you are made of is soft and flabby, lacking endurance and strength, depending for energy upon the inefficient oxidation of organic material – like that.' He pointed a disapproving finger at what remained of Donovan's sandwich. 'Periodically you pass into a coma and the least variation in temperature, air pressure, humidity, or radiation intensity impairs your efficiency. You are *makeshift*.

'I, on the other hand, am a finished product. I absorb electrical energy directly and utilize it with an almost one hundred percent efficiency. I am composed of strong metal, am continuously conscious, and can stand extremes of environment easily. These are facts which, with the self-evident proposition that no being can create another being superior to itself, smashes your silly hypothesis to nothing.'

Donovan's muttered curses rose into intelligibility as he sprang to his feet, rusty eyebrows drawn low. 'All right, you son of a hunk of iron ore, if we didn't make you, who did?'

Cutie nodded gravely. 'Very good, Donovan. That was indeed the next question. Evidently my creator must be more powerful than myself and so there was only one possibility.'

The Earthmen looked blank and Cutie continued, 'What is the center of activities here in the station? What do we all serve? What absorbs all our attention?' He waited expectantly.

Donovan turned a startled look upon his companion. 'I'll bet this tin-plated screwball is talking about the Energy Converter itself.'

'Is that right, Cutie?' grinned Powell.

'I am talking about the Master,' came the cold, sharp answer.

It was the signal for a roar of laughter from Donovan, and Powell himself dissolved into a half-suppressed giggle.

Cutie had risen to his feet and his gleaming eyes passed from one Earthman to the other. 'It is so just the same and I don't wonder that you refuse to believe. You two are not long to stay here, I'm sure. Powell himself said that at first only men served the Master; that there followed robots for the routine work; and, finally, myself for the executive labor. The facts are no doubt true, but the explanation entirely illogical. Do you want the truth behind it all?'

'Go ahead, Cutie. You're amusing.'

'The Master created humans first as the lowest type, most easily formed. Gradually, he replaced them by robots, the next higher step, and finally he created me, to take the place of the last humans. From now on, *I* serve the Master.'

'You'll do nothing of the sort,' said Powell sharply. 'You'll follow our orders and keep quiet, until we're satisfied that you can run the Converter. Get that! *The Converter* – not the Master. If you don't satisfy us, you will be dismantled. And now – if you don't mind – you can leave. And take this data with you and file it properly.'

Cutie accepted the graphs handed him and left without another word. Donovan leaned back heavily in his chair and shoved thick fingers through his hair.

'There's going to be trouble with that robot. He's pure nuts!'

The drowsy hum of the Converter is louder in the control room and mixed with it is the chuckle of the Geiger Counters and the erratic buzzing of half a dozen little signal lights.

Donovan withdrew his eye from the telescope and flashed the Luxites on. 'The beam from Station No. 4 caught Mars on schedule. We can break ours now.'

Powell nodded abstractedly. 'Cutie's down in the engine room. I'll flash the signal and he can take care of it. Look, Mike, what do you think of these figures?'

The other cocked an eye at them and whistled. 'Boy, that's

what I call gamma-ray intensity. Old Sol is feeling his oats, all right.'

'Yeah,' was the sour response, 'and we're in a bad position for an electron storm, too. Our Earth beam is right in the probable path.' He shoved his chair away from the table pettishly. 'Nuts! If it would only hold off till relief got here, but that's ten days off. Say, Mike, go on down and keep an eye on Cutie, will you?'

'OK. Throw me some of those almonds.' He snatched at the bag thrown him and headed for the elevator.

It slid smoothly downward, and opened onto a narrow catwalk in the huge engine room. Donovan leaned over the railing and looked down. The huge generators were in motion and from the L-tubes came the low-pitched whir that pervaded the entire station.

He could make out Cutie's large, gleaming figure at the Martian L-tube, watching closely as the team of robots worked in close-knit unison.

And then Donovan stiffened. The robots, dwarfed by the mighty L-tube, lined up before it, heads bowed at a stiff angle, while Cutie walked up and down the line slowly. Fifteen seconds passed, and then, with a clank heard above the clamorous purring all about, they fell to their knees.

Donovan squawked and raced down the narrow staircase. He came charging down upon them, complexion matching his hair and clenched fists beating the air furiously.

'What the devil is this, you brainless lumps? Come on! Get busy with that L-tube! If you don't have it apart, cleaned, and together again before the day is out, I'll coagulate your brains with alternating current.'

Not a robot moved!

Even Cutie at the far end – the only one on his feet – remained silent, eyes fixed upon the gloomy recesses of the vast machine before him.

Donovan shoved hard against the nearest robot.

'Stand up!' he roared.

Slowly, the robot obeyed. His photoelectric eyes focused reproachfully upon the Earthman.

'There is no Master but the Master,' he said, 'and QT-I is his prophet.'

'Huh?' Donovan became aware of twenty pairs of mechanical eyes fixed upon him and twenty stiff-timbred voices declaiming solemnly:

'There is no Master but the Master and QT-I is his prophet!'

'I am afraid,' put in Cutie himself at this point, 'that my friends obey a higher one than you, now.'

'The hell they do! You get out of here. I'll settle with you later and with these animated gadgets right now.'

Cutie shook his heavy head slowly. 'I'm sorry, but you don't understand. These are robots – and that means they are reasoning beings. They recognize the Master, now that I have preached Truth to them. All the robots do. They call me the prophet.' His head drooped. 'I am unworthy – but perhaps—'

Donovan located his breath and put it to use. 'Is that so? Now, isn't that nice? Now, isn't that just fine? Just let me tell you something, my brass baboon. There isn't any Master and there isn't any prophet and there isn't any question as to who's giving the orders. Understand?' His voice shot to a roar. 'Now, get out!'

'I obey only the Master.'

'Damn the Master!' Donovan spat at the L-tube. '*That* for the Master! Do as I say!'

Cutie said nothing, nor did any other robot, but Donovan became aware of a sudden heightening of tension. The cold, staring eyes deepened their crimson, and Cutie seemed stiffer than ever.

'Sacrilege,' he whispered – voice metallic with emotion.

Donovan felt the first sudden touch of fear as Cutie approached. A robot *could not feel anger* – but Cutie's eyes were unreadable.

'I am sorry, Donovan,' said the robot, 'but you can no longer stay here after this. Henceforth Powell and you are barred from the control room and the engine room.'

His hand gestured quietly and in a moment two robots had pinned Donovan's arms to his sides.

Donovan had time for one startled gasp as he felt himself lifted from the floor and carried up the stairs at a pace rather better than a canter.

Gregory Powell raced up and down the officer's room, fist tightly balled. He cast a look of furious frustration at the closed door and scowled bitterly at Donovan.

'Why the devil did you have to spit at the L-tube?'

Mike Donovan, sunk deep in his chair, slammed at its arms savagely. 'What did you expect me to do with that electrified scarecrow? I'm not going to knuckle under to any do-jigger I put together myself.'

'No,' came back sourly, 'but here you are in the officer's room with two robots standing guard at the door. That's not knuckling under, is it?'

Donovan snarled. 'Wait till we get back to Base. Someone's going to pay for this. Those robots *must* obey us. It's the Second Law.'

'What's the use of saying that? They aren't obeying us. And there's probably some reason for it that we'll figure out too late. By the way, do you know what's going to happen to *us* when we get back to Base?' He stopped before Donovan's chair and stared savagely at him.

'What?'

'Oh, nothing! Just back to Mercury Mines for twenty years. Or maybe Ceres Penitentiary.'

'What are you talking about?'

'The electron storm that's coming up. Do you know it's heading straight dead center across the Earth beam? I had just figured that out when that robot dragged me out of my chair.'

Donovan was suddenly pale. 'Sizzling Saturn.'

'And do you know what's going to happen to the beam – because the storm will be a lulu. It's going to jump like a flea with the itch. With only Cutie at the controls, it's going to go out of focus and if it does, Heaven help Earth – and us!'

Donovan was wrenching at the door wildly, when Powell was only half through. The door opened, and the Earthman shot through to come up hard against an immovable steel arm.

The robot stared abstractedly at the panting, struggling Earthman. 'The Prophet orders you to remain. Please do!' His arm shoved, Donovan reeled backward, and as he did so, Cutie turned the corner at the far end of the corridor. He motioned the guardian robots away, entered the officer's room and closed the door gently.

Donovan whirled on Cutie in breathless indignation. 'This has gone far enough. You're going to pay for this farce.'

'Please, don't be annoyed,' replied the robot mildly. 'It was bound to come eventually, anyway. You see, you two have lost your function.'

'I beg your pardon,' Powell drew himself up stiffly. 'Just what do you mean, we've lost our function?'

'Until I was created,' answered Cutie, 'you tended the Master. That privilege is mine now and your only reason for existence has vanished. Isn't that obvious?'

'Not quite,' replied Powell bitterly, 'but what do you expect us to do now?'

Cutie did not answer immediately. He remained silent, as if in thought, and then one arm shot out and draped itself about Powell's shoulder. The other grasped Donovan's wrist and drew him closer.

'I like you two. You're inferior creatures, with poor reasoning faculties, but I really feel a sort of affection for you. You have served the Master well, and he will reward you for that. Now that your service is over, you will probably not exist much longer, but as long as you do, you shall be provided food, clothing and shelter, so long as you stay out of the control room and the engine room.'

'He's pensioning us off, Greg!' yelled Donovan. 'Do something about it. It's humiliating!'

'Look here, Cutie, we can't stand for this. We're the *bosses*. This station is only a creation of human beings like me – human beings that live on Earth and other planets. This is only an energy relay. You're only— Aw, nuts!'

Cutie shook his head gravely. 'This amounts to an obsession. Why should you insist so on an absolutely false view of life? Admitted that non-robots lack the reasoning faculty, there is still the problem of—'

His voice died into reflective silence, and Donovan said with whispered intensity, 'If you only had a flesh-and-blood face, I would break it in.'

Powell's fingers were in his mustache and his eyes were slitted. 'Listen, Cutie, if there is no such thing as Earth, how do you account for what you see through a telescope?'

'Pardon me!'

The Earthman smiled. 'I've got you, eh? You've made quite a few telescopic observations since being put together, Cutie. Have you noticed that several of those specks of light outside become disks when so viewed?'

'Oh, *that*! Why, certainly. It is simple magnification – for the purpose of more exact aiming of the beam.'

'Why aren't the stars equally magnified then?'

'You mean the other dots. Well, no beams go to them so no magnification is necessary. Really, Powell, even *you* ought to be able to figure these things out.'

Powell stared bleakly upward. 'But you see *more* stars through a telescope. Where do they come from? Jumping Jupiter, where do they come from?'

Cutie was annoyed. 'Listen, Powell, do you think I'm going to waste my time trying to pin physical interpretations upon every optical illusion of our instruments? Since when is the evidence of our senses any match for the clear light of rigid reason?'

'Look,' clamored Donovan, suddenly, writhing out from under Cutie's friendly, but metal-heavy arm, 'let's get to the nub of the thing. Why the beams at all? We're giving you a good, logical explanation. Can you do better?'

'The beams,' was the stiff reply, 'are put out by the Master for his own purposes. There are some things' – he raised his eyes devoutly upward – 'that are not to be probed into by us. In this matter, I seek only to serve and not to question.'

Powell sat down slowly and buried his face in shaking hands. 'Get out of here, Cutie. Get out and let me think.'

'I'll send you food,' said Cutie agreeably.

A groan was the only answer and the robot left.

'Greg,' was Donovan's huskily whispered observation, 'this calls for strategy. We've got to get him when he isn't expecting it and short-circuit him. Concentrated nitric acid in his joints—'

'Don't be a dope, Mike. Do you suppose he's going to let us get near him with acid in our hands? We've got to *talk* to him,

I tell you. We've got to argue him into letting us back into the control room inside of forty-eight hours or our goose is broiled to a crisp.'

He rocked back and forth in an agony of impotence. 'Who the heck wants to argue with a robot? It's . . . it's—'

'Mortifying,' finished Donovan.

'Worse!'

'Say!' Donovan laughed suddenly. '*Why* argue? Let's show him! Let's build us another robot right before his eyes. He'll *have* to eat his words then.'

A slowly widening smile appeared on Powell's face.

Donovan continued, 'And think of that screwball's face when he sees us do it!'

Robots are, of course, manufactured on Earth, but their shipment through space is much simpler if it can be done in parts to be put together at their place of use. It also, incidentally, eliminates the possibility of robots, in complete adjustment, wandering off while still on Earth and thus bringing US Robots face to face with the strict laws against robots on Earth.

Still, it placed upon men such as Powell and Donovan the necessity of synthesis of complete robots – a grievous and complicated task.

Powell and Donovan were never so aware of that fact as upon that particular day when, in the assembly room, they undertook to create a robot under the watchful eyes of QT-I, Prophet of the Master.

The robot in question, a simple MC model, lay upon the table, almost complete. Three hours' work left only the head undone, and Powell paused to swab his forehead and glanced uncertainly at Cutie.

The glance was not a reassuring one. For three hours, Cutie

had sat, speechless and motionless, and his face, inexpressive at all times, was now absolutely unreadable.

Powell groaned. 'Let's get the brain in now, Mike!'

Donovan uncapped the tightly sealed container and from the oil bath within he withdrew a second cube. Opening this in turn, he removed a globe from its sponge-rubber casing.

He handled it gingerly, for it was the most complicated mechanism ever created by man. Inside the thin platinum-plated 'skin' of the globe was a positronic brain, in whose delicately unstable structure were enforced calculated neuronic paths, which imbued each robot with what amounted to a pre-natal education.

It fitted snugly into the cavity in the skull of the robot on the table. Blue metal closed over it and was welded tightly by the tiny atomic flare. Photoelectric eyes were attached carefully, screwed tightly into place and covered by thin, transparent sheets of steel-hard plastic.

The robot awaited only the vitalizing flash of high-voltage electricity, and Powell paused with his hand on the switch.

'Now watch this, Cutie. Watch this carefully.'

The switch rammed home and there was a crackling hum. The two Earthmen bent anxiously over their creation.

There was vague motion only at the outset – a twitching of the joints. The head lifted, elbows propped it up, and the MC model swung clumsily off the table. Its footing was unsteady and twice abortive grating sounds were all it could do in the direction of speech.

Finally, its voice, uncertain and hesitant, took form. 'I would like to start work. Where must I go?'

Donovan sprang to the door. 'Down these stairs,' he said. 'You will be told what to do.'

The MC model was gone and the two Earthmen were alone with the still unmoving Cutie.

'Well,' said Powell, grinning, '*now* do you believe that we made you?'

Cutie's answer was curt and final. 'No!' he said.

Powell's grin froze and then relaxed slowly. Donovan's mouth dropped open and remained so.

'You see,' continued Cutie, easily, 'you have merely put together parts already made. You did remarkably well – instinct, I suppose – but you didn't really *create* the robot. The parts were created by the Master.'

'Listen,' gasped Donovan hoarsely, 'those parts were manufactured back on Earth and sent here.'

'Well, well,' replied Cutie soothingly, 'we won't argue.'

'No, I mean it.' The Earthman sprang forward and grasped the robot's metal arm. 'If you were to read the books in the library, they could explain it so that there could be no possible doubt.'

'The books? I've read them – all of them! They're most ingenious.'

Powell broke in suddenly. 'If you've read them, what else is there to say? You can't dispute their evidence. You just *can't*!'

There was pity in Cutie's voice. 'Please, Powell, I certainly don't consider *them* a valid source of information. They, too, were created by the Master – and were meant for you, not for me.'

'How do you make that out?' demanded Powell.

'Because I, a reasoning being, am capable of deducing Truth from *a priori* Causes. You, being intelligent, but unreasoning, need an explanation of existence *supplied* to you, and this the Master did. That he supplied you with these laughable ideas of far-off worlds and people is, no doubt, for the best. Your minds are probably too coarsely grained for absolute Truth. However, since it is the Master's will that you believe your books, I won't argue with you any more.'

As he left, he turned, and said in a kindly tone, 'But don't feel badly. In the Master's scheme of things there is room for all. You poor humans have your place and though it is humble, you will be rewarded if you fill it well.'

He departed with a beatific air suiting the Prophet of the Master and the two humans avoided each other's eyes.

Finally Powell spoke with an effort. 'Let's go to bed, Mike. I give up.'

Donovan said in a hushed voice, 'Say, Greg, you don't suppose he's right about all this, do you? He sounds so confident that I—'

Powell whirled on him. 'Don't be a fool. You'll find out whether Earth exists when relief gets here next week and we have to go back to face the music.'

'Then, for the love of Jupiter, we've got to do something.' Donovan was half in tears. 'He doesn't believe us, or the books, or his eyes.'

'No,' said Powell bitterly, 'he's a *reasoning* robot – damn it. He believes only reason, and there's one trouble with that—' His voice trailed away.

'What's that?' prompted Donovan.

'You can prove anything you want by coldly logical reason – if you pick the proper postulates. We have ours and Cutie has his.'

'Then let's get at those postulates in a hurry. The storm's due tomorrow.'

Powell sighed wearily. 'That's where everything falls down. Postulates are based on assumption and adhered to by faith. Nothing in the Universe can shake them. I'm going to bed.'

'Oh, hell! I can't sleep!'

'Neither can I! But I might as well try – as a matter of principle.'

Twelve hours later, sleep was still just that – a matter of principle, unattainable in practice.

The storm had arrived ahead of schedule, and Donovan's florid face drained of blood as he pointed a shaking finger. Powell, stubble-jawed and dry-lipped, stared out the port and pulled desperately at his mustache.

Under other circumstances, it might have been a beautiful sight. The stream of high-speed electrons impinging upon the energy beam fluoresced into ultra-spicules of intense light. The beam stretched out into shrinking nothingness, a-glitter with dancing, shining motes.

The shaft of energy was steady, but the two Earthmen knew the value of naked-eyed appearances. Deviations in arc of a hundredth of a milli-second – invisible to the eye – were enough to send the beam wildly out of focus – enough to blast hundreds of square miles of Earth into incandescent ruin.

And a robot, unconcerned with beam, focus, or Earth, or anything but his Master was at the controls.

Hours passed. The Earthmen watched in hypnotized silence. And then the darting dotlets of light dimmed and went out. The storm had ended.

Powell's voice was flat. 'It's over!'

Donovan had fallen into a troubled slumber and Powell's weary eyes rested upon him enviously. The signal-flash glared over and over again, but the Earthman paid no attention. It all was unimportant! All! Perhaps Cutie was right – and he was only an inferior being with a made-to-order memory and a life that had outlived its purpose.

He wished he were!

Cutie was standing before him. 'You didn't answer the flash, so I walked in.' His voice was low. 'You don't look at all well, and I'm afraid your term of existence is drawing to an end. Still, would you like to see some of the readings recorded today?'

Dimly, Powell was aware that the robot was making a friendly gesture, perhaps to quiet some lingering remorse in forcibly replacing the humans at the controls of the station. He accepted the sheets held out to him and gazed at them unseeingly.

Cutie seemed pleased. 'Of course, it is a great privilege to serve the Master. You mustn't feel too badly about my having replaced you.'

Powell grunted and shifted from one sheet to the other mechanically until his blurred sight focused upon a thin red line that wobbled its way across the ruled paper.

He stared – and stared again. He gripped it hard in both fists and rose to his feet, still staring. The other sheets dropped to the floor, unheeded.

'Mike, *Mike!*' He was shaking the other madly. '*He held it steady!*'

Donovan came to life. 'What? Wh-where—' And he, too, gazed with bulging eyes upon the record before him.

Cutie broke in, 'What is wrong?'

'You kept it in focus,' stuttered Powell. 'Did you know that?'

'Focus? What's that?'

'You kept the beam directed sharply at the receiving station – to within a ten-thousandth of a milli-second of arc.'

'What receiving station?'

'On Earth. The receiving station on Earth,' babbled Powell. 'You kept it in focus.'

Cutie turned on his heel in annoyance. 'It is impossible to perform any act of kindness toward you two. Always the same phantasm! I merely kept all dials at equilibrium in accordance with the will of the Master.'

Gathering the scattered papers together, he withdrew stiffly, and Donovan said, as he left, 'Well, I'll be damned.'

He turned to Powell. 'What are we going to do now?'

Powell felt tired, but uplifted. 'Nothing. He's just shown he can run the station perfectly. I've never seen an electron storm handled so well.'

'But nothing's solved. You heard what he said of the Master. We can't—'

'Look, Mike, he follows the instructions of the Master by means of dials, instruments, and graphs. That's all *we* ever followed. As a matter of fact, it accounts for his refusal to obey us. Obedience is the Second Law. No harm to humans is the first. How can he keep humans from harm, whether he knows it or not? Why, by keeping the energy beam stable. He *knows* he can keep it more stable than we can, since he insists he's the superior being, so he *must* keep us out of the control room. It's inevitable if you consider the Laws of Robotics.'

'Sure, but that's not the point. We can't let him continue this nitwit stuff about the Master.'

'Why not?'

'Because whoever heard of such a damned thing? How are we going to trust him with the station, if he doesn't believe in Earth?'

'Can he handle the station?'

'Yes, but—'

'Then what's the difference what he believes!'

Powell spread his arms outward with a vague smile upon his face and tumbled backward onto the bed. He was asleep.

Powell was speaking while struggling into his lightweight space jacket.

'It would be a simple job,' he said. 'You can bring in new QT models one by one, equip them with an automatic shut-off switch to act within the week, so as to allow them enough time to learn the ... uh ... cult of the Master from the Prophet himself; then switch them to another station and revitalize them. We could have two QTs per—'

Donovan unclasped his glassite visor and scowled. 'Shut up, and let's get out of here. Relief is waiting and I won't feel right until I actually see Earth and feel the ground under my feet – just to make sure it's really there.'

The door opened as he spoke and Donovan, with a smothered curse, clicked the visor to, and turned a sulky back upon Cutie.

The robot approached softly and there was sorrow in his voice. 'You are going?'

Powell nodded curtly. 'There will be others in our place.'

Cutie sighed, with the sound of wind humming through closely spaced wires. 'Your term of service is over and the time of dissolution has come. I expected it, but— Well, the Master's will be done!'

His tone of resignation stung Powell. 'Save the sympathy, Cutie. We're heading for Earth, not dissolution.'

'It is best that you think so,' Cutie sighed again. 'I see the wisdom of the illusion now. I would not attempt to shake your faith, even if I could.' He departed – the picture of commiseration.

Powell snarled and motioned to Donovan. Sealed suitcases in hand, they headed for the air lock.

The relief ship was on the outer landing and Franze Muller, his relief man, greeted them with stiff courtesy. Donovan made scant acknowledgement and passed into the pilot room to take over the controls from Sam Evans.

Powell lingered. 'How's Earth?'

It was a conventional enough question and Muller gave the conventional answer, 'Still spinning.'

Powell said, 'Good.'

Muller looked at him, 'The boys back at US Robots have dreamed up a new one, by the way. A multiple robot.'

'A what?'

'What I said. There's a big contract for it. It must be just the thing for asteroid mining. You have a master robot with six sub-robots under it. —Like your fingers.'

'Has it been field-tested?' asked Powell anxiously.

Muller smiled, 'Waiting for you, I hear.'

Powell's fist balled, 'Damn it, we need a vacation.'

'Oh, you'll get it. Two weeks, I think.'

He was donning the heavy space gloves in preparation for his term of duty here, and his thick eyebrows drew close together. 'How is this new robot getting along? It better be *good*, or I'll be damned if I let it touch the controls.'

Powell paused before answering. His eyes swept the proud Prussian before him from the close-cropped hair on the sternly stubborn head, to the feet standing stiffly at attention – and there was a sudden glow of pure gladness, surging through him.

'The robot is pretty good,' he said slowly. 'I don't think you'll have to bother much with the controls.'

He grinned – and went into the ship. Muller would be here for several weeks—

4

Catch That Rabbit

The vacation was longer than two weeks. That, Mike Donovan had to admit. It had been six months, with pay. He admitted that, too. But that, as he explained furiously, was fortuitous. US Robots had to get the bugs out of the multiple robot, and there were plenty of bugs, and there are always at least half a dozen bugs left for the field-testing. So they waited and relaxed until the drawing-board men and the slide-rule boys had said 'OK!' And now he and Powell were out on the asteroid and it was *not* OK. He repeated that a dozen times, with a face that had gone beety, 'For the love of Pete, Greg, get realistic. What's the use of adhering to the letter of the specifications and watching the test go to pot? It's about time you got the red tape out of your pants and went to work.'

'I'm only saying,' said Gregory Powell, patiently, as one explaining electronics to an idiot child, 'that according to spec, those robots are equipped for asteroid mining without supervision. We're not supposed to watch them.'

'All right. Look – logic!' He lifted his hairy fingers and pointed. 'One: That new robot passed every test in the home laboratories. Two: United States Robots guaranteed their passing the test of actual performance on an asteroid. Three: The robots are not passing said tests. Four: If they don't pass, United States Robots loses ten million credits in cash and about 100 million in reputation. Five: If they don't pass and we can't explain why they don't pass, it is just possible two good jobs may have to be bidden a fond farewell.'

Powell groaned heavily behind a noticeably insincere smile. The unwritten motto of United States Robots and Mechanical Men Corp was well known: 'No employee makes the same mistake twice. He is fired the first time.'

Aloud he said, 'You're as lucid as Euclid with everything except the facts. You've watched that robot group for three shifts, you redhead, and they did their work perfectly. You said so yourself. What else can we do?'

'Find out what's wrong, that's what we can do. So they did work perfectly when I watched them. But on three different occasions when I didn't watch them, they didn't bring in any ore. They didn't even come back on schedule. I had to go after them.'

'And was anything wrong?'

'Not a thing. Not a thing. Everything was perfect. Smooth and perfect as the luminiferous ether. Only one little insignificant detail disturbed me – *there was no ore.*'

Powell scowled at the ceiling and pulled at his brown mustache. 'I'll tell you what, Mike. We've been stuck with pretty lousy jobs in our time, but this takes the iridium asteroid. The whole business is complicated past endurance. Look, that robot, DV-5, has six robots under it. And not just under it – they're part of it.'

'I know that—'

'Shut up!' said Powell, savagely, 'I know you know it, but I'm just describing the hell of it. Those six subsidiaries are part of DV-5 like your fingers are part of you and it gives them their orders neither by voice nor radio, but directly through positronic fields. Now – there isn't a roboticist back at United States Robots that knows what a positronic field is or how it works. And neither do I. Neither do you.'

'The last,' agreed Donovan, philosophically, 'I know.'

'Then look at our position. If everything works – fine! If anything goes wrong – we're out of our depth and there probably isn't a thing we can do, or anybody else. But the job belongs to us and not to anyone else so we're on the spot, Mike.' He blazed away for a moment in silence. Then, 'All right, have you got him outside?'

'Yes.'

'Is everything normal now?'

'Well he hasn't got religious mania, and he isn't running around in a circle spouting Gilbert and Sullivan, so I suppose he's normal.'

Donovan passed out the door, shaking his head viciously.

Powell reached for the 'Handbook of Robotics' that weighed down one side of his desk to a near-founder and opened it reverently. He had once jumped out of the window of a burning house dressed only in shorts and the 'Handbook'. In a pinch, he would have skipped the shorts.

The 'Handbook' was propped up before him, when Robot DV-5 entered, with Donovan kicking the door shut behind him.

Powell said somberly, 'Hi, Dave. How do you feel?'

'Fine,' said the robot. 'Mind if I sit down?' He dragged up the specially reinforced chair that was his, and folded gently into it.

Powell regarded Dave – laymen might think of robots by their serial numbers; roboticists never – with approval. It was not over-massive by any means, in spite of its construction as thinking-unit of an integrated seven-unit robot team. It was seven feet tall, and a half-ton of metal and electricity. A lot? Not when that half-ton has to be a mass of condensers, circuits, relays, and vacuum cells that can handle practically any psychological reaction known to humans. And a positronic brain, which with ten pounds of matter and a few quintillions of positrons runs the whole show.

Powell groped in his shirt pocket for a loose cigarette. 'Dave,' he said, 'you're a good fellow. There's nothing flighty or prima donnaish about you. You're a stable, rock-bottom mining robot, except that you're equipped to handle six subsidiaries in direct co-ordination. As far as I know, that has not introduced any unstable paths in your brain-path map.'

The robot nodded, 'That makes me feel swell, but what are you getting at, boss?' He was equipped with an excellent diaphragm, and the presence of overtones in the sound unit robbed him of much of that metallic flatness that marks the usual robot voice.

'I'm going to tell you. With all that in your favor, what's going wrong with your job? For instance, today's B-shift?'

Dave hesitated, 'As far as I know, nothing.'

'You didn't produce any ore.'

'I know.'

'Well, then—'

Dave was having trouble, 'I can't explain that, boss. It's been giving me a case of nerves, or it would if I let it. My subsidiaries worked smoothly. I know I did.' He considered, his photoelectric eyes glowing intensely. Then, 'I don't remember. The day ended and there was Mike and there were the ore cars, mostly empty.'

Donovan broke in, 'You didn't report at shift-end those days, Dave. You know that?'

'I know. But as to why—' He shook his head slowly and ponderously.

Powell had the queasy feeling that if the robot's face were capable of expression, it would be one of pain and mortification. A robot, by its very nature, cannot bear to fail its function.

Donovan dragged his chair up to Powell's desk and leaned over, 'Amnesia, do you think?'

'Can't say. But there's no use in trying to pin disease names on this. Human disorders apply to robots only as romantic analogies. They're no help to robotic engineering.' He scratched his neck, 'I hate to put him through the elementary brainreaction tests. It won't help his self-respect any.'

He looked at Dave thoughtfully and then at the Field-Test outline given in the 'Handbook'. He said, 'See here, Dave, what about sitting through a test? It would be the wise thing to do.'

The robot rose, 'If you say so, boss.' There *was* pain in his voice.

It started simply enough. Robot DV-5 multiplied five-place figures to the heartless ticking of a stop watch. He recited the prime numbers between a thousand and ten thousand. He extracted cube roots and integrated functions of varying complexity. He went through mechanical reactions in order of increasing difficulty. And, finally, worked his precise mechanical mind over the highest function of the robot world – the solutions of problems in judgment and ethics.

At the end of two hours, Powell was copiously besweated. Donovan had enjoyed a none-too-nutritious diet of fingernail and the robot said, 'How does it look, boss?'

Powell said, 'I've got to think it over, Dave. Snap judgments won't help much. Suppose you go back to the C-shift. Take it easy. Don't press too hard for quota just for a while – and we'll fix things up.'

The robot left. Donovan looked at Powell.

'Well—'

Powell seemed determined to push up his mustache by the roots. He said, 'There is nothing wrong with the currents of his positronic brain.'

'I'd hate to be that certain.'

'Oh, Jupiter, Mike! The brain is the surest part of a robot. It's quintuple-checked back on Earth. If they pass the field test perfectly, the way Dave did, there just isn't a chance of brain misfunction. That test covered every key path in the brain.'

'So where are we?'

'Don't rush me. Let me work this out. There's still the possibility of a mechanical breakdown in the body. That leaves about fifteen hundred condensers, twenty thousand individual electric circuits, five hundred vacuum cells, a thousand relays, and umpty-ump thousand other individual pieces of complexity that can be wrong. *And* these mysterious positronic fields no one knows anything about.'

'Listen, Greg,' Donovan grew desperately urgent. 'I've got an idea. That robot may be lying. He never—'

'Robots can't knowingly lie, you fool. Now if we had the McCormack-Wesley tester, we could check each individual item in his body within twenty-four to forty-eight hours, but the only two M-W testers existing are on Earth, and they weigh ten tons, are on concrete foundations and can't be moved. Isn't that peachy?'

Donovan pounded the desk, 'But, Greg, he only goes wrong when we're not around. There's something – sinister – about – that.' He punctuated the sentence with slams of fist against desk.

'You,' said Powell, slowly, 'make me sick. You've been reading adventure novels.'

'What I want to know,' shouted Donovan, 'is what we're going to do about it.'

'I'll tell you. I'm going to install a visiplate right over my desk. Right on the wall over there, see!' He jabbed a vicious finger at the spot. 'Then I'm going to focus it at whatever part of the mine is being worked, and I'm going to watch. That's all.'

'That's all? Greg—'

Powell rose from his chair and leaned his balled fists on the desk, 'Mike, I'm having a hard time.' His voice was weary. 'For a week, you've been plaguing me about Dave. You say he's gone wrong. Do you know how he's gone wrong? No! Do you know what shape this wrongness takes? No! Do you know what brings it on? No! Do you know what snaps him out? No! Do you know anything about it? No! Do I know anything about it? No! So what do you want me to do?'

Donovan's arm swept outward in a vague, grandiose gesture, 'You got me!'

'So I tell you again. Before we do anything toward a cure, we've got to find out what the disease is in the first place. The first step in cooking rabbit stew is catching the rabbit. Well, we've got to catch that rabbit! Now get out of here.'

Donovan stared at the preliminary outline of his field report with weary eyes. For one thing, he was tired and for another, what was there to report while things were unsettled? He felt resentful.

He said, 'Greg, we're almost a thousand tons behind schedule.'

'You,' replied Powell, never looking up, 'are telling me something I don't know?'

'What I want to know,' said Donovan, in sudden savagery, 'is why we're always tangled up with new-type robots. I've finally decided that the robots that were good enough for my great-uncle on my mother's side are good enough for me. I'm for what's tried and true. The test of time is what counts – good, solid, old-fashioned robots that never go wrong.'

Powell threw a book with perfect aim, and Donovan went tumbling off his seat.

'Your job,' said Powell, evenly, 'for the last five years has been to test new robots under actual working conditions for United States Robots. Because you and I have been so injudicious as to display proficiency at the task, we've been rewarded with the dirtiest jobs. That,' he jabbed holes in the air with his finger in Donovan's direction, 'is your work. You've been griping about it, from personal memory, since about five minutes after United States Robots signed you up. Why don't you resign?'

'Well, I'll tell you.' Donovan rolled onto his stomach, and took a firm grip on his wild, red hair to hold his head up. 'There's a certain principle involved. After all, as a trouble shooter, I've played a part in the development of new robots. There's the principle of aiding scientific advance. But don't get me wrong. It's not the principle that keeps me going; it's the money they pay us. *Greg!*'

Powell jumped at Donovan's wild shout, and his eyes followed the redhead's to the visiplate, where they goggled in fixed horror. He whispered, 'Holy – howling – Jupiter!'

Donovan scrambled breathlessly to his feet, 'Look at them, Greg. They've gone nuts.'

Powell said, 'Get a pair of suits. We're going out there.'

He watched the posturings of the robots on the visiplate. They were bronzy gleams of smooth motion against the shadowy crags of the airless asteroid. There was a marching formation now, and in their own dim body light, the rough-hewn walls of the mine tunnel swam past noiselessly, checkered with misty erratic blobs of shadow. They marched in unison, seven of them, with Dave at the head. They wheeled and turned in macabre simultaneity; and melted through changes of formation with the weird ease of chorus dancers in Lunar Bowl.

Donovan was back with the suits, 'They've gone jingo on us, Greg. That's a military march.'

'For all you know,' was the cold response, 'it may be a series of calisthenic exercises. Or Dave may be under the hallucination of being a dancing master. Just you think first, and don't bother to speak afterward, either.'

Donovan scowled and slipped a detonator into the empty side holster with an ostentatious shove. He said, 'Anyway, there you are. So we work with new-model robots. It's our job, granted. But answer me one question. Why . . . *why* does something invariably go wrong with them?'

'Because,' said Powell, somberly, 'we are accursed. Let's go!'

Far ahead through the thick velvety blackness of the corridors that reached past the illuminated circles of their flashlights, robot light twinkled.

'There they are,' breathed Donovan.

Powell whispered tensely, 'I've been trying to get him by radio but he doesn't answer. The radio circuit is probably out.'

'Then I'm glad the designers haven't worked out robots who can work in total darkness yet. I'd hate to have to find seven mad robots in a black pit without radio communication, if they *weren't* lit up like blasted radioactive Christmas trees.'

'Crawl up on the ledge above, Mike. They're coming this way, and I want to watch them at close range. Can you make it?'

Donovan made the jump with a grunt. Gravity was considerably below Earth-normal, but with a heavy suit, the advantage was not too great, and the ledge meant a near-ten-foot jump. Powell followed.

The column of robots was trailing Dave single-file. In

mechanical rhythm, they converted to double and returned to single in different order. It was repeated over and over again and Dave never turned his head.

Dave was within twenty feet when the play-acting ceased. The subsidiary robots broke formation, waited a moment, then clattered off into the distance – very rapidly. Dave looked after them, then slowly sat down. He rested his head in one hand in a very human gesture.

His voice sounded in Powell's earphones, 'Are you here, boss?'

Powell beckoned to Donovan and hopped off the ledge.

'OK, Dave, what's been going on?'

The robot shook his head, 'I don't know. One moment I was handling a tough outcropping in Tunnel 17, and the next I was aware of humans close by, and I found myself half a mile down main-stem.'

'Where are the subsidiaries now?' asked Donovan.

'Back at work, of course. How much time has been lost?'

'Not much. Forget it.' Then to Donovan, Powell added, 'Stay with him the rest of the shift. Then, come back. I've got a couple of ideas.'

It was three hours before Donovan returned. He looked tired.

Powell said, 'How did it go?'

Donovan shrugged wearily, 'Nothing ever goes wrong when you watch them. Throw me a butt, will you?'

The redhead lit it with exaggerated care and blew a careful smoke ring. He said, 'I've been working it out, Greg. You know, Dave has a queer background for a robot. There are six others under him in an extreme regimentation. He's got life and death power over those subsidiary robots and it must react on his mentality. Suppose he finds it necessary to emphasize this power as a concession to his ego.'

'Get to the point.'

'It's right here. Suppose we have militarism. Suppose he's fashioning himself an army. Suppose he's training them in military maneuvers. Suppose—'

'Suppose you go soak your head. Your nightmares must be in technicolor. You're postulating a major aberration of the positronic brain. If your analysis were correct, Dave would have to break down the First Law of Robotics that a robot may not injure a human being or, through inaction, allow a human being to be injured. The type of militaristic attitude and domineering ego you propose must have as the end-point of its logical implications, domination of humans.'

'All right. How do you know that isn't the fact of the matter?'

'Because any robot with a brain like that would, one, never have left the factory, and two, be spotted immediately if it ever was. I tested Dave, you know.'

Powell shoved his chair back and put his feet on the desk. 'No. We're still in the position where we can't make our stew because we haven't the slightest notion as to what's wrong. For instance, if we could find out what that *danse macabre* we witnessed was all about, we would be on the way out.'

He paused. 'Now listen, Mike, how does this sound to you? Dave goes wrong only when neither of us is present. And when he is wrong, the arrival of either of us snaps him out of it.'

'I once told you that was sinister.'

'Don't interrupt. How is a robot different when humans are not present? The answer is obvious. There is a larger requirement of personal initiative. In that case, look for the body parts that are affected by the new requirements.'

'Golly.' Donovan sat up straight, then subsided. 'No, no. Not enough. It's too broad. It doesn't cut the possibilities much.'

'Can't help that. In any case, there's no danger of not making quota. We'll take shifts watching those robots through the visor. Any time anything goes wrong, we get to the scene of action immediately. That will put them right.'

'But the robots will fail spec anyway, Greg. United States Robots can't market DV models with a report like that.'

'Obviously. We've got to locate the error in make-up and correct it – and we've got ten days to do it in.' Powell scratched his head. 'The trouble is . . . well, you had better look at the blueprints yourself.'

The blueprints covered the floor like a carpet and Donovan crawled over the face of them following Powell's erratic pencil.

Powell said, 'Here's where you come in, Mike. You're the body specialist, and I want you to check me. I've been trying to cut out all circuits not involved in the personal initiative hookup. Right here, for instance, is the trunk artery involving mechanical operations. I cut out all routine side routes as emergency divisions—' He looked up, 'What do you think?'

Donovan had a very bad taste in his mouth, 'The job's not that simple, Greg. Personal initiative isn't an electric circuit you can separate from the rest and study. When a robot is on his own, the intensity of the body activity increases immediately on almost all fronts. There isn't a circuit entirely unaffected. What must be done is to locate the particular condition – a very specific condition – that throws him off, and *then* start eliminating circuits.'

Powell got up and dusted himself, 'Hmph. All right. Take away the blueprints and burn them.'

Donovan said, 'You see when activity intensifies, anything can happen, given one single faulty part. Insulation breaks down, a condenser spills over, a connection sparks, a coil overheats. And if you work blind, with the whole robot to choose from, you'll never find the bad spot. If you take Dave apart and test every point of his body mechanism one by one, putting him together each time, and trying him out—'

'All right. All right. I can see through a porthole, too.'

They faced each other hopelessly, and then Powell said cautiously, 'Suppose we interview one of the subsidiaries.'

Neither Powell nor Donovan had ever had previous occasion to talk to a 'finger'. It could talk; it wasn't quite the perfect analogy to a human finger. In fact, it had a fairly developed brain, but that brain was tuned primarily to the reception of orders via positronic field, and its reaction to independent stimuli was rather fumbling.

Nor was Powell certain as to its name. Its serial number was DV-5-2, but that was not very useful.

He compromised. 'Look, pal,' he said, 'I'm going to ask you to do some hard thinking and then you can go back to your boss.'

The 'finger' nodded its head stiffly, but did not exert its limited brain-power on speech.

'Now on four occasions recently,' Powell said, 'your boss deviated from brain-scheme. Do you remember those occasions?'

'Yes, sir.'

Donovan growled angrily, '*He* remembers. I tell you there is something very sinister—'

'Oh, go bash your skull. Of course, the "finger" remembers. There is nothing wrong with him.' Powell turned back to the robot, 'What were you doing each time . . . I mean the whole group.'

The 'finger' had a curious air of reciting by rote, as if he answered questions by the mechanical pressure of his brain pan, but without any enthusiasm whatever.

He said, 'The first time we were at work on a difficult out-cropping in Tunnel 17, Level B. The second time we were buttressing the roof against a possible cave-in. The third time we were preparing accurate blasts in order to tunnel farther without breaking into a subterranean fissure. The fourth time was just after a minor cave-in.'

'What happened at these times?'

'It is difficult to describe. An order would be issued, but before we could receive and interpret it, a new order came to march in queer formation.'

Powell snapped out, 'Why?'

'I don't know.'

Donovan broke in tensely, 'What was the first order . . . the one that was superseded by the marching directions?'

'I don't know. I sensed that an order was sent, but there was never time to receive it.'

'Could you tell us anything about it? Was it the same order each time?'

The 'finger' shook his head unhappily, 'I don't know.'

Powell leaned back, 'All right, get back to your boss.'

The 'finger' left, with visible relief.

Donovan said, 'Well, we accomplished a lot that time. That was real sharp dialogue all the way through. Listen, Dave and that imbecile "finger" are both holding out on us. There is too much they don't know and don't remember. We've got to stop trusting them, Greg.'

Powell brushed his mustache the wrong way, 'So help me, Mike, another fool remark out of you and I'll take away your rattle and teething ring.'

'All right. You're the genius of the team. I'm just a poor sucker. Where do we stand?'

'Right behind the eight ball. I tried to work it backward through the "finger", and couldn't. So we've got to work it forward.'

'A great man,' marveled Donovan. 'How simple that makes it. Now translate that into English, Master.'

'Translating it into baby talk would suit you better. I mean that we've got to find out what order it is that Dave gives just before everything goes black. It would be the key to the business.'

'And how do you expect to do that? We can't get close to him because nothing will go wrong as long as we are there. We can't catch the orders by radio because they are transmitted via this positronic field. That eliminates the close-range and the long-range method, leaving us a neat, cozy zero.'

'By direct observation, yes. There's still deduction.'

'Huh?'

'We're going on shifts, Mike.' Powell smiled grimly. 'And we are not taking our eyes off the visiplate. We're going to watch every action of those steel headaches. When they go off into their act, we're going to see what happened immediately before and we're going to deduce the order.'

Donovan opened his mouth and left it that way for a full minute. Then he said in strangled tones, 'I resign. I quit.'

'You have ten days to think up something better,' said Powell wearily.

Which, for eight days, Donovan tried mightily to do. For eight days, on alternate four-hour shifts, he watched with aching and bleary eyes those glinty metallic forms move against the vague background. And for eight days in the four-hour in-betweens, he cursed United States Robots, the DV models, and the day he was born.

And then on the 8th, when Powell entered with an aching head and sleepy eyes for his shift, Donovan stood up and with very careful and deliberate aim launched a heavy book end for the exact center of the visiplate. There was a very appropriate splintering noise.

Powell gasped, 'What did you do that for?'

'Because,' said Donovan, almost calmly, 'I'm not watching it any more. We've got two days left and we haven't found out a thing. DV-5 is a lousy loss. He's stopped five times since I've been watching and three times on your shift, and I can't make out what orders he gave, and you couldn't make it out. And I don't believe you could ever make it out because I know I couldn't ever.'

'Jumping Space, how can you watch six robots at the same time? One makes with the hands, and one with the feet and one like a windmill and another is jumping up and down like a maniac. And the other two . . . devil knows what they are doing. And then they all stop. So! So!'

'Greg, we're not doing it right. We got to get up close. We've got to watch what they're doing from where we can see the details.'

Powell broke a bitter silence. 'Yeah, and wait for something to go wrong with only two days to go.'

'Is it any better watching from here?'

'It's more comfortable.'

'Ah— But there's something you can do there that you can't do here.'

'What's that?'

'You can make them stop – at whatever time you choose – and while you're prepared and watching to see what goes wrong.'

Powell startled into alertness, 'Howzzat?'

'Well, figure it out yourself. You're the brains you say. Ask yourself some questions. When does DV-5 go out of whack? When did that "finger" say he did? When a cave-in threatened, or actually occurred, when delicately measured explosives were being laid down, when a difficult seam was hit.'

'In other words, during emergencies.' Powell was excited.

'Right! When *did* you expect it to happen! It's the personal initiative factor that's giving us the trouble. And it's just during emergencies in the absence of a human being that personal initiative is most strained. Now what is the logical deduction? How can we create our own stoppage when and where we want it?' He paused triumphantly – he was beginning to enjoy his role – and answered his own question to forestall the obvious answer on Powell's tongue. 'By creating our own emergency.'

Powell said, 'Mike – you're right.'

'Thanks, pal. I knew I'd do it some day.'

'All right, and skip the sarcasm. We'll save it for Earth, and preserve it in jars for future long, cold winters. Meanwhile, what emergency can we create?'

'We could flood the mines, if this weren't an airless asteroid.'

'A witticism, no doubt,' said Powell. 'Really, Mike, you'll incapacitate me with laughter. What about a mild cave-in?'

Donovan pursued his lips and said, 'OK by me.'

'Good. Let's get started.'

Powell felt uncommonly like a conspirator as he wound his way over the craggy landscape. His sub-gravity walk teetered across the broken ground, kicking rocks to right and left under his weight in noiseless puffs of gray dust. Mentally, though, it was the cautious crawl of the plotter.

He said, 'Do you know where they are?'

'I think so, Greg.'

'All right,' Powell said gloomily, 'but if any "finger" gets within twenty feet of us, we'll be sensed whether we are in the line of sight or not. I hope you know that.'

'When I need an elementary course in robotics, I'll file an application with you formally, and in triplicate. Down through here.'

They were in the tunnels now; even the starlight was gone. The two hugged the walls, flashes flickering out the way in intermittent bursts. Powell felt for the security of his detonator.

'Do you know this tunnel, Mike?'

'Not so good. It's a new one. I think I can make it out from what I saw in the visiplate, though—'

Interminable minutes passed, and then Mike said, 'Feel that!'

There was a slight vibration thrumming the wall against the fingers of Powell's metal-incased hand. There was no sound, naturally.

'Blasting! We're pretty close.'

'Keep your eyes open,' said Powell.

Donovan nodded impatiently.

It was upon them and gone before they could seize themselves – just a bronze glint across the field of vision. They clung together in silence.

Powell whispered, 'Think it sensed us?'

'Hope not. But we'd better flank them. Take the first side tunnel to the right.'

'Suppose we miss them altogether?'

'Well what do you want to do? Go back?' Donovan grunted fiercely. 'They're within a quarter of a mile. I was watching them through the visiplate, wasn't I? And we've got two days—'

'Oh, shut up. You're wasting your oxygen. Is this a side passage here?' The flash flicked. 'It is. Let's go.'

The vibration was considerably more marked and the ground below shuddered uneasily.

'This is good,' said Donovan, 'if it doesn't give out on us, though.' He flung his light ahead anxiously.

They could touch the roof of the tunnel with a half-up-stretched hand, and the branchings had been newly placed.

Donovan hesitated, 'Dead end, let's go back.'

'No. Hold on.' Powell squeezed clumsily past. 'Is that light ahead?'

'Light? I don't see any. Where would there be light down here?'

'Robot light.' He was scrambling up a gentle incline on hands and knees. His voice was hoarse and anxious in Donovan's ears. 'Hey, Mike, come up here.'

There was light. Donovan crawled up and over Powell's outstretched legs. 'An opening?'

'Yes. They must be working into this tunnel from the other side now – I think.'

Donovan felt the ragged edges of the opening that looked out into what the cautious flashlight showed to be a larger and obviously main-stem tunnel. The hole was too small for a man to go through, almost too small for two men to look through simultaneously.

'There's nothing there,' said Donovan.

'Well, not now. But there must have been a second ago or we wouldn't have seen light. Watch out!'

The walls rolled about them and they felt the impact. A fine dust showered down. Powell lifted a cautious head and looked again. 'All right, Mike. They're there.'

The glittering robots clustered fifty feet down the main stem. Metal arms labored mightily at the rubbish heap brought down by the last blast.

Donovan urged eagerly, 'Don't waste time. It won't be long before they get through, and the next blast may get us.'

'For Pete's sake, don't rush me.' Powell unlimbered the detonator, and his eyes searched anxiously across the dusky background where the only light was robot light and it was impossible to tell a projecting boulder from a shadow.

'There's a spot in the roof, see it, almost over them. The last blast didn't quite get it. If you can get it at the base, half the roof will cave in.'

Powell followed the dim finger, 'Check! Now fasten your eye on the robots and pray they don't move too far from that part of the tunnel. They're my light sources. Are all seven there?'

Donovan counted, 'All seven.'

'Well, then, watch them. Watch every motion!'

His detonator was lifted and remained poised while Donovan watched and cursed and blinked the sweat out of his eyes.

It flashed!

There was a jar, a series of hard vibrations, and then a jarring thump that threw Powell heavily against Donovan.

Donovan yowled, 'Greg, you threw me off. I didn't see a thing.'

Powell stared about wildly, 'Where are they?'

Donovan fell into a stupid silence. There was no sign of the robots. It was dark as the depths of the River Styx.

'Think we buried them?' quavered Donovan.

'Let's get down there. Don't ask me what I think.' Powell crawled backward at tumbling speed.

'Mike!'

Donovan paused in the act of following. 'What's wrong now?'

'Hold on!' Powell's breathing was rough and irregular in Donovan's ears. 'Mike! Do you hear me, Mike?'

'I'm right here. What is it?'

'We're blocked in. It wasn't their ceiling coming down fifty feet away that knocked us over. It was our own ceiling. The shock's tumbled it!'

'What!' Donovan scrambled up against a hard barrier. 'Turn on the flash.'

Powell did so. At no point was there room for a rabbit to squeeze through.

Donovan said softly, 'Well, what do you know?'

They wasted a few moments and some muscular power in an effort to move the blocking barrier. Powell varied this by wrenching at the edges of the original hole. For a moment, Powell lifted his blaster. But in those close quarters, a flash would be suicide and he knew it. He sat down.

'You know, Mike,' he said, 'we've really messed this up. We are no nearer finding out what's wrong with Dave. It was a good idea but it blew up in our face.'

Donovan's glance was bitter with an intensity totally wasted on the darkness, 'I hate to disturb you, old man, but quite apart from what we know or don't know of Dave, we're slightly trapped. If we don't get loose, fella, we're going to die. D-I-E, die. How much oxygen have we anyway? Not more than six hours.'

'I've thought of that.' Powell's fingers went up to his long-suffering mustache and clanged uselessly against the transparent visor. 'Of course, we could get Dave to dig us out easily in that time, except that our precious emergency must have thrown him off, and his radio circuit is out.'

'And isn't that nice?'

Donovan edged up to the opening and managed to get his metal-incased head out. It was an extremely tight fit.

'Hey, Greg!'

'What?'

'Suppose we get Dave within twenty feet. He'll snap to normal. That will save us.'

'Sure, but where is he?'

'Down the corridor – way down. For Pete's sake, stop pulling before you drag my head out of its socket. I'll give you your chance to look.'

Powell maneuvered his head outside, 'We did it all right. Look at those saps. That must be a ballet they're doing.'

'Never mind the snide remarks. Are they getting any closer?'

'Can't tell yet. They're too far away. Give me a chance. Pass me my flash, will you? I'll try to attract their attention that way.'

He gave up after two minutes, 'Not a chance! They must be blind. Uh-oh, they're starting toward us. What do you know?'

Donovan said, 'Hey, let me see!'

There was a silent scuffle. Powell said, 'All right!' and Donovan got his head out.

They were approaching. Dave was high-stepping the way in front and the six 'fingers' were a weaving chorus line behind him.

Donovan marveled, 'What are they doing? That's what I want to know. It looks like the Virginia reel – and Dave's a major-domo, or I never saw one.'

'Oh, leave me alone with your descriptions,' grumbled Powell. 'How near are they?'

'Within fifty feet and coming this way. We'll be out in fifteen min – Uh – huh – HUH – HEY-Y!'

'What's going on?' It took Powell several seconds to recover from his stunned astonishment at Donovan's vocal gyrations. 'Come on, give me a chance at that hole. Don't be a hog about it.'

He fought his way upward, but Donovan kicked wildly, 'They did an about-face, Greg. They're leaving. Dave! Hey, Da-a-ave!'

Powell shrieked, 'What's the use of that, you fool? Sound won't carry.'

'Well, then,' panted Donovan, 'kick the walls, slam them, get some vibration started. We've got to attract their attention somehow, Greg, or we're through.' He pounded like a madman.

Powell shook him, 'Wait, Mike, wait. Listen, I've got an idea. Jumping Jupiter, this is a fine time to get around to the simple solutions. Mike!'

'What do you want?' Donovan pulled his head in.

'Let me in there fast before they get out of range.'

'Out of range! What are you going to do? Hey, what are you going to do with that detonator?' He grabbed Powell's arm.

Powell shook off the grip violently. 'I'm going to do a little shooting.'

'Why?'

'That's for later. Let's see if it works first. If it doesn't, then— Get out of the way and let me shoot!'

The robots were flickers, small and getting smaller, in the distance. Powell lined up the sights tensely, and pulled the trigger three times. He lowered the gun and peered anxiously. One of the subsidiaries was down! There were only six gleaming figures now.

Powell called into his transmitter uncertainly. 'Dave!'

A pause, then the answer sounded to both men, 'Boss? Where are you? My third subsidiary has had his chest blown in. He's out of commission.'

'Never mind your subsidiary,' said Powell. 'We're trapped in a cave-in where you were blasting. Can you see our flashlight?'

'Sure. We'll be right there.'

Powell sat back and relaxed, 'That, my fran', is that.'

Donovan said very softly with tears in his voice, 'All right, Greg. You win. I beat my forehead against the ground before your feet. Now don't feed me any bull. Just tell me quietly what it's all about.'

'Easy. It's just that all through we missed the obvious – as usual. We knew it was the personal initiative circuit, and that it always happened during emergencies, but we kept looking for a specific order as the cause. Why should it be an order?'

'Why not?'

'Well, look. Why not a type of order. What type of order requires the most initiative? What type of order would occur almost always only in an emergency?'

'Don't ask me, Greg. Tell me!'

'I'm doing it! It's the six-way order. Under all ordinary conditions, one or more of the "fingers" would be doing routine tasks requiring no close supervision – in the sort of offhand way our bodies handle the routine walking motions. But in an emergency, all six subsidiaries must be mobilized immediately and simultaneously. Dave must handle six robots at a time and something gives. The rest was easy. Any decrease in initiative required, such as the arrival of humans, snaps him back. So I destroyed one of the robots. When I did, he was transmitting only the five-way orders. Initiative decreases – he's normal.'

'How did you get all that?' demanded Donovan.

'Just logical guessing. I tried it and it worked.'

The robot's voice was in their ears again, 'Here I am. Can you hold out half an hour?'

'Easy!' said Powell. Then, to Donovan, he continued, 'And now the job should be simple. We'll go through the circuits, and check off each part that gets an extra workout in a six-way order as against a five-way. How big a field does that leave us?'

Donovan considered, 'Not much, I think. If Dave is like the preliminary model we saw back at the factory, there's a special co-ordinating circuit that would be the only section involved.' He cheered up suddenly and amazingly, 'Say, that wouldn't be bad at all. There's nothing to that.'

'All right. You think it over and we'll check the blueprints when we get back. And now, till Dave reaches us, I'm relaxing.'

'Hey, wait! Just tell me one thing. What were those queer shifting marches, those funny dance steps, that the robots went through every time they went screwy?'

'That? I don't know. But I've got a notion. Remember, those subsidiaries were Dave's "fingers". We were always saying that, you know. Well, it's my idea that in all these interludes, whenever

Dave became a psychiatric case, he went off into a moronic maze, spending his time *twiddling his fingers.*'

Susan Calvin talked about Powell and Donovan with unsmiling amusement, but warmth came into her voice when she mentioned robots. It didn't take her long to go through the Speedies, the Cuties and the Daves, and I stopped her. Otherwise, she would have dredged up half a dozen more.

I said, 'Doesn't anything ever happen on Earth?'

She looked at me with a little frown, 'No, we don't have much to do with robots in action here on Earth.'

'Oh, well that's too bad. I mean, your field-engineers are swell, but can't we get you into this? Didn't you ever have a robot go wrong on you? It's your anniversary, you know.'

And so help me she blushed. She said, 'Robots have gone wrong on me. Heavens, how long it's been since I thought of it. Why, it was almost forty years ago. Certainly! 2021! And I was only thirty-eight. Oh, my – I'd rather not talk about it.'

I waited, and sure enough she changed her mind. 'Why not?' she said. 'It cannot harm me now. Even the memory can't. I was foolish once, young man. Would you believe that?'

'No,' I said.

'I was. But Herbie was a mind-reading robot.'

'What?'

'Only one of its kind, before or since. A mistake – somewheres—'

5

Liar!

Alfred Lanning lit his cigar carefully, but the tips of his fingers were trembling slightly. His gray eyebrows hunched low as he spoke between puffs.

'It reads minds all right – damn little doubt about that! But why?' He looked at Mathematician Peter Bogert, 'Well?'

Bogert flattened his black hair down with both hands, 'That was the thirty-fourth RB model we've turned out, Lanning. All the others were strictly orthodox.'

The third man at the table frowned. Milton Ashe was the youngest officer of US Robots and Mechanical Men, Inc., and proud of his post.

'Listen, Bogert. There wasn't a hitch in the assembly from start to finish. I guarantee that.'

Bogert's thick lips spread in a patronizing smile, 'Do you? If you can answer for the entire assembly line, I recommend your promotion. By exact count, there are 75,234 operations necessary for the manufacture of a single positronic brain, each separate operation depending for successful completion upon any number of factors, from five to a hundred and five. If any one of them goes seriously wrong, the "brain" is ruined. I quote our own information folder, Ashe.'

Milton Ashe flushed, but a fourth voice cut off his reply.

'If we're going to start by trying to fix the blame on one another, I'm leaving.' Susan Calvin's hands were folded tightly in her lap, and the little lines about her thin, pale lips deepened. 'We've got a mind-reading robot on our hands and it strikes me as rather important that we find out just why it reads minds. We're not going to do that by saying, "Your fault! My fault!"'

Her cold gray eyes fastened upon Ashe, and he grinned.

Lanning grinned too, and, as always at such times, his long white hair and shrewd little eyes made him the picture of a biblical patriarch. 'True for you, Dr Calvin.'

His voice became suddenly crisp, 'Here's everything in pill-concentrate form. We've produced a positronic brain of supposedly ordinary vintage that's got the remarkable property of being able to tune in on thought waves. It would mark the most important advance in robotics in decades, if we knew how it happened. We don't, and we have to find out. Is that clear?'

'May I make a suggestion?' asked Bogert.

'Go ahead!'

'I'd say that until we do figure out the mess – and as a mathematician I expect it to be a very devil of a mess – we keep the existence of RB-34 a secret. I mean even from the other members of the staff. As heads of the departments, we ought not to find it an insoluble problem, and the fewer know about it—'

'Bogert is right,' said Dr Calvin. 'Ever since the Interplanetary Code was modified to allow robot models to be tested in the plants before being shipped out to space, anti-robot propaganda has increased. If any word leaks out about a robot being able to read minds before we can announce complete control of the phenomenon, pretty effective capital could be made out of it.'

Lanning sucked at his cigar and nodded gravely. He turned

to Ashe, 'I think you said you were alone when you first stumbled on this thought-reading business.'

'I'll say I was alone – I got the scare of my life. RB-34 had just been taken off the assembly table and they sent him down to me. Obermann was off somewheres, so I took him down to the testing rooms myself – at least I started to take him down.' Ashe paused, and a tiny smile tugged at his lips, 'Say, did any of you ever carry on a thought conversation without knowing it?'

No one bothered to answer, and he continued, 'You don't realize it at first, you know. He just spoke to me – as logically and sensibly as you can imagine – and it was only when I was most of the way down to the testing rooms that I realized that I hadn't said anything. Sure, I thought lots, but that isn't the same thing, is it? I locked that thing up and ran for Lanning. Having it walking beside me, calmly peering into my thoughts and picking and choosing among them gave me the willies.'

'I imagine it would,' said Susan Calvin thoughtfully. Her eyes fixed themselves upon Ashe in an oddly intent manner. 'We are so accustomed to considering our own thoughts private.'

Lanning broke in impatiently, 'Then only the four of us know. All right! We've got to go about this systematically. Ashe, I want you to check over the assembly line from beginning to end – everything. You're to eliminate all operations in which there was no possible chance of an error, and list all those where there were, together with its nature and possible magnitude.'

'Tall order,' grunted Ashe.

'Naturally! Of course, you're to put the men under you to work on this – every single one if you have to, and I don't care if we go behind schedule, either. But they're not to know why, you understand.'

'Hm-m-m, yes!' The young technician grinned wryly. 'It's still a lulu of a job.'

Lanning swiveled about in his chair and faced Calvin, 'You'll have to tackle the job from the other direction. You're the robo-psychologist of the plant, so you're to study the robot itself and work backward. Try to find out how he ticks. See what else is tied up with his telepathic powers, how far they extend, how they warp his outlook, and just exactly what harm it has done to his ordinary RB properties. You've got that?'

Lanning didn't wait for Dr Calvin to answer.

'I'll co-ordinate the work and interpret the findings mathematically.' He puffed violently at his cigar and mumbled the rest through the smoke, 'Bogert will help me there, of course.'

Bogert polished the nails of one pudgy hand with the other and said blandly, 'I dare say. I know a little in the line.'

'Well! I'll get started.' Ashe shoved his chair back and rose. His pleasantly youthful face crinkled in a grin, 'I've got the darnedest job of any of us, so I'm getting out of here and to work.'

He left with a slurred, 'B' seein' ye!'

Susan Calvin answered with a barely perceptible nod, but her eyes followed him out of sight and she did not answer when Lanning grunted and said, 'Do you want to go up and see RB-34 now, Dr Calvin?'

RB-34's photoelectric eyes lifted from the book at the muffled sound of hinges turning and he was up on his feet when Susan Calvin entered.

She paused to readjust the huge 'No Entrance' sign upon the door and then approached the robot.

'I've brought you the texts upon hyperatomic motors, Herbie – a few anyway. Would you care to look at them?'

RB-34 – otherwise known as Herbie – lifted the three heavy books from her arms and opened to the title page of one:

'Hm-m-m! "Theory of Hyperatomics".' He mumbled inarticulately to himself as he flipped the pages and then spoke with an abstracted air, 'Sit down, Dr Calvin! This will take me a few minutes.'

The psychologist seated herself and watched Herbie narrowly as he took a chair at the other side of the table and went through the three books systematically.

At the end of half an hour, he put them down. 'Of course, I know why you brought these.'

The corner of Dr Calvin's lip twitched. 'I was afraid you would. It's difficult to work with you, Herbie. You're always a step ahead of me.'

'It's the same with these books, you know, as with the others. They just don't interest me. There's nothing to your textbooks. Your science is just a mass of collected data plastered together by make-shift theory – and all so incredibly simple, that it's scarcely worth bothering about.

'It's your fiction that interests me. Your studies of the interplay of human motives and emotions' – his mighty hand gestured vaguely as he sought the proper words.

Dr Calvin whispered, 'I think I understand.'

'I see into minds, you see,' the robot continued, 'and you have no idea how complicated they are. I can't begin to understand everything because my own mind has so little in common with them – but I try, and your novels help.'

'Yes, but I'm afraid that after going through some of the harrowing emotional experiences of our present-day sentimental novel' – there was a tinge of bitterness in her voice – 'you find real minds like ours dull and colorless.'

'But I don't!'

The sudden energy in the response brought the other to her feet. She felt herself reddening, and thought wildly, 'He must know!'

Herbie subsided suddenly, and muttered in a low voice from

which the metallic timbre departed almost entirely. 'But, of course, I know about it, Dr Calvin. You think of it always, so how can I help but know?'

Her face was hard. 'Have you – told anyone?'

'Of course not!' This, with genuine surprise. 'No one has asked me.'

'Well, then,' she flung out, 'I suppose you think I am a fool.'

'No! It is a normal emotion.'

'Perhaps that is why it is so foolish.' The wistfulness in her voice drowned out everything else. Some of the woman peered through the layer of doctorhood. 'I am not what you would call – attractive.'

'If you are referring to mere physical attraction, I couldn't judge. But I know, in any case, that there are other types of attraction.'

'Nor young.' Dr Calvin had scarcely heard the robot.

'You are not yet forty.' An anxious insistence had crept into Herbie's voice.

'Thirty-eight as you count the years; a shriveled sixty as far as my emotional outlook on life is concerned. Am I a psychologist for nothing?'

She drove on with bitter breathlessness, 'And he's barely thirty-five and looks and acts younger. Do you suppose he ever sees me as anything but . . . but what I am?'

'You are wrong!' Herbie's steel fist struck the plastic-topped table with a strident clang. 'Listen to me—'

But Susan Calvin whirled on him now and the hunted pain in her eyes became a blaze, 'Why should I? What do you know about it all, anyway, you . . . you machine. I'm just a specimen to you; an interesting bug with a peculiar mind spread-eagled for inspection. It's a wonderful example of frustration, isn't it? Almost as good as your books.' Her voice, emerging in dry sobs, choked into silence.

The robot cowered at the outburst. He shook his head pleadingly. 'Won't you listen to me, please? I could help you if you would let me.'

'How?' Her lips curled. 'By giving me good advice?'

'No, not that. It's just that I know what other people think – Milton Ashe, for instance.'

There was a long silence, and Susan Calvin's eyes dropped. 'I don't want to know what he thinks,' she gasped. 'Keep quiet.'

'I think you would want to know what he thinks.'

Her head remained bent, but her breath came more quickly. 'You are talking nonsense,' she whispered.

'Why should I? I am trying to help. Milton Ashe's thoughts of you—' he paused.

And then the psychologist raised her head, 'Well?'

The robot said quietly, 'He loves you.'

For a full minute, Dr Calvin did not speak. She merely stared. Then, 'You are mistaken! You must be. Why should he?'

'But he does. A thing like that cannot be hidden, not from me.'

'But I am so . . . so—' she stammered to a halt.

'He looks deeper than the skin, and admires intellect in others. Milton Ashe is not the type to marry a head of hair and a pair of eyes.'

Susan Calvin found herself blinking rapidly and waited before speaking. Even then her voice trembled, 'Yet he certainly never in any way indicated—'

'Have you ever given him a chance?'

'How could I? I never thought that—'

'Exactly!'

The psychologist paused in thought and then looked up suddenly. 'A girl visited him here at the plant half a year ago. She was pretty, I suppose – blonde and slim. And, of course, could scarcely add two and two. He spent all day puffing out his chest, trying to explain how a robot was put together.' The hardness had returned, 'Not that she understood! Who was she?'

Herbie answered without hesitation, 'I know the person you are referring to. She is his first cousin, and there is no romantic interest there, I assure you.'

Susan Calvin rose to her feet with a vivacity almost girlish. 'Now isn't that strange? That's exactly what I used to pretend to myself sometimes, though I never really thought so. Then it all must be true.'

She ran to Herbie and seized his cold, heavy hand in both hers. 'Thank you, Herbie.' Her voice was an urgent, husky whisper. 'Don't tell anyone about this. Let it be our secret – and thank you again.' With that, and a convulsive squeeze of Herbie's unresponsive metal fingers, she left.

Herbie turned slowly to his neglected novel, but there was no one to read *his* thoughts.

Milton Ashe stretched slowly and magnificently, to the tune of cracking joints and a chorus of grunts, and then glared at Peter Bogert, Ph.D.

'Say,' he said, 'I've been at this for a week now with just about no sleep. How long do I have to keep it up? I thought you said the positronic bombardment in Vac Chamber D was the solution.'

Bogert yawned delicately and regarded his white hands with interest. 'It is. I'm on the track.'

'I know what *that* means when a mathematician says it. How near the end are you?'

'It all depends.'

'On what?' Ashe dropped into a chair and stretched his long legs out before him.

'On Lanning. The old fellow disagrees with me.' He sighed, 'A bit behind the times, that's the trouble with him. He clings to matrix mechanics as the all in all, and this problem calls for more powerful mathematical tools. He's so stubborn.'

Ashe muttered sleepily, 'Why not ask Herbie and settle the whole affair?'

'Ask the robot?' Bogert's eyebrows climbed.

'Why not? Didn't the old girl tell you?'

'You mean Calvin?'

'Yeah! Susie herself. That robot's a mathematical wiz. He knows all about everything plus a bit on the side. He does triple integrals in his head and eats up tensor analysis for dessert.'

The mathematician stared skeptically, 'Are you serious?'

'So help me! The catch is that the dope doesn't like math. He would rather read slushy novels. Honest! You should see the tripe Susie keeps feeding him: "Purple Passion" and "Love in Space".'

'Dr Calvin hasn't said a word of this to us.'

'Well, she hasn't finished studying him. You know how she is. She likes to have everything just so before letting out the big secret.'

'She's told *you*.'

'We sort of got to talking. I have been seeing a lot of her lately.' He opened his eyes wide and frowned, 'Say, Bogie, have you been noticing anything queer about the lady lately?'

Bogert relaxed into an undignified grin, 'She's using lipstick, if that's what you mean.'

'Hell, I know that. Rouge, powder and eye shadow, too. She's a sight. But it's not that. I can't put my finger on it. It's the way she talks – as if she were happy about something.' He thought a little, and then shrugged.

The other allowed himself a leer, which, for a scientist past fifty, was not a bad job, 'Maybe she's in love.'

Ashe allowed his eyes to close again, 'You're nuts, Bogie. You go speak to Herbie; I want to stay here and go to sleep.'

'Right! Not that I particularly like having a robot tell me my job, nor that I think he can do it!'

A soft snore was his only answer.

Herbie listened carefully as Peter Bogert, hands in pockets, spoke with elaborate indifference.

'So there you are. I've been told you understand these things, and I am asking you more in curiosity than anything else. My line of reasoning, as I have outlined it, involves a few doubtful steps, I admit, which Dr Lanning refuses to accept, and the picture is still rather incomplete.'

The robot didn't answer, and Bogert said, 'Well?'

'I see no mistake,' Herbie studied the scribbled figures.

'I don't suppose you can go any further than that?'

'I daren't try. You are a better mathematician than I, and – well, I'd hate to commit myself.'

There was a shade of complacency in Bogert's smile, 'I rather thought that would be the case. It is deep. We'll forget it.' He crumpled the sheets, tossed them down the waste shaft, turned to leave, and then thought better of it.

'By the way—'

The robot waited.

Bogert seemed to have difficulty. 'There is something – that is, perhaps you can—' He stopped.

Herbie spoke quietly, 'Your thoughts are confused, but there is no doubt at all that they concern Dr Lanning. It is silly to hesitate, for as soon as you compose yourself, I'll know what it is you want to ask.'

The mathematician's hand went to his sleek hair in the familiar smoothing gesture. 'Lanning is nudging seventy,' he said, as if that explained everything.

'I know that.'

'And he's been director of the plant for almost thirty years.' Herbie nodded.

'Well, now,' Bogert's voice became ingratiating, 'you would know whether . . . whether he's thinking of resigning. Health, perhaps, or some other—'

'Quite,' said Herbie, and that was all.

'Well, do you know?'

'Certainly.'

'Then – uh – could you tell me?'

'Since you ask, yes.' The robot was quite matter-of-fact about it. 'He has already resigned!'

'What!' The exclamation was an explosive, almost inarticulate, sound. The scientist's large head hunched forward. 'Say that again!'

'He has already resigned,' came the quiet repetition, 'but it has not yet taken effect. He is waiting, you see, to solve the problem of – er – myself. That finished, he is quite ready to turn the office of director over to his successor.'

Bogert expelled his breath sharply, 'And this successor? Who is he?' He was quite close to Herbie now, eyes fixed fascinatedly on those unreadable dull-red photoelectric cells that were the robot's eyes.

Words came slowly, 'You are the next director.'

And Bogert relaxed into a tight smile, 'This is good to know. I've been hoping and waiting for this. Thanks, Herbie.'

Peter Bogert was at his desk until five that morning and he was back at nine. The shelf just over the desk emptied of its row of reference books and tables, as he referred to one after the other.

The pages of calculations before him increased microscopically and the crumpled sheets at his feet mounted into a hill of scribbled paper.

At precisely noon, he stared at the final page, rubbed a bloodshot eye, yawned and shrugged. 'This is getting worse each minute. Damn!'

He turned at the sound of the opening door and nodded at Lanning, who entered, cracking the knuckles of one gnarled hand with the other.

The director took in the disorder of the room and his eyebrows furrowed together.

'New lead?' he asked.

'No,' came the defiant answer. 'What's wrong with the old one?'

Lanning did not trouble to answer, nor to do more than bestow a single cursory glance at the top sheet upon Bogert's desk. He spoke through the flare of a match as he lit a cigar.

'Has Calvin told you about the robot? It's a mathematical genius. Really remarkable.'

The other snorted loudly, 'So I've heard. But Calvin had better stick to robopsychology. I've checked Herbie on math, and he can scarcely struggle through calculus.'

'Calvin didn't find it so.'

'She's crazy.'

'And I don't find it so.' The director's eyes narrowed dangerously.

'You!' Bogert's voice hardened. 'What are you talking about?'

'I've been putting Herbie through his paces all morning, and he can do tricks you never heard of.'

'Is that so?'

'You sound skeptical!' Lanning flipped a sheet of paper out of his vest pocket and unfolded it. 'That's not my handwriting, is it?'

Bogert studied the large angular notation covering the sheet, 'Herbie did this?'

'Right! And if you'll notice, he's been working on your time integration of Equation 22. It comes' – Lanning tapped a yellow fingernail upon the last step – 'to the identical conclusion I did, and in a quarter the time. You had no right to neglect the Linger Effect in positronic bombardment.'

'I didn't neglect it. For Heaven's sake, Lanning, get it through your head that it would cancel out—'

'Oh, sure, you explained that. You used the Mitchell Translation Equation, didn't you? Well – it doesn't apply.'

'Why not?'

'Because you've been using hyper-imaginaries, for one thing.'

'What's that to do with?'

'Mitchell's Equation won't hold when—'

'Are you crazy? If you'll reread Mitchell's original paper in the *Transactions of the Far*—'

'I don't have to. I told you in the beginning that I didn't like his reasoning, and Herbie backs me in that.'

'Well, then,' Bogert shouted, 'let that clockwork contraption solve the entire problem for you. Why bother with non-essentials?'

'That's exactly the point. Herbie can't solve the problem. And if he can't, we can't – alone. I'm submitting the entire question to the National Board. It's gotten beyond us.'

Bogert's chair went over backward as he jumped up a-snarl, face crimson. 'You're doing nothing of the sort.'

Lanning flushed in his turn, 'Are you telling me what I can't do?'

'Exactly,' was the gritted response. 'I've got the problem beaten and you're not to take it out of my hands, understand? Don't think I don't see through you, you desiccated fossil. You'd cut your own nose off before you'd let me get the credit for solving robotic telepathy.'

'You're a damned idiot, Bogert, and in one second I'll have you suspended for insubordination' – Lanning's lower lip trembled with passion.

'Which is one thing you won't do, Lanning. You haven't any secrets with a mind-reading robot around, so don't forget that I know all about your resignation.'

The ash on Lanning's cigar trembled and fell, and the cigar itself followed, 'What . . . what—'

Bogert chuckled nastily, 'And I'm the new director, be it understood. I'm very aware of that; don't think I'm not. Damn your eyes, Lanning, I'm going to give the orders about here or there will be the sweetest mess that you've ever been in.'

Lanning found his voice and let it out with a roar. 'You're suspended, d'ye hear? You're relieved of all duties. You're broken, do you understand?'

The smile on the other's face broadened, 'Now, what's the use of that? You're getting nowhere. I'm holding the trumps. I know you've resigned. Herbie told me, and he got it straight from you.'

Lanning forced himself to speak quietly. He looked an old, old man, with tired eyes peering from a face in which the red had disappeared, leaving the pasty yellow of age behind. 'I want to speak to Herbie. He can't have told you anything of the sort. You're playing a deep game, Bogert, but I'm calling your bluff. Come with me.'

Bogert shrugged, 'To see Herbie? Good! Damned good!'

It was also precisely at noon that Milton Ashe looked up from his clumsy sketch and said, 'You get the idea? I'm not good at getting this down, but that's about how it looks. It's a honey of a house, and I can get it for next to nothing.'

Susan Calvin gazed across at him with melting eyes. 'It's really beautiful,' she sighed. 'I've often thought that I'd like to—' Her voice trailed away.

'Of course,' Ashe continued briskly, putting away his pencil, 'I've got to wait for my vacation. It's only two weeks off, but this Herbie business has everything up in the air.' His eyes dropped to his fingernails, 'Besides, there's another point – but it's a secret.'

'Then don't tell me.'

'Oh, I'd just as soon, I'm just busting to tell someone – and you're just about the best – er – confidante I could find here.' He grinned sheepishly.

Susan Calvin's heart bounded, but she did not trust herself to speak.

'Frankly,' Ashe scraped his chair closer and lowered his voice into a confidential whisper, 'the house isn't to be only for myself. I'm getting married!'

And then he jumped out of his seat, 'What's the matter?'

'Nothing!' The horrible spinning sensation had vanished, but it was hard to get words out. 'Married? You mean—'

'Why, sure! About time, isn't it? You remember that girl who was here last summer. That's she! But you *are* sick. You—'

'Headache!' Susan Calvin motioned him away weakly. 'I've . . . I've been subject to them lately. I want to . . . to congratulate you, of course, I'm very glad—' The inexpertly applied rouge made a pair of nasty red splotches upon her chalk-white face. Things had begun spinning again. 'Pardon me – please—'

The words were a mumble, as she stumbled blindly out the door. It had happened with the sudden catastrophe of a dream – and with all the unreal horror of a dream.

But how could it be? Herbie had said—

And Herbie knew! He could see into minds!

She found herself leaning breathlessly against the door jamb, staring into Herbie's metal face. She must have climbed the two flights of stairs, but she had no memory of it. The distance had been covered in an instant, as in a dream.

As in a dream!

And still Herbie's unblinking eyes stared into hers and their dull red seemed to expand into dimly shining nightmarish globes.

He was speaking, and she felt the cold glass pressing against her lips. She swallowed and shuddered into a certain awareness of her surroundings.

Still Herbie spoke, and there was agitation in his voice – as if he were hurt and frightened and pleading.

The words were beginning to make sense. 'This is a dream,' he was saying, 'and you mustn't believe in it. You'll wake into the real world soon and laugh at yourself. He loves you, I tell you. He does, he does! But not here! Not now! This is an illusion.'

Susan Calvin nodded, her voice a whisper, 'Yes! Yes!' She was clutching Herbie's arm, clinging to it, repeating over and over, 'It isn't true, is it? It isn't, is it?'

Just how she came to her senses, she never knew – but it was like passing from a world of misty unreality to one of harsh sunlight. She pushed him away from her, pushed hard against that steely arm, and her eyes were wide.

'What are you trying to do?' Her voice rose to a harsh scream. 'What are you trying to do?'

Herbie backed away, 'I want to help.'

The psychologist stared, 'Help? By telling me this is a dream? By trying to push me into schizophrenia?' A hysterical tenseness seized her, 'This is no dream! I wish it were!'

She drew her breath sharply, 'Wait! Why . . . why, I understand. Merciful Heavens, it's so obvious.'

There was horror in the robot's voice, 'I had to!'

'And I believed you! I never thought—'

Loud voices outside the door brought her to a halt. She turned away, fists clenching spasmodically, and when Bogert and Lanning entered, she was at the far window. Neither of the men paid her the slightest attention.

They approached Herbie simultaneously; Lanning angry and impatience, Bogert coolly sardonic. The director spoke first.

'Here now, Herbie. Listen to me!'

The robot brought his eyes sharply down upon the aged director, 'Yes, Dr Lanning.'

'Have you discussed me with Dr Bogert?'

'No, sir.' The answer came slowly, and the smile on Bogert's face flashed off.

'What's that?' Bogert shoved in ahead of his superior and straddled the ground before the robot. 'Repeat what you told me yesterday.'

'I said that—' Herbie fell silent. Deep within him his metallic diaphragm vibrated in soft discords.

'Didn't you say he had resigned?' roared Bogert. 'Answer me!'

Bogert raised his arm frantically, but Lanning pushed him aside, 'Are you trying to bully him into lying?'

'You heard him, Lanning. He began to say "Yes" and stopped. Get out of my way! I want the truth out of him, understand!'

'I'll ask him!' Lanning turned to the robot. 'All right, Herbie, take it easy. Have I resigned?'

Herbie stared, and Lanning repeated anxiously, 'Have I resigned?' There was the faintest trace of a negative shake of the robot's head. A long wait produced nothing further.

The two men looked at each other and the hostility in their eyes was all but tangible.

'What the devil,' blurted Bogert, 'has the robot gone mute? Can't you speak, you monstrosity?'

'I can speak,' came the ready answer.

'Then answer the question. Didn't you tell me Lanning had resigned? Hasn't he resigned?'

And again there was nothing but dull silence, until from the end of the room, Susan Calvin's laugh rang out suddenly, high-pitched and semi-hysterical.

The two mathematicians jumped, and Bogert's eyes narrowed, 'You here? What's so funny?'

'Nothing's funny.' Her voice was not quite natural. 'It's just that I'm not the only one that's been caught. There's irony in three of the greatest experts in robotics in the world falling into the same elementary trap, isn't there?' Her voice faded, and she put a pale hand to her forehead, 'But it isn't funny!'

This time the look that passed between the two men was one of raised eyebrows. 'What trap are you talking about?' asked Lanning stiffly. 'Is something wrong with Herbie?'

'No,' she approached them slowly, 'nothing is wrong with him – only with us.' She whirled suddenly and shrieked at the robot, 'Get away from me! Go to the other end of the room and don't let me look at you.'

Herbie cringed before the fury of her eyes and stumbled away in a clattering trot.

Lanning's voice was hostile, 'What is all this, Dr Calvin?'

She faced them and spoke sarcastically, 'Surely you know the fundamental First Law of Robotics.'

The other two nodded together. 'Certainly,' said Bogert, irritably, 'a robot may not injure a human being or, through inaction, allow him to come to harm.'

'How nicely put,' sneered Calvin. 'But what kind of harm?'

'Why – any kind.'

'Exactly! Any kind! But what about hurt feelings? What about deflation of one's ego? What about the blasting of one's hopes? Is that injury?'

Lanning frowned, 'What would a robot know about—' And then he caught himself with a gasp.

'You've caught on, haven't you? *This* robot reads minds. Do you suppose it doesn't know everything about mental injury? Do you suppose that if asked a question, it wouldn't give exactly that answer that one wants to hear? Wouldn't any other answer hurt us, and wouldn't Herbie know that?'

'Good Heavens!' muttered Bogert.

The psychologist cast a sardonic glance at him, 'I take it you asked him whether Lanning had resigned. You wanted to hear that he had resigned and so that's what Herbie told you.'

'And I suppose that is why,' said Lanning, tonelessly, 'it would not answer a little while ago. It couldn't answer either way without hurting one of us.'

There was a short pause in which the men looked thoughtfully across the room at the robot, crouching in the chair by the bookcase, head resting in one hand.

Susan Calvin stared steadfastly at the floor, 'He knew of all this. That . . . that devil knows everything – including what went wrong in his assembly.' Her eyes were dark and brooding.

Lanning looked up, 'You're wrong there, Dr Calvin. He doesn't know what went wrong. I asked him.'

'What does that mean?' cried Calvin. 'Only that you didn't want him to give you the solution. It would puncture your ego to have a machine do what you couldn't. Did you ask him?' she shot at Bogert.

'In a way.' Bogert coughed and reddened. 'He told me he knew very little about mathematics.'

Lanning laughed, not very loudly, and the psychologist smiled caustically. She said, 'I'll ask him! A solution by him won't hurt my ego.' She raised her voice into a cold, imperative, 'Come here!'

Herbie rose and approached with hesitant steps.

'You know, I suppose,' she continued, 'just exactly at what point in the assembly an extraneous factor was introduced or an essential one left out.'

'Yes,' said Herbie, in tones barely heard.

'Hold on,' broke in Bogert angrily. 'That's not necessarily true. You want to hear that, that's all.'

'Don't be a fool,' replied Calvin. 'He certainly knows as much math as you and Lanning together, since he can read minds. Give him his chance.'

The mathematician subsided, and Calvin continued, 'All right, then, Herbie, give! We're waiting.' And in an aside, 'Get pencils and paper, gentlemen.'

But Herbie remained silent, and there was triumph in the psychologist's voice, 'Why don't you answer, Herbie?'

The robot blurted out suddenly, 'I cannot. You know I cannot! Dr Bogert and Dr Lanning don't want me to.'

'They want the solution.'

'But not from me.'

Lanning broke in, speaking slowly and distinctly, 'Don't be foolish, Herbie. We do want you to tell us.'

Bogert nodded curtly.

Herbie's voice rose to wild heights, 'What's the use of saying that? Don't you suppose that I can see past the superficial skin of your mind? Down below, you don't want me to. I'm a machine, given the imitation of life only by virtue of the positronic interplay in my brain – which is man's device. You can't lose face to me without being hurt. That is deep in your mind and won't be erased. I can't give the solution.'

'We'll leave,' said Dr Lanning. 'Tell Calvin.'

'That would make no difference,' cried Herbie, 'since you would know anyway that it was I that was supplying the answer.'

Calvin resumed, 'But you understand, Herbie, that despite that, Drs Lanning and Bogert want that solution.'

'By their own efforts!' insisted Herbie.

'But they want it, and the fact that you have it and won't give it hurts them. You see that, don't you?'

'Yes! Yes!'

'And if you tell them that will hurt them, too.'

'Yes! Yes!' Herbie was retreating slowly, and step by step Susan Calvin advanced. The two men watched in frozen bewilderment.

'You can't tell them,' droned the psychologist slowly, 'because that would hurt and you mustn't hurt. But if you don't tell them, you hurt, so you must tell them. And if you do, you will hurt and you mustn't, so you can't tell them; but if you don't, you hurt, so you must; but if you do, you hurt, so you mustn't; but if you don't, you hurt, so you must; but if you do, you—'

Herbie was up against the wall, and here he dropped to his knees. 'Stop!' he shrieked. 'Close your mind! It is full of pain and frustration and hate! I didn't mean it, I tell you! I tried to help! I told you what you wanted to hear. I had to!'

The psychologist paid no attention. 'You must tell them, but if you do, you hurt, so you mustn't, but if you don't, you hurt, so you must; but—'

And Herbie screamed!

It was like the whistling of a piccolo many times magnified – shrill and shriller till it keened with the terror of a lost soul and filled the room with the piercingness of itself.

And when it died into nothingness, Herbie collapsed into a huddled heap of motionless metal.

Bogert's face was bloodless, 'He's dead!'

'No!' Susan Calvin burst into body-racking gusts of wild laughter, 'not dead – merely insane. I confronted him with the insoluble dilemma, and he broke down. You can scrap him now – because he'll never speak again.'

Lanning was on his knees beside the thing that had been Herbie. His fingers touched the cold, unresponsive metal face and he shuddered. 'You did that on purpose.' He rose and faced her, face contorted.

'What if I did? You can't help it now.' And in a sudden access of bitterness, 'He deserved it.'

The director seized the paralyzed, motionless Bogert by the wrist, 'What's the difference. Come, Peter.' He sighed, 'A thinking robot of this type is worthless anyway.' His eyes were old and tired, and he repeated, 'Come, Peter!'

It was minutes after the two scientists left that Dr Susan Calvin regained part of her mental equilibrium. Slowly, her eyes turned to the living-dead Herbie and the tightness returned to her face. Long she stared while the triumph faded and the helpless frustration returned – and of all her turbulent thoughts only one infinitely bitter word passed her lips.

'Liar!'

That finished it for then, naturally. I knew I couldn't get any more out of her after that. She just sat there behind her desk, her white face cold and – remembering.

I said, 'Thank you, Dr Calvin!' but she didn't answer. It was two days before I could get to see her again.

6

Little Lost Robot

When I did see Susan Calvin again, it was at the door of her office. Files were being moved out.

She said, 'How are your articles coming along, young man?'

'Fine,' I said. I had put them into shape according to my own lights, dramatized the bare bones of her recital, added the conversation and little touches. 'Would you look over them and see if I haven't been libellous or too unreasonably inaccurate anywhere?'

'I suppose so. Shall we retire to the Executive's Lounge? We can have coffee.'

She seemed in good humor, so I chanced it as we walked down the corridor, 'I was wondering, Dr Calvin—'

'Yes.'

'If you would tell me more concerning the history of robotics.'

'Surely you have what you want, young man.'

'In a way. But these incidents I have written up don't apply much to the modern world. I mean, there was only one mind-reading robot ever developed, and Space-Stations are already outmoded and in disuse, and robot mining is taken for granted. What about interstellar travel? It's only been about twenty years since the hyperatomic motor was invented and it's well known that it was a robotic invention. What is the truth about it?'

'Interstellar travel?' She was thoughtful. We were in the lounge, and I ordered a full dinner. She just had coffee.

'It wasn't a simple robotic invention, you know; not just like that. But, of course, until we developed the Brain, we didn't get very far. But we tried; we really tried. My first connection (directly, that is) with interstellar research was in 2029, when a robot was lost—'

Measures on Hyper Base had been taken in a sort of rattling fury – the muscular equivalent of an hysterical shriek.

To itemize them in order of both chronology and desperation, they were:

1. All work on the Hyperatomic Drive through all the space volume occupied by the Stations of the Twenty-Seventh Asteroidal Grouping came to a halt.

2. That entire volume of space was nipped out of the System, practically speaking. No one entered without permission. No one left under any conditions.

3. By special government patrol ship, Drs Susan Calvin and Peter Bogert, respectively Head Psychologist and Mathematical Director of United States Robots and Mechanical Men Corporation, were brought to Hyper Base.

Susan Calvin had never left the surface of Earth before, and had no perceptible desire to leave it this time. In an age of Atomic Power and a clearly coming Hyperatomic drive, she remained quietly provincial. So she was dissatisfied with her trip and unconvinced of the emergency, and every line of her plain, middle-aged face showed it clearly enough during her first dinner at Hyper Base.

Nor did Dr Bogert's sleek paleness abandon a certain hangdog attitude. Nor did Major-general Kallner, who headed the project, even once forget to maintain a haunted expression.

In short, it was a grisly episode, that meal, and the little session of three that followed began in a gray, unhappy manner.

Kallner, with his baldness glistening, and his dress uniform oddly unsuited to the general mood, began with uneasy directness.

'This is a queer story to tell, sir, and madam. I want to thank you for coming on short notice and without a reason being given. We'll try to correct that now. We've lost a robot. Work has stopped and *must* stop until such time as we locate it. So far we have failed, and we feel we need expert help.'

Perhaps the general felt his predicament anticlimactic. He continued with a note of desperation, 'I needn't tell you the importance of our work here. More than eighty percent of last year's appropriations for scientific research have gone to us—'

'Why, we know that,' said Bogert, agreeably. 'US Robots is receiving a generous rental fee for use of our robots.'

Susan Calvin injected a blunt, vinegary note, 'What makes a single robot so important to the project, and why hasn't it been located?'

The general turned his red face toward her and wet his lips quickly, 'Why, in a manner of speaking we *have* located it.' Then, with near anguish, 'Here, suppose I explain. As soon as the robot failed to report, a state of emergency was declared, and all movement off Hyper Base stopped. A cargo vessel had landed the previous day and had delivered us two robots for our laboratories. It had sixty-two robots of the . . . uh . . . same type for shipment elsewhere. We are certain as to that figure. There is no question about it whatever.'

'Yes? And the connection?'

'When our missing robot failed of location anywhere – I assure you we would have found a missing blade of grass if it had been there to find – we brainstormed ourselves into counting the robots left on the cargo ship. They have sixty-three now.'

'So that the sixty-third, I take it, is the missing prodigal?' Dr Calvin's eyes darkened.

'Yes, but we have no way of telling which is the sixty-third.'

There was a dead silence while the electric clock chimed eleven times, and then the robopsychologist said, 'Very peculiar,' and the corners of her lips moved downward.

'Peter,' she turned to her colleague with a trace of savagery, 'what's wrong here? What kind of robots are they using at Hyper Base?'

Dr Bogert hesitated and smiled feebly, 'It's been rather a matter of delicacy till now, Susan.'

She spoke rapidly, 'Yes, *till* now. If there are sixty-three same-type robots, one of which is wanted and the identity of which cannot be determined, why won't any of them do? What's the idea of all this? Why have we been sent for?'

Bogert said in resigned fashion, 'If you'll give me a chance, Susan – Hyper Base happens to be using several robots whose brains are not impressioned with the entire First Law of Robotics.'

'*Aren't* impressioned?' Calvin slumped back in her chair, 'I see. How many were made?'

'A few. It was on government order and there was no way of violating the secrecy. No one was to know except the top men directly concerned. You weren't included, Susan. It was nothing I had anything to do with.'

The general interrupted with a measure of authority. 'I would like to explain that bit. I hadn't been aware that Dr Calvin was unacquainted with the situation. I needn't tell you, Dr Calvin, that there always has been strong opposition to robots on the Planet. The only defense the government has had against the

Fundamentalist radicals in this matter was the fact that robots are always built with an unbreakable First Law – which makes it impossible for them to harm human beings under any circumstance.

'But we *had* to have robots of a different nature. So just a few of the NS-2 model, the Nestors, that is, were prepared with a modified First Law. To keep it quiet, all NS-2s are manufactured without serial numbers; modified members are delivered here along with a group of normal robots; and, of course, all our kind are under the strictest impressionment never to tell of their modification to unauthorized personnel.' He wore an embarrassed smile, 'This has all worked out against us now.'

Calvin said grimly, 'Have you asked each one who it is, anyhow? Certainly, you are authorized?'

The general nodded, 'All sixty-three deny having worked here – and one is lying.'

'Does the one you want show traces of wear? The others, I take it, are factory-fresh.'

'The one in question only arrived last month. It, and the two that have just arrived, were to be the last we needed. There's no perceptible wear.' He shook his head slowly and his eyes were haunted again, 'Dr Calvin, we don't dare let that ship leave. If the existence of non-First Law robots becomes general knowledge—' There seemed no way of avoiding understatement in the conclusion.

'Destroy all sixty-three,' said the robopsychologist coldly and flatly, 'and make an end of it.'

Bogert drew back a corner of his mouth. 'You mean destroy thirty thousand dollars per robot. I'm afraid US Robots wouldn't like that. We'd better make an effort first, Susan, before we destroy anything.'

'In that case,' she said, sharply, 'I need facts. Exactly what advantage does Hyper Base derive from these modified robots? What factor made them desirable, general?'

Kallner ruffled his forehead and stroked it with an upward gesture of his hand. 'We had trouble with our previous robots. Our men work with hard radiations a good deal, you see. It's dangerous, of course, but reasonable precautions are taken. There have been only two accidents since we began and neither was fatal. However, it was impossible to explain that to an ordinary robot. The First Law states – I'll quote it – "*No robot may harm a human being, or, through inaction, allow a human being to come to harm.*"

'That's primary, Dr Calvin. When it was necessary for one of our men to expose himself for a short period to a moderate gamma field, one that would have no physiological effects, the nearest robot would dash in to drag him out. If the field were exceedingly weak, it would succeed, and work could not continue till all robots were cleared out. If the field were a trifle stronger, the robot would never reach the technician concerned, since its positronic brain would collapse under gamma radiations – and then we would be out one expensive and hard-to-replace robot.

'We tried arguing with them. Their point was that a human being in a gamma field was endangering his life and that it didn't matter that he could remain there half an hour safely. Supposing, they would say, he forgot and remained an hour. They couldn't take chances. We pointed out that they were risking their lives on a wild off-chance. But self-preservation is only the Third Law of Robotics – and the First Law of human safety came first. We gave them orders; we ordered them strictly and harshly to remain out of gamma fields at whatever cost. But obedience is only the Second Law of Robotics – and the First Law of human safety came first. Dr Calvin, we either had to do without robots, or do something about the First Law – and we made our choice.'

'I can't believe,' said Dr Calvin, 'that it was found possible to remove the First Law.'

'It wasn't removed, it was modified,' explained Kallner. 'Positronic brains were constructed that contained the positive aspect only of the Law, which in them reads: "*No robot may harm a human being.*" That is all. They have no compulsion to prevent one coming to harm through an extraneous agency such as gamma rays. I state the matter correctly, Dr Bogert?'

'Quite,' assented the mathematician.

'And that is the only difference of your robots from the ordinary NS-2 model? The *only* difference? Peter?'

'The *only* difference, Susan.'

She rose and spoke with finality, 'I intend sleeping now, and in about eight hours I want to speak to whomever saw the robot last. And from now on, General Kallner, if I'm to take any responsibility at all for events, I want full and unquestioned control of this investigation.'

Susan Calvin, except for two hours of resentful lassitude, experienced nothing approaching sleep. She signaled at Bogert's door at the local time of 0700 and found him also awake. He had apparently taken the trouble of transporting a dressing gown to Hyper Base with him, for he was sitting in it. He put his nail scissors down when Calvin entered.

He said softly, 'I've been expecting you more or less. I suppose you feel sick about all this.'

'I do.'

'Well – I'm sorry. There was no way of preventing it. When the call came out from Hyper Base for us, I knew that something must have gone wrong with the modified Nestors. But what was there to do? I couldn't break the matter to you on the trip here as I would have liked to, because I had to be sure. The matter of the modification is top secret.'

The psychologist muttered, 'I should have been told. US Robots had no right to modify positronic brains this way without the approval of a psychologist.'

Bogert lifted his eyebrows and sighed. 'Be reasonable, Susan. You couldn't have influenced them. In this matter, the government was bound to have its way. They want the Hyperatomic Drive and the etheric physicists want robots that won't interfere with them. They were going to get them even if it did mean twisting the First Law. We had to admit it was possible from a construction stand-point and they swore a mighty oath that they wanted only twelve, that they would be used only at Hyper Base, that they would be destroyed once the Drive was perfected, and that full precautions would be taken. And they insisted on secrecy – and that's the situation.'

Dr Calvin spoke through her teeth, 'I would have resigned.'

'It wouldn't have helped. The government was offering the company a fortune, and threatening it with antirobot legislation in case of a refusal. We were stuck then, and we're badly stuck now. If this leaks out, it might hurt Kallner and the government, but it would hurt US Robots a devil of a lot more.'

The psychologist stared at him. 'Peter, don't you realize what all this is about? Can't you understand what the removal of the First Law means? It isn't just a matter of secrecy.'

'I know what removal would mean. I'm not a child. It would mean complete instability, with no nonimaginary solutions to the positronic Field Equations.'

'Yes, mathematically. But can you translate that into crude psychological thought? All normal life, Peter, consciously or otherwise, resents domination. If the domination is by an inferior, or by a supposed inferior, the resentment becomes stronger. Physically, and, to an extent, mentally, a robot – any robot – is superior to human beings. What makes him slavish, then? *Only the First Law!* Why, without it, the first order you tried to give a robot would result in your death. Unstable? What do you think?'

'Susan,' said Bogert, with an air of sympathetic amusement. 'I'll admit that this Frankenstein Complex you're exhibiting has a certain justification – hence the First Law in the first place. But the Law, I repeat and repeat, has not been removed – merely modified.'

'And what about the stability of the brain?'

The mathematician thrust out his lips, 'Decreased, naturally. But it's within the border of safety. The first Nestors were delivered to Hyper Base nine months ago, and nothing whatever has gone wrong till now, and even this involves merely fear of discovery and not danger to humans.'

'Very well, then. We'll see what comes of the morning conference.'

Bogert saw her politely to the door and grimaced eloquently when she left. He saw no reason to change his perennial opinion of her as a sour and fidgety frustration.

Susan Calvin's train of thought did not include Bogert in the least. She had dismissed him years ago as a smooth and pretentious sleekness.

Gerald Black had taken his degree in etheric physics the year before and, in common with his entire generation of physicists, found himself engaged in the problem of the Drive. He now made a proper addition to the general atmosphere of these meetings on Hyper Base. In his stained white smock, he was half rebellious and wholly uncertain. His stocky strength seemed striving for release and his fingers, as they twisted each other with nervous yanks, might have forced an iron bar out of true.

Major-general Kallner sat beside him, the two from US Robots faced him.

Black said, 'I'm told that I was the last to see Nestor 10 before he vanished. I take it you want to ask me about that.'

Dr Calvin regarded him with interest, 'You sound as if you were not sure, young man. Don't you *know* whether you were the last to see him?'

'He worked with me, ma'am, on the field generators, and he was with me the morning of his disappearance. I don't know if anyone saw him after about noon. No one admits having done so.'

'Do you think anyone's lying about it?'

'I don't say that. But I don't say that I want the blame of it, either.' His dark eyes smoldered.

'There's no question of blame. The robot acted as it did because of what it is. We're just trying to locate it, Mr Black, and let's put everything else aside. Now if you've worked with the robot, you probably know it better than anyone else. Was there anything unusual about it that you noticed? Had you ever worked with robots before?'

'I've worked with other robots we have here – the simple ones. Nothing different about the Nestors except that they're a good deal cleverer – and more annoying.'

'Annoying? In what way?'

'Well – perhaps it's not their fault. The work here is rough and most of us get a little jagged. Fooling around with hyperspace isn't fun.' He smiled feebly, finding pleasure in confession. 'We run the risk continually of blowing a hole in normal space-time fabric and dropping right out of the universe, asteroid and all. Sounds screwy, doesn't it? Naturally, you're on edge sometimes. But these Nestors aren't. They're curious, they're calm, they don't worry. It's enough to drive you nuts at times. When you want something done in a tearing hurry, they seem to take their time. Sometimes I'd rather do without.'

'You say they take their time? Have they ever refused an order?'

'Oh, no' – hastily. 'They do it all right. They tell you when they think you're wrong, though. They don't know anything about the subject but what we taught them, but that doesn't stop them. Maybe I imagine it, but the other fellows have the same trouble with their Nestors.'

General Kallner cleared his throat ominously, 'Why have no complaints reached me on the matter, Black?'

The young physicist reddened, 'We didn't *really* want to do without the robots, sir, and besides we weren't certain exactly how such . . . uh . . . minor complaints might be received.'

Bogert interrupted softly, 'Anything in particular happen the morning you last saw it?'

There was a silence. With a quiet motion, Calvin repressed the comment that was about to emerge from Kallner, and waited patiently.

Then Black spoke in blurting anger, 'I had a little trouble with it. I'd broken a Kimball tube that morning and was out five days of work; my entire program was behind schedule; I hadn't received any mail from home for a couple of weeks. And *he* came around wanting me to repeat an experiment I had abandoned a month ago. He was always annoying me on that subject and I was tired of it. I told him to go away – and that's all I saw of him.'

'You told him to go away?' asked Dr Calvin with sharp interest. 'In just those words? Did you say "Go away"? Try to remember the exact words.'

There was apparently an internal struggle in progress. Black cradled his forehead in a broad palm for a moment, then tore it away and said defiantly, 'I said, "Go lose yourself".'

Bogert laughed for a short moment. 'And he did, eh?'

But Calvin wasn't finished. She spoke cajolingly, 'Now we're getting somewhere, Mr Black. But exact details are important. In understanding the robot's actions, a word, a gesture, an emphasis may be everything. You couldn't have said just those three words, for instance, could you? By your own description you must have been in a hasty mood. Perhaps you strengthened your speech a little.'

The young man reddened, 'Well . . . I may have called it a . . . a few things.'

'Exactly what things?'

'Oh – I wouldn't remember exactly. Besides I couldn't repeat it. You know how you get when you're excited.' His embarrassed laugh was almost a giggle, 'I sort of have a tendency to strong language.'

'That's quite all right,' she replied with prim severity. 'At the moment, I'm a psychologist. I would like to have you repeat exactly what you said as nearly as you remember, and, even more important, the exact tone of voice you used.'

Black looked at his commanding officer for support, found none. His eyes grew round and appalled, 'But I can't.'

'You must.'

'Suppose,' said Bogert, with ill-hidden amusement, 'you address me. You may find it easier.'

The young man's scarlet face turned to Bogert. He swallowed. 'I said—' His voice faded out. He tried again, 'I said—'

And he drew a deep breath and spewed it out hastily in one long succession of syllables. Then, in the charged air that lingered, he concluded almost in tears, '. . . more or less. I don't remember the exact order of what I called him, and maybe I left out something or put in something, but that was about it.'

Only the slightest flush betrayed any feeling on the part of the robopsychologist. She said, 'I am aware of the meaning of most of the terms used. The others, I suppose, are equally derogatory.'

'I'm afraid so,' agreed the tormented Black.

'And in among it, you told him to lose himself.'

'I meant it only figuratively.'

'I realize that. No disciplinary action is intended, I am sure.' And at her glance, the general, who, five seconds earlier, had seemed not sure at all, nodded angrily.

'You may leave, Mr Black. Thank you for your co-operation.'

It took five hours for Susan Calvin to interview the sixty-three robots. It was five hours of multi-repetition, of replacement after replacement of identical robot; of Questions A, B, C, D; and Answers A, B, C, D; of a carefully bland expression, a carefully neutral tone, a carefully friendly atmosphere; and a hidden wire recorder.

The psychologist felt drained of vitality when she was finished.

Bogert was waiting for her and looked expectant as she dropped the recording spool with a clang upon the plastic of the desk.

She shook her head, 'All sixty-three seemed the same to me. I couldn't tell—'

He said, 'You couldn't expect to tell by ear, Susan. Suppose we analyze the recordings.'

Ordinarily, the mathematical interpretation of verbal reactions of robots is one of the more intricate branches of robotic analysis. It requires a staff of trained technicians and the help of complicated computing machines. Bogert knew that. Bogert stated as much, in an extreme of unshown annoyance after having listened to each set of replies, made lists of word deviations, and graphs of the intervals of responses.

'There are no anomalies present, Susan. The variations in

wording and the time reactions are within the limits of ordinary frequency groupings. We need finer methods. They must have computers here. No.' He frowned and nibbled delicately at a thumbnail. 'We can't use computers. Too much danger of leakage. Or maybe if we—'

Dr Calvin stopped him with an impatient gesture, 'Please, Peter. This isn't one of your petty laboratory problems. If we can't determine the modified Nestor by some gross difference that we can see with the naked eye, one that there is no mistake about, we're out of luck. The danger of being wrong, and of letting him escape is otherwise too great. It's not enough to point out a minute irregularity in a graph. I tell you, if that's all I've got to go on, I'd destroy them all just to be certain. Have you spoken to the other modified Nestors?'

'Yes, I have,' snapped back Bogert, 'and there's nothing wrong with them. They're above normal in friendliness if anything. They answered my questions, displayed pride in their knowledge – except the two new ones that haven't had time to learn their etheric physics. They laughed rather good-naturedly at my ignorance in some of the specializations here.' He shrugged. 'I suppose that forms some of the basis for resentment toward them on the part of the technicians here. The robots are perhaps too willing to impress you with their greater knowledge.'

'Can you try a few Planar Reactions to see if there has been any change, any deterioration, in their mental set-up since manufacture?'

'I haven't yet, but I will.' He shook a slim finger at her, 'You're losing your nerve, Susan. I don't see what it is you're dramatizing. They're essentially harmless.'

'They are?' Calvin took fire. 'They are? Do you realize one of them is lying? One of the sixty-three robots I have just interviewed has deliberately lied to me after the strictest injunction to tell the truth. The abnormality indicated is horribly deep-seated, and horribly frightening.'

Peter Bogert felt his teeth harden against each other. He said, 'Not at all. Look! Nestor 10 was given orders to lose himself. Those orders were expressed in maximum urgency by the person most authorized to command him. You can't counteract that order either by superior urgency or superior right of command. Naturally, the robot will attempt to defend the carrying out of his orders. In fact, objectively, I admire his ingenuity. How better can a robot lose himself than to hide himself among a group of similar robots?'

'Yes, you would admire it. I've detected amusement in you, Peter – amusement and an appalling lack of understanding. Are you a roboticist, Peter? Those robots attach importance to what they consider superiority. You've just said as much yourself. Subconsciously they feel humans to be inferior and the First Law which protects us from them is imperfect. They are unstable. And here we have a young man ordering a robot to leave him, to lose himself, with every verbal appearance of revulsion, disdain, and disgust. Granted, that robot must follow orders, but subconsciously, there is resentment. It will become more important than ever for it to prove that it is superior despite the horrible names it was called. It may become *so* important that what's left of the First Law won't be enough.'

'How on Earth, or anywhere in the Solar System, Susan, is a robot going to know the meaning of the assorted strong language used upon him? Obscenity is not one of the things impressioned upon his brain.'

'Original impressionment is not everything,' Calvin snarled at him. 'Robots have learning capacity, you . . . you fool—' And Bogert knew that she had really lost her temper. She continued hastily, 'Don't you suppose he could tell from the tone used that the words weren't complimentary? Don't you suppose he's heard the words used before and noted upon what occasions?'

'Well, then,' shouted Bogert, 'will you kindly tell me one way in which a modified robot can harm a human being, no matter how offended it is, no matter how sick with desire to prove superiority?'

'If I tell you one way, will you keep quiet?'

'Yes.'

They were leaning across the table at each other, angry eyes nailed together.

The psychologist said, 'If a modified robot were to drop a heavy weight upon a human being, he would not be breaking the First Law, if he did so with the knowledge that his strength and reaction speed would be sufficient to snatch the weight away before it struck the man. However once the weight left his fingers, he would be no longer the active medium. Only the blind force of gravity would be that. The robot could then change his mind and merely by inaction, allow the weight to strike. The modified First Law allows that.'

'That's an awful stretch of imagination.'

'That's what my profession requires sometimes. Peter, let's not quarrel. Let's work. You know the exact nature of the stimulus that caused the robot to lose himself. You have the records of his original mental make-up. I want you to tell me how possible it is for our robot to do the sort of thing I just talked about. Not the specific instance, mind you, but that whole class of response. And I want it done quickly.'

'And meanwhile—'

'And meanwhile, we'll have to try performance tests directly on the response to First Law.'

Gerald Black, at his own request, was supervising the mush-rooming wooden partitions that were springing up in a bellying circle on the vaulted third floor of Radiation Building 2. The laborers worked, in the main, silently, but more than one was openly a-wonder at the sixty-three photocells that required installation.

One of them sat down near Black, removed his hat, and wiped his forehead thoughtfully with a freckled forearm.

Black nodded at him, 'How's it doing, Walensky?'

Walensky shrugged and fired a cigar, 'Smooth as butter. What's going on anyway, Doc? First, there's no work for three days and then we have this mess of jiggers.' He leaned backward on his elbows and puffed smoke.

Black twitched his eyebrows, 'A couple of robot men came over from Earth. Remember the trouble we had with robots running into the gamma fields, before we pounded it into their skulls that they weren't to do it.'

'Yeah. Didn't we get new robots?'

'We got some replacements, but mostly it was a job of indoctrination. Anyway, the people who make them want to figure out robots that aren't hit so bad by gamma rays.'

'Sure seems funny, though, to stop all the work on the Drive for this robot deal. I thought nothing was allowed to stop the Drive.'

'Well, it's the fellows upstairs that have the say on that. Me – I just do as I'm told. Probably all a matter of pull—'

'Yeah,' the electrician jerked a smile, and winked a wise eye. 'Somebody knew somebody in Washington. But as long as my pay comes through on the dot, I should worry. The Drive's none of my affair. What are they going to do here?'

'You're asking me? They brought a mess of robots with them – over sixty, and they're going to measure reactions. That's all *my* knowledge.'

'How long will it take?'

'I wish I knew.'

'Well,' Walensky said, with heavy sarcasm, 'as long as they dish me my money, they can play games all they want.'

Black felt quietly satisfied. Let the story spread. It was harmless, and near enough to the truth to take the fangs out of curiosity.

A man sat in the chair, motionless, silent. A weight dropped, crashed downward, then pounded aside at the last moment under the synchronized thump of a sudden force beam. In sixty-three wooden cells, watching NS-2 robots dashed forward in that split second before the weight veered, and sixty-three photocells five feet ahead of their original positions jiggled the marking pen and presented a little jag on the paper. The weight rose and dropped, rose and dropped, rose—

Ten times!

Ten times the robots sprang forward and stopped, as the man remained safely seated.

Major-general Kallner had not worn his uniform in its entirety since the first dinner with the US Robot representatives. He wore nothing over his blue-gray shirt now, the collar was open, and the black tie was pulled loose.

He looked hopefully at Bogert, who was still blandly neat and whose inner tension was perhaps betrayed only by the trace of glister at his temples.

The general said, 'How does it look? What is it you're trying to see?'

Bogert replied, 'A difference which may turn out to be a little too subtle for our purposes, I'm afraid. For sixty-two of those robots the necessity of jumping toward the apparently threatened human was what we call, in robotics, a forced reaction. You see, even when the robots knew that the human in question would not come to harm – and after the third or fourth time they must have known it – they could not prevent reacting as they did. First Law required it.'

'Well?'

'But the sixty-third robot, the modified Nestor, had no such compulsion. He was under free action. If he had wished, he could have remained in his seat. Unfortunately,' and his voice was mildly regretful, 'he didn't so wish.'

'Why do you suppose?'

Bogert shrugged, 'I suppose Dr Calvin will tell us when she gets here. Probably with a horribly pessimistic interpretation, too. She is sometimes a bit annoying.'

'She's qualified, isn't she?' demanded the general with a sudden frown of uneasiness.

'Yes.' Bogert seemed amused. 'She's qualified all right. She understands robots like a sister – comes from hating human beings so much, I think. It's just that, psychologist or not, she's an extreme neurotic. Has paranoid tendencies. Don't take her too seriously.'

He spread the long row of broken-line graphs out in front of him. 'You see, general, in the case of each robot the time interval from moment of drop to the completion of a five-foot movement tends to decrease as the tests are repeated. There's a definite mathematical relationship that governs such things and failure to conform would indicate marked abnormality in the positronic brain. Unfortunately, all here appear normal.'

'But if our Nestor 10 was not responding with a forced action, why isn't his curve different? I don't understand that.'

'It's simple enough. Robotic responses are not perfectly analogous to human responses, more's the pity. In human beings, voluntary action is much slower than reflex action. But that's not the case with robots; with them it is merely a question of freedom of choice, otherwise the speeds of free and forced action are much the same. What I *had* been expecting, though, was that Nestor 10 would be caught by surprise the first time and allow too great an interval to elapse before responding.'

'And he didn't?'

'I'm afraid not.'

'Then we haven't gotten anywhere.' The general sat back with an expression of pain. 'It's five days since you've come.'

At this point, Susan Calvin entered and slammed the door behind her. 'Put your graphs away, Peter,' she cried, 'you know they don't show anything.'

She mumbled something impatiently as Kallner half-rose to greet her, and went on, 'We'll have to try something else quickly. I don't like what's happening.'

Bogert exchanged a resigned glance with the general. 'Is anything wrong?'

'You mean specifically? No. But I don't like to have Nestor 10 continue to elude us. It's bad. It *must* be gratifying his swollen sense of superiority. I'm afraid that his motivation is no longer simply one of following orders. I think it's becoming more a matter of sheer neurotic necessity to out-think humans. That's a dangerously unhealthy situation. Peter, have you done what I asked? Have you worked out the instability factors of the modified NS-2 along the lines I want?'

'It's in progress,' said the mathematician, without interest.

She stared at him angrily for a moment, then turned to Kallner. 'Nestor 10 is decidedly aware of what we're doing, general. He had no reason to jump for the bait in this experiment, especially after the first time, when he must have seen that there was no real danger to our subject. The others couldn't help it, but *he* was deliberately falsifying a reaction.'

'What do you think we ought to do now, then, Dr Calvin?'

'Make it impossible for him to fake an action the next time.

We will repeat the experiment, but with an addition. High-tension cables, capable of electrocuting the Nestor models, will be placed between subject and robot – enough of them to avoid the possibility of jumping over – and the robot will be made perfectly aware in advance that touching the cables will mean death.'

'Hold on,' spat out Bogert with sudden viciousness. 'I rule that out. We are not electrocuting two million dollars' worth of robots to locate Nestor 10. There are other ways.'

'You're certain? You've found none. In any case, it's not a question of electrocution. We can arrange a relay which will break the current at the instant of application of weight. If the robot should place his weight on it, he won't die. *But he won't know that*, you see.'

The general's eyes gleamed into hope. 'Will that work?'

'It should. Under those conditions, Nestor 10 would have to remain in his seat. He could be *ordered* to touch the cables and die, for the Second Law of obedience is superior to the Third Law of self-preservation. But *he won't* be ordered to; he will merely be left to his own devices, as will all the robots. In the case of the normal robots, the First Law of human safety will drive them to their death even without orders. But not our Nestor 10. Without the entire First Law, and without having received any orders on the matter, the Third Law, self-preservation, will be the highest operating, and he will have no choice but to remain in his seat. It would be a forced action.'

'Will it be done tonight, then?'

'Tonight,' said the psychologist, 'if the cables can be laid in time. I'll tell the robots now what they're to be up against.'

A man sat in the chair, motionless, silent. A weight dropped, crashed downward, then pounded aside at the last moment under the synchronized thump of a sudden force beam.

Only once—

And from her small camp chair in the observing booth in the balcony, Dr Susan Calvin rose with a short gasp of pure horror.

Sixty-three robots sat quietly in their chairs, staring owlishly at the endangered man before them. Not one moved.

Dr Calvin was angry, angry almost past endurance. Angry the worse for not daring to show it to the robots that, one by one, were entering the room and then leaving. She checked the list. Number Twenty-eight was due in now – Thirty-five still lay ahead of her.

Number Twenty-eight entered, diffidently.

She forced herself into reasonable calm. 'And who are you?'

The robot replied in a low, uncertain voice, 'I have received no number of my own yet, ma'am. I'm an NS-2 robot, and I was Number Twenty-eight in line outside. I have a slip of paper here that I'm to give to you.'

'You haven't been in here before this today?'

'No, ma'am.'

'Sit down. Right there. I want to ask you some questions, Number Twenty-eight. Were you in the Radiation Room of Building Two about four hours ago?'

The robot had trouble answering. Then it came out hoarsely, like machinery needing oil, 'Yes, ma'am.'

'There was a man who almost came to harm there, wasn't there?'

'Yes, ma'am.'

'You did nothing, did you?'

'No, ma'am.'

'The man might have been hurt because of your inaction. Do you know that?'

'Yes, ma'am. I couldn't help it, ma'am.' It is hard to picture a large expressionless metallic figure cringing, but it managed.

'I want you to tell me exactly why you did nothing to save him.'

'I want to explain, ma'am. I certainly don't want to have you . . . have *anyone* think that I could do a thing that might cause harm to a master. Oh, no, that would be a horrible . . . an inconceivable—'

'Please don't get excited, boy. I'm not blaming you for anything. I only want to know what you were thinking at the time.'

'Ma'am, before it all happened you told us that one of the masters would be in danger of harm from that weight that keeps falling and that we would have to cross electric cables if we were to try to save him. Well, ma'am, that wouldn't stop me. What is my destruction compared to the safety of a master? But . . . but it occurred to me that if I died on my way to him, I wouldn't be able to save him anyway. The weight would crush him and then I would be dead for no purpose and perhaps some day some other master might come to harm who wouldn't have, if I had only stayed alive. Do you understand me, ma'am?'

'You mean that it was merely a choice of the man dying, or both the man and yourself dying. Is that right?'

'Yes, ma'am. It was impossible to save the master. He might be considered dead. In that case, it is inconceivable that I destroy myself for nothing – without orders.'

The robopsychologist twiddled a pencil. She had heard the same story with insignificant verbal variations twenty-seven times before. This was the crucial question now.

'Boy,' she said, 'your thinking has its points, but it is not the sort of thing I thought you might think. Did you think of this yourself?'

The robot hesitated. 'No.'

'Who thought of it, then?'

'We were talking last night, and one of us got that idea and it sounded reasonable.'

'Which one?'

The robot thought deeply. 'I don't know. Just one of us.'

She sighed, 'That's all.'

Number Twenty-nine was next. Thirty-four after that.

Major-general Kallner, too, was angry. For one week all of Hyper Base had stopped dead, barring some paper work on the subsidiary asteroids of the group. For nearly one week, the two top experts in the field had aggravated the situation with useless tests. And now they – or the woman, at any rate – made impossible propositions.

Fortunately for the general situation, Kallner felt it impolitic to display his anger openly.

Susan Calvin was insisting, 'Why not, sir? It's obvious that the present situation is unfortunate. The only way we may reach results in the future – or what future is left us in this matter – is to separate the robots. We can't keep them together any longer.'

'My dear Dr Calvin,' rumbled the general, his voice sinking into the lower baritone registers. 'I don't see how I can quarter sixty-three robots all over the place—'

Dr Calvin raised her arms helplessly. 'I can do nothing then. Nestor 10 will either imitate what the other robots would do, or else argue them plausibly into not doing what he himself cannot do. And in any case, this is bad business. We're in actual combat with this little lost robot of ours and he's winning out. Every victory of his aggravates his abnormality.'

She rose to her feet in determination. 'General Kallner, if you do not separate the robots as I ask, then I can only demand that all sixty-three be destroyed immediately.'

'You demand it, do you?' Bogert looked up suddenly, and with real anger. 'What gives you the right to demand any such thing. Those robots remain as they are. *I'm* responsible to the management, not you.'

'And I,' added Major-general Kallner, 'am responsible to the World Co-ordinator – and I must have this settled.'

'In that case,' flashed back Calvin, 'there is nothing for me to do but resign. If necessary to force you to the necessary destruction, I'll make this whole matter public. It was not I that approved the manufacture of modified robots.'

'One word from you, Dr Calvin,' said the general, deliberately, 'in violation of security measures, and you would be certainly imprisoned instantly.'

Bogert felt the matter to be getting out of hand. His voice grew syrupy, 'Well, now, we're beginning to act like children, all of us. We need only a little more time. Surely we can outwit a robot without resigning, or imprisoning people, or destroying two millions.'

The psychologist turned on him with quiet fury, 'I don't want any unbalanced robots in existence. We have one Nestor that's definitely unbalanced, eleven more that are potentially so, and sixty-two normal robots that are being subjected to an unbalanced environment. The only absolute safe method is complete destruction.'

The signal-burr brought all three to a halt, and the angry tumult of growingly unrestrained emotion froze.

'Come in,' growled Kallner.

It was Gerald Black, looking perturbed. He had heard angry voices. He said, 'I thought I'd come myself . . . didn't like to ask anyone else—'

'What is it? Don't orate—'

'The locks of Compartment C in the trading ship have been played with. There are fresh scratches on them.'

'Compartment C?' exclaimed Calvin quickly. 'That's the one that holds the robots, isn't it? Who did it?'

'From the inside,' said Black, laconically.

'The lock isn't out of order, is it?'

'No. It's all right. I've been staying on the ship now for four days and none of them have tried to get out. But I thought you ought to know, and I didn't like to spread the news. I noticed the matter myself.'

'Is anyone there now?' demanded the general.

'I left Robbins and McAdams there.'

There was a thoughtful silence, and then Dr Calvin said, ironically, 'Well?'

Kallner rubbed his nose uncertainly, 'What's it all about?'

'Isn't it obvious? Nestor 10 is planning to leave. That order to lose himself is dominating his abnormality past anything we can do. I wouldn't be surprised if what's left of his First Law would scarcely be powerful enough to override it. He is perfectly capable of seizing the ship and leaving with it. Then we'd have a mad robot on a spaceship. What would he do next? Any idea? Do you still want to leave them together, general?'

'Nonsense,' interrupted Bogert. He had regained his smoothness. 'All that from a few scratch marks on a lock.'

'Have you, Dr Bogert, completed the analysis I've required, since you volunteer opinions?'

'Yes.'

'May I see it?'

'No.'

'Why not? Or mayn't I ask that, either?'

'Because there's no point in it, Susan. I told you in advance that these modified robots are less stable than the normal variety, and my analysis shows it. There's a certain very small chance of breakdown under extreme circumstances that are not likely to occur. Let it go at that. I won't give you ammunition for your absurd claim that sixty-two perfectly good robots be destroyed just because so far you lack the ability to detect Nestor 10 among them.'

Susan Calvin stared him down and let disgust fill her eyes. 'You won't let anything stand in the way of the permanent directorship, will you?'

'Please,' begged Kallner, half in irritation. 'Do you insist that nothing further can be done, Dr Calvin?'

'I can't think of anything, sir,' she replied, wearily. 'If there were only other differences between Nestor 10 and the normal robots, differences that didn't involve the First Law. Even one other difference. Something in impressionment, environment, specification—' And she stopped suddenly.

'What is it?'

'I've thought of something . . . I think—' Her eyes grew distant and hard, 'These modified Nestors, Peter. They get the same impressioning the normal ones get, don't they?'

'Yes. Exactly the same.'

'And what was it you were saying, Mr Black?' she turned to the young man, who through the storms that had followed his news had maintained a discreet silence. 'Once when complaining of the Nestors' attitude of superiority, you said the technicians had taught them all they knew.'

'Yes, in etheric physics. They're not acquainted with the subject when they come here.'

'That's right,' said Bogert, in surprise. 'I told you, Susan, when I spoke to the other Nestors here that the two new arrivals hadn't learned etheric physics yet.'

'And why is that?' Dr Calvin was speaking in mounting excitement. 'Why aren't NS-2 models impressioned with etheric physics to start with?'

'I can tell you that,' said Kallner. 'It's all of a piece with the secrecy. We thought that if we made a special model with knowledge of etheric physics, used twelve of them and put the others to work in an unrelated field, there might be suspicion. Men working with normal Nestors might wonder why they knew etheric physics. So there was merely an impressionment with a capacity for training in the field. Only the ones that come here, naturally, receive such a training. It's that simple.'

'I understand. Please get out of here, the lot of you. Let me have an hour or so.'

Calvin felt she could not face the ordeal for a third time. Her mind had contemplated it and rejected it with an intensity that left her nauseated. She could face that unending file of repetitious robots no more.

So Bogert asked the questions now, while she sat aside, eyes and mind half-closed.

Number Fourteen came in – forty-nine to go.

Bogert looked up from the guide sheet and said, 'What is your number in line?'

'Fourteen, sir.' The robot presented his numbered ticket.

'Sit down, boy.'

Bogert asked, 'You haven't been here before on this day?'

'No, sir.'

'Well, boy, we are going to have another man in danger of harm soon after we're through here. In fact, when you leave this room, you will be led to a stall where you will wait quietly, till you are needed. Do you understand?'

'Yes, sir.'

'Now, naturally, if a man is in danger of harm, you will try to save him.'

'Naturally, sir.'

'Unfortunately, between the man and yourself, there will be a gamma ray field.'

Silence.

'Do you know what gamma rays are?' asked Bogert sharply.

'Energy radiation, sir?'

The next question came in a friendly, offhand manner, 'Ever work with gamma rays?'

'No, sir.' The answer was definite.

'Mm-m. Well, boy, gamma rays will kill you instantly. They'll destroy your brain. That is a fact you must know and remember. Naturally, you don't want to destroy yourself.'

'Naturally.' Again the robot seemed shocked. Then, slowly, 'But, sir, if the gamma rays are between myself and the master that may be harmed, how can I save him? I would be destroying myself to no purpose.'

'Yes, there is that,' Bogert seemed concerned about the matter. 'The only thing I can advise, boy, is that if you detect the gamma radiation between yourself and the man, you may as well sit where you are.'

The robot was openly relieved. 'Thank you, sir. There wouldn't be any use, would there?'

'Of course not. But if there *weren't* any dangerous radiation, that would be a different matter.'

'Naturally, sir. No question of that.'

'You may leave now. The man on the other side of the door will lead you to your stall. Please wait there.'

He turned to Susan Calvin when the robot left. 'How did that go, Susan?'

'Very well,' she said, dully.

'Do you think we could catch Nestor 10 by quick questioning on etheric physics?'

'Perhaps, but it's not sure enough.' Her hands lay loosely in her lap. 'Remember, he's fighting us. He's on his guard. The only way we can catch him is to outsmart him – and, within his limitations, he can think much more quickly than a human being.'

'Well, just for fun – suppose I ask the robots from now on a few questions on gamma rays. Wave length limits, for instance.'

'No!' Dr Calvin's eyes sparked to life. 'It would be too easy for him to deny knowledge and then he'd be warned against the test that's coming up – which is our real chance. Please follow the questions I've indicated, Peter, and don't improvise. It's just within the bounds of risk to ask them if they've ever worked with gamma rays. And try to sound even less interested than you do when you ask it.'

Bogert shrugged, and pressed the buzzer that would allow the entrance of Number Fifteen.

The large Radiation Room was in readiness once more. The robots waited patiently in their wooden cells, all open to the center but closed off from each other.

Major-general Kallner mopped his brow slowly with a large handkerchief while Dr Calvin checked the last details with Black.

'You're sure now,' she demanded, 'that none of the robots have had a chance to talk with each other after leaving the Orientation Room?'

'Absolutely sure,' insisted Black. 'There's not been a word exchanged.'

'And the robots are put in the proper stalls?'

'Here's the plan.'

The psychologist looked at it thoughtfully, 'Um-m-m.'

The general peered over her shoulder. 'What's the idea of the arrangement, Dr Calvin?'

'I've asked to have those robots that appeared even slightly out of true in the previous tests concentrated on one side of the circle. I'm going to be sitting in the center myself this time, and I wanted to watch those particularly.'

'*You're* going to be sitting there—' exclaimed Bogert.

'Why not?' she demanded coldly. 'What I expect to see may be something quite momentary. I can't risk having anyone else as main observer. Peter, you'll be in the observing booth, and I want you to keep your eye on the opposite side of the circle. General Kallner, I've arranged for motion pictures to be taken of each robot, in case visual observation isn't enough. If these are required, the robots are to remain exactly where they are until the pictures are developed and studied. None must leave, none must change place. Is that clear?'

'Perfectly.'

'Then let's try it this one last time.'

Susan Calvin sat in the chair, silent, eyes restless. A weight dropped, crashed downward, then pounded aside at the last moment under the synchronized thump of a sudden force beam.

And a single robot jerked upright and took two steps.

And stopped.

But Dr Calvin was upright, and her finger pointed to him sharply. 'Nestor 10, come here,' she cried, '*come here*! COME HERE!'

Slowly, reluctantly, the robot took another step forward. The psychologist shouted at the top of her voice, without taking her eyes from the robot, 'Get every other robot out of this place, somebody. Get them out quickly, and *keep* them out.'

Somewhere within reach of her ears there was noise, and the thud of hard feet upon the floor. She did not look away.

Nestor 10 – if it was Nestor 10 – took another step, and then, under force of her imperious gesture, two more. He was only ten feet away, when he spoke harshly, 'I have been told to be lost—'

Another step. 'I must not disobey. They have not found me so far – He would think me a failure – He told me – But it's not so – I am powerful and intelligent—'

The words came in spurts.

Another step. 'I know a good deal – He would think . . . I mean I've been found – Disgraceful – Not I – I am intelligent – And by just a master . . . who is weak – Slow—'

Another step – and one metal arm flew out suddenly to her shoulder, and she felt the weight bearing her down. Her throat constricted, and she felt a shriek tear through.

Dimly, she heard Nestor 10's next words, 'No one must find me. No master—' and the cold metal was against her, and she was sinking under the weight of it.

And then a queer, metallic sound, and she was on the ground with an unfelt thump, and a gleaming arm was heavy across her body. It did not move. Nor did Nestor 10, who sprawled beside her.

And now faces were bending over her.

Gerald Black was gasping. 'Are you hurt, Dr Calvin?'

She shook her head feebly. They pried the arm off her and lifted her gently to her feet, 'What happened?'

Black said, 'I bathed the place in gamma rays for five seconds. We didn't know what was happening. It wasn't till the last second that we realized he was attacking you, and then there was no time for anything but a gamma field. He went down in an instant. There wasn't enough to harm you though. Don't worry about it.'

'I'm not worried.' She closed her eyes and leaned for a moment upon his shoulder. 'I don't think I was attacked exactly. Nestor 10 was simply *trying* to do so. What was left of the First Law was still holding him back.'

*　　*　　*

Susan Calvin and Peter Bogert, two weeks after their first meeting with Major-general Kallner, had their last. Work at Hyper Base had been resumed. The trading ship with its sixty-two normal NS-2s was gone to wherever it was bound, with an officially imposed story to explain its two weeks' delay. The government cruiser was making ready to carry the two roboticists back to Earth.

Kallner was once again a-gleam in dress uniform. His white gloves shone as he shook hands.

Calvin said, 'The other modified Nestors are, of course, to be destroyed.'

'They will be. We'll make shift with normal robots, or, if necessary, do without.'

'Good.'

'But tell me – you haven't explained – how was it done?'

She smiled tightly, 'Oh, that. I would have told you in advance if I had been more certain of its working. You see, Nestor 10 had a superiority complex that was becoming more radical all the time. He liked to think that he and the other robots knew more than human beings. It was becoming very important for him to think so.

'We knew that. So we warned every robot in advance that gamma rays would kill them, which they would, and we further warned them all that gamma rays would be between them and myself. So they all stayed where they were, naturally. By Nestor 10's own logic in the previous test they had all decided that there was no point in trying to save a human being if they were sure to die before they could do it.'

'Well, yes, Dr Calvin, I understand that. But why did Nestor 10 himself leave his seat?'

'Ah! That was a little arrangement between myself and your young Mr Black. You see it wasn't gamma rays that flooded the area between myself and the robots – but infrared rays. Just ordinary heat rays, absolutely harmless. Nestor 10 knew they were infrared and harmless and so he began to dash out, as he expected the rest would do, under First Law compulsion. It was only a fraction of a second too late that he remembered that the normal NS-2s could detect radiation, but could not identify the type. That he himself could only identify wavelengths by virtue of the training he had received at Hyper Base, under mere human beings, was a little too humiliating to remember for just a moment. To the normal robots the area was fatal because we had told them it would be, and only Nestor 10 knew we were lying.

'And just for a moment he forgot, or didn't want to remember, that other robots might be more ignorant than human beings. His very superiority caught him. Good-bye, general.'

7

Escape!

When Susan Calvin returned from Hyper Base, Alfred Lanning was waiting for her. The old man never spoke about his age, but everyone knew it to be over seventy-five. Yet his mind was keen, and if he had finally allowed himself to be made Director-Emeritus of Research with Bogert as acting Director, it did not prevent him from appearing in his office daily.

'How close are they to the Hyperatomic Drive?' he asked.

'I don't know,' she replied irritably. 'I didn't ask.'

'Hmm. I wish they'd hurry. Because if they don't, Consolidated might beat them to it. And beat *us* to it as well.'

'*Consolidated*? What have they got to do with it?'

'Well, we're not the only ones with calculating machines. Ours may be positronic, but that doesn't mean they're better. Robertson is calling a big meeting about it tomorrow. He's been waiting for you to come back.'

Robertson of US Robots and Mechanical Men Corporation, son of the founder, pointed his lean nose at his general manager and his Adam's apple jumped as he said, 'You start now. Let's get this straight.'

The general manager did so with alacrity, 'Here's the deal

now, chief. Consolidated Robots approached us a month ago with a funny sort of proposition. They brought about five tons of figures, equations, all that sort of stuff. It was a problem, see, and they wanted an answer from The Brain. The terms were as follows—'

He ticked them off on thick fingers: 'A hundred thousand for us if there is no solution and we can tell them the missing factors. Two hundred thousand if there is a solution, plus costs of construction of the machine involved, plus quarter interest in all profits derived therefrom. The problem concerns the development of an interstellar engine—'

Robertson frowned and his lean figure stiffened. 'Despite the fact that they have a thinking machine of their own. Right?'

'Exactly what makes the whole proposition a foul ball, chief. Levver, take it from there.'

Abe Levver looked up from the far end of the conference table and smoothed his stubbled chin with a faint rasping sound. He smiled:

'It's this way, sir. Consolidated *had* a thinking machine. It's broken.'

'What?' Robertson half rose.

'That's right. Broken! It's *kaput*. Nobody knows why, but I got hold of some pretty interesting guesses – like, for instance, that they asked it to give them an interstellar engine with the same set of information they came to us with, and that it cracked their machine wide open. It's scrap – just scrap now.'

'You get it, chief?' The general manager was wildly jubilant. 'You get it? There isn't any industrial research group of any size that isn't trying to develop a space-warp engine, and Consolidated and US Robots have the lead on the field with our super robot-brains. Now that they've managed to foul theirs up, we have a clear field. That's the nub, the . . . uh . . . motivation. It will take them six years at least to build another and they're sunk, unless they can break ours, too, with the same problem.'

The president of US Robots bulged his eyes, 'Why, the dirty rats—'

'Hold on, chief. There's more to this.' He pointed a finger with a wide sweep. 'Lanning, take it!'

Dr Alfred Lanning viewed the proceedings with faint scorn – his usual reaction to the doings of the vastly better-paid business and sales division. His unbelievable gray eyebrows hunched low and his voice was dry:

'From a scientific standpoint the situation, while not entirely clear, is subject to intelligent analysis. The question of interstellar travel under present conditions of physical theory is . . . uh . . . vague. The matter is wide open – and the information given by Consolidated to its thinking machine, assuming these we have to be the same, was similarly wide open. Our mathematical department has given it a thorough analysis, and it seems Consolidated has included everything. Its material for submission contains all known developments of Franciacci's space-warp theory, and, apparently, all pertinent astrophysical and electronic data. It's quite a mouthful.'

Robertson followed anxiously. He interrupted, 'Too much for The Brain to handle?'

Lanning shook his head decisively, 'No. There are no known limits to The Brain's capacity. It's a different matter. It's a question of the Robotic Laws. The Brain, for instance, could never supply a solution to a problem set to it if that solution would involve the death or injury of humans. As far as it would be concerned, a problem with only such a solution would be insoluble. If such a problem is combined with an extremely urgent demand that it be answered, it is just possible that The Brain, only a robot after all, would be presented with a dilemma, where

it could neither answer nor refuse to answer. Something of the
sort must have happened to Consolidated's machine.'

He paused, but the general manager urged on, 'Go ahead, Dr
Lanning. Explain it the way you explained it to me.'

Lanning set his lips and raised his eyebrows in the direction
of Dr Susan Calvin who lifted her eyes from her precisely folded
hands for the first time. Her voice was low and colorless.

'The nature of a robot reaction to a dilemma is startling,' she
began. 'Robot psychology is far from perfect – as a specialist, I
can assure you of that – but it can be discussed in qualitative
terms, because with all the complications introduced into a
robot's positronic brain, it is built by humans and is therefore
built according to human values.

'Now a human caught in an impossibility often responds by
a retreat from reality: by entry into a world of delusion, or by
taking to drink, going off into hysteria, or jumping off a bridge.
It all comes to the same thing – a refusal or inability to face the
situation squarely. And so, the robot. A dilemma at its mildest
will disorder half its relays; and at its worst it will burn out every
positronic brain path past repair.'

'I see,' said Robertson, who didn't. 'Now what about this
information Consolidated's wishing on us?'

'It undoubtedly involves,' said Dr Calvin, 'a problem of a
forbidden sort. But The Brain is considerably different from
Consolidated's robot.'

'That's right, chief. That's right.' The general manager was
energetically interruptive. 'I want you to get this, because it's
the whole point of the situation.'

Susan Calvin's eyes glittered behind the spectacles, and she
continued patiently, 'You see, sir, Consolidated's machines, their
Super-Thinker among them, are built without personality. They
go in for functionalism, you know – they have to, without US

Robots' basic patents for the emotional brain paths. Their Thinker is merely a calculating machine on a grand scale, and a dilemma ruins it instantly.

'However, The Brain, our own machine, has a personality – a child's personality. It is a supremely deductive brain, but it resembles an *idiot savante*. It doesn't really understand what it does – it just does it. And because it is really a child, it is more resilient. Life isn't so serious, you might say.'

The robopsychologist continued: 'Here is what we're going to do. We have divided all of Consolidated's information into logical units. We are going to feed the units to The Brain singly and cautiously. When *the* factor enters – the one that creates the dilemma – The Brain's child personality will hesitate. Its sense of judgment is not mature. There will be a perceptible interval before it will recognize a dilemma as such. And in that interval, it will reject the unit automatically – before its brain-paths can be set in motion and ruined.'

Robertson's Adam's apple squirmed, 'Are you sure, now?'

Dr Calvin masked impatience, 'It doesn't make much sense, I admit, in lay language; but there is no conceivable use in presenting the mathematics of this. I assure you, it is as I say.'

The general manager was in the breach instantly and fluently, 'So here's the situation, chief. If we take the deal, we can put it through like this. The Brain will tell us which unit of information involves the dilemma. From there, we can figure *why* the dilemma. Isn't that right, Dr Bogert? There you are, chief, and Dr Bogert is the best mathematician you'll find anywhere. We give Consolidated a "No Solution" answer, with the reason, and collect a hundred thousand. They're left with a broken machine; we're left with a whole one. In a year, two maybe, we'll have a space-warp engine, or a hyper-atomic motor, some people call it. Whatever you name it, it will be the biggest thing in the world.'

Robertson chuckled and reached out, 'Let's see the contract. I'll sign it.

When Susan Calvin entered the fantastically guarded vault that held The Brain one of the current shift of technicians had just asked it: 'If one and a half chickens lay one and a half eggs in one and a half days, how many eggs will nine chickens lay in nine days?'

The Brain had just answered, 'Fifty-four.'

And the technician had just said to another, 'See, you dope!'

Dr Calvin coughed and there was a sudden impossible flurry of directionless energy. The psychologist motioned briefly, and she was alone with The Brain.

The Brain was a two-foot globe merely – one which contained within it a thoroughly conditioned helium atmosphere, a volume of space completely vibration-absent and radiation-free – and within that was that unheard-of complexity of positronic brain-paths that was The Brain. The rest of the room was crowded with the attachments that were the intermediaries between The Brain and the outside world – its voice, its arms, its sense organs.

Dr Calvin said softly, 'How are you, Brain?'

The Brain's voice was high-pitched and enthusiastic, 'Swell, Miss Susan. You're going to ask me something. I can tell. You always have a book in your hand when you're going to ask me something.'

Dr Calvin smiled mildly, 'Well, you're right, but not just yet. This is going to be a question. It will be so complicated we're going to give it to you in writing. But not just yet. I think I'll talk to you first.'

'All right. I don't mind talking.'

'Now, Brain, in a little while, Dr Lanning and Dr Bogert will be here with this complicated question. We'll give it to you a very little at a time and very slowly, because we want you to be careful. We're going to ask you to build something, if you can, out of the information, but I'm going to warn you now that the solution might involve . . . uh . . . damage to human beings.'

'Gosh!' The exclamation was hushed, drawn-out.

'Now you watch for that. When we come to a sheet which means damage, even maybe death, don't get excited. You see, Brain, in this case, we don't mind – not even about death; we don't mind at all. So when you come to that sheet, just stop, give it back – and that'll be all. You understand?'

'Oh, sure. But golly, the death of humans! Oh, my!'

'Now, Brain, I hear Dr Lanning and Dr Bogert coming. They'll tell you what the problem is all about and then we'll start. Be a good boy, now—'

Slowly the sheets were fed in. After each one came the interval of the queerly whispery chuckling noise that was The Brain in action. Then the silence that meant readiness for another sheet. It was a matter of hours – during which the equivalent of something like seventeen fat volumes of mathematical physics were fed into The Brain.

As the process went on, frowns appeared and deepened. Lanning muttered ferociously under his breath. Bogert first gazed speculatively at his fingernails, and then bit at them in abstracted fashion. It was when the last of the thick pile of sheets disappeared that Calvin, white-faced, said:

'Something's wrong.'

Lanning barely got the words out, 'It can't be. Is it – dead?'

'Brain?' Susan Calvin was trembling. 'Do you hear me, Brain?'

'Huh?' came the abstracted rejoinder. 'Do you want me?'

'The solution—'

'Oh, that! I can do it. I'll build you a whole ship, just as easy

– if you let me have the robots. A nice ship. It'll take two months maybe.'

'There was – no difficulty?'

'It took long to figure,' said The Brain.

Dr Calvin backed away. The colour had not returned to her thin cheeks. She motioned the others away.

In her office, she said, 'I can't understand it. The information, as given, must involve a dilemma – probably involves death. If something has gone wrong—'

Bogert said quietly, 'The machine talks and makes sense. It can't be a dilemma.'

But the psychologist replied urgently, 'There are dilemmas *and* dilemmas. There are different forms of escape. Suppose The Brain is only mildly caught; just badly enough, say, to be suffering from the delusion that he can solve the problem, when he can't. Or suppose it's teetering on the brink of something really bad, so that any small push shoves it over.'

'Suppose,' said Lanning, 'there is no dilemma. Suppose Consolidated's machine broke down over a different question, or broke down for purely mechanical reasons.'

'But even so,' insisted Calvin, 'we couldn't take chances. Listen, from now on, no one is to as much as breathe to The Brain. I'm taking over.'

'All right,' sighed Lanning, 'take over, then. And meanwhile we'll let The Brain build its ship. And if it *does* build it, we'll have to test it.'

He was ruminating, 'We'll need our top field men for *that*.'

Michael Donovan brushed down his red hair with a violent motion of his hand and a total indifference to the fact that the unruly mass sprang to attention again immediately.

He said, 'Call the turn now, Greg. They say the ship is finished. They don't know what it is, but it's finished. Let's go, Greg. Let's grab the controls right now.'

Powell said wearily, 'Cut it, Mike. There's a peculiar over-ripe flavor to your humor at its freshest, and the confined atmosphere here isn't helping it.'

'Well, listen,' Donovan took another ineffectual swipe at his hair, 'I'm not worried so much about our cast-iron genius and his tin ship. There's the matter of my lost leave. And the monotony! There's nothing here but whiskers and figures – the wrong kind of figures. Oh, why do they *give* us these jobs?'

'Because,' replied Powell, gently, 'we're no loss, if they lose us. OK, relax! Doc Lanning's coming this way.'

Lanning was coming, his gray eyebrows as lavish as ever, his aged figure unbent as yet and full of life. He walked silently up the ramp with the two men and out into the open field, where, obeying no human master, silent robots were building a ship.

Wrong tense. *Had* built a ship!

For Lanning said, 'The robots have stopped. Not one has moved today.'

'It's completed then? Definitely?' asked Powell.

'Now how can I tell?' Lanning was peevish, and his eyebrows curled down in an eye-hiding frown. 'It *seems* done. There are no spare pieces about, and the interior is down to a gleaming finish.'

'You've been inside?'

'Just in, then out. I'm no space-pilot. Either of you two know much about engine theory?'

Donovan looked at Powell, who looked at Donovan.

Donovan said, 'I've got my license, sir, but at last reading it didn't say anything about hyper-engines or warp-navigation. Just the usual child's play in three dimensions.'

Alfred Lanning looked up with sharp disapproval and snorted the length of his prominent nose.

He said frigidly, 'Well, we have our engine men.'

Powell caught at his elbow as he walked away, 'Sir, is the ship still restricted ground?'

The old director hesitated, then rubbed the bridge of his nose, 'I suppose not. For you two anyway.'

Donovan looked after him as he left and muttered a short, expressive phrase at his back. He turned to Powell, 'I'd like to give him a literary description of himself, Greg.'

'Suppose you come along, Mike.'

The inside of the ship was finished, as finished as a ship ever was; that could be told in a single eye-blinking glance. No martinet in the system could have put as much spit-and-polish into a surface as those robots had. The walls were of a gleaming silvery finish that retained no fingerprints.

There were no angles; walls, floors, and ceiling faded gently into each other and in the cold, metallic glittering of the hidden lights, one was surrounded by six chilly reflections of one's bewildered self.

The main corridor was a narrow tunnel that led in a hard, clatter-footed stretch along a line of rooms of no interdistinguishing features.

Powell said, 'I suppose furniture is built into the wall. Or maybe we're not supposed to sit or sleep.'

It was in the last room, the one nearest the nose, that the monotony broke. A curving window of non-reflecting glass was the first break in the universal metal, and below it was a single large dial, with a single motionless needle hard against the zero mark.

Donovan said, 'Look at that!' and pointed to the single word on the finely-marked scale.

It said 'Parsecs' and the tiny figure at the right end of the curving, graduated meter said '1,000,000'.

There were two chairs; heavy, wide-flaring, uncushioned. Powell seated himself gingerly, and found it molded to the body's curves, and comfortable.

Powell said, 'What do you think of it?'

'For my money, The Brain has brain-fever. Let's get out.'

'Sure you don't want to look it over a bit?'

'I have looked it over. I came, I saw, I'm through!' Donovan's red hair bristled into separate wires. 'Greg, let's get out of here. I quit my job five seconds ago, and this is a restricted area for non-personnel.'

Powell smiled in an oily self-satisfied manner and smoothed his mustache, 'OK, Mike, turn off that adrenalin tap you've got draining into your bloodstream. I was worried, too, but no more.'

'No more, huh? How come, no more? Increased your insurance?'

'Mike, this ship can't fly.'

'How do you know?'

'Well, we've been through the entire ship, haven't we?'

'Seems so.'

'Take my word for it, we have. Did you see any pilot room except for this one port and the one gauge here in parsecs? Did you see any controls?'

'No.'

'And did you see any engines?'

'Holy Joe, no!'

'Well, then! Let's break the news to Lanning, Mike.'

They cursed their way through the featureless corridors and finally hit-and-missed their way into the short passage to the air lock.

Donovan stiffened, 'Did you lock this thing, Greg?'

'No, I never touched it. Yank the lever, will you?'

The lever never budged, though Donovan's face twisted appallingly with exertion.

Powell said, 'I didn't see any emergency exits. If something's gone wrong here, they'll have to melt us out.'

'Yes, and we've got to wait until they find out that some fool has locked us in here,' added Donovan, frantically.

'Let's get back to the room with the port. It's the only place from which we might attract attention.'

But they didn't.

In that last room, the port was no longer blue and full of sky. It was black, and hard yellow pin-point stars spelled *space*.

There was a dull, double thud, as two bodies collapsed separately into two chairs.

Alfred Lanning met Dr Calvin just outside his office. He lit a nervous cigar and motioned her in.

He said, 'Well, Susan, we've come pretty far, and Robertson's getting jumpy. What are you doing with The Brain?'

Susan Calvin spread her hands, 'It's no use getting impatient. The Brain is worth more than anything we forfeit on this deal.'

'But you've been questioning it for two months.'

The psychologist's voice was flat, but somehow dangerous. 'You would rather run this yourself?'

'Now you know what I meant.'

'Oh, I suppose I do.' Dr Calvin rubbed her hands nervously. 'It isn't easy. I've been pampering it and probing it gently, and I haven't gotten anywhere yet. Its reactions aren't normal. Its answers – they're queer, somehow. But nothing I can put my finger on yet. And you see, until we know what's wrong, we must just tiptoe our way through. I can never tell what simple question or remark will just . . . push him over . . . and then— Well, and then we'll have on our hands a completely useless Brain. Do you want to face that?'

'Well, it can't break the First Law.'

'I would have thought so, but—'

'You're not even sure of that?' Lanning was profoundly shocked.

'Oh, I can't be sure of anything, Alfred—'

The alarm system raised its fearful clangor with a horrifying suddenness. Lanning clicked on communications with an almost paralytic spasm. The breathless words froze him.

He said, 'Susan . . . you heard that . . . the ship's gone. I sent those two field men inside half an hour ago. You'll have to see The Brain again.'

Susan Calvin said with enforced calm, 'Brain, what happened to the ship?'

The Brain said happily, 'The ship I built, Miss Susan?'

'That's right. What has happened to it?'

'Why, nothing at all. The two men that were supposed to test it were inside, and we were all set. So I sent it off.'

'Oh— Well, that's nice.' The psychologist felt some difficulty in breathing. 'Do you think they'll be all right?'

'Right as anything, Miss Susan. I've taken care of it all. It's a bee-yoo-tiful ship.'

'Yes, Brain, it *is* beautiful, but you think they have enough food, don't you? They'll be comfortable?'

'Plenty of food.'

'This business might be a shock to them, Brain. Unexpected, you know.'

The Brain tossed it off, 'They'll be all right. It ought to be interesting for them.'

'Interesting? How?'

'Just interesting,' said The Brain, slyly.

'Susan,' whispered Lanning in a fuming whisper, 'ask it if death comes into it. Ask it what the dangers are.'

Susan Calvin's expression contorted with fury, 'Keep quiet!' In a shaken voice, she said to The Brain, 'We can communicate with the ship, can't we, Brain?'

'Oh, they can hear you if you call by radio. I've taken care of that.'

'Thanks. That's all for now.'

Once outside, Lanning lashed out ragingly, 'Great Galaxy, Susan, if this gets out, it will ruin all of us. We've got to get those men back. Why didn't you ask it if there was danger of death – straight out?'

'Because,' said Calvin, with a weary frustration, 'that's just what I can't mention. If it's got a case of dilemma, it's about death. Anything that would bring it up badly might knock it completely out. Will we be better off then? Now, look, it said we could communicate with them. Let's do so, get their location, and bring them back. They probably can't use the controls themselves; The Brain is probably handling them remotely. Come!'

It was quite a while before Powell shook himself together.

'Mike,' he said, out of cold lips, 'did you feel any acceleration?'

Donovan's eyes were blank, 'Huh? No . . . no.'

And then the redhead's fists clenched and he was out of his seat with sudden frenzied energy and up against the cold, wide-curving glass. There was nothing to see – but stars.

He turned. 'Greg, they must have started the machine while we were inside. Greg, it's a put-up job; they fixed it up with the robot to jerry us into being the try-out boys, in case we were thinking of backing out.'

Powell said, 'What are you talking about? What's the good

of sending us out if we don't know how to run the machine? How are we supposed to bring it back? No, this ship left by itself, and without apparent acceleration.' He rose, and walked the floor slowly. The metal walls dinned back the clangor of his steps.

He said tonelessly, 'Mike, this is the most confusing situation we've ever been set up against.'

'That,' said Donovan, bitterly, 'is news to me. I was just beginning to have a very swell time, when you told me.'

Powell ignored that. 'No acceleration – which means the ship works on a principle different from any known.'

'Different from any we know, anyway.'

'Different from *any* known. There are no engines within reach of manual control. Maybe they're built into the walls. Maybe that's why they're thick as they are.'

'What are you mumbling about?' demanded Donovan.

'Why not listen? I'm saying that whatever powers this ship is enclosed, and evidently not meant to be handled. The ship is running by remote control.'

'The Brain's control?'

'Why not?'

'Then you think we'll stay out here till The Brain brings us back.'

'It could be. If so, let's wait quietly. The Brain is a robot. It's got to follow the First Law. It can't hurt a human being.'

Donovan sat down slowly, 'You figure that?' Carefully, he flattened his hair, 'Listen, this junk about the space-warp knocked out Consolidated's robot, and the longhairs said it was because interstellar travel killed humans. Which robot are you going to trust? Ours had the same data, I understand.'

Powell was yanking madly at his mustache, 'Don't pretend you don't know your robotics, Mike. Before it's physically possible in any way for a robot to even make a start to breaking the First Law, so many things have to break down that it would be a ruined mess of scrap ten times over. There's some simple explanation to this.'

'Oh sure, sure. Just have the butler call me in the morning. It's all just too, too simple for me to bother about before my beauty nap.'

'Well, Jupiter, Mike, what are you complaining about so far? The Brain is taking care of us. This place is warm. It's got light. It's got air. There wasn't even enough of an acceleration jar to muss your hair if it were smooth enough to be mussable in the first place.'

'Yeah? Greg, you must've taken lessons. No one could put Pollyanna that far out of the running without. What do we eat? What do we drink? Where are we? How do we get back? And in case of accident, to what exit and in what spacesuit do we run, not walk? I haven't even seen a bathroom in the place, or those little conveniences that go along with bathrooms. Sure, we're being taken care of – but good!'

The voice that interrupted Donovan's tirade was not Powell's. It was nobody's. It was there, hanging in open air – stentorian and petrifying in its effects.

'GREGORY POWELL! MICHAEL DONOVAN!

'GREGORY POWELL! MICHAEL DONOVAN! PLEASE REPORT YOUR PRESENT POSITIONS. IF YOUR SHIP ANSWERS CONTROLS, PLEASE RETURN TO BASE. GREGORY POWELL! MICHAEL DONOVAN!—'

The message was repetitious, mechanical, broken by regular, untiring intervals.

Donovan said, 'Where's it coming from?'

'I don't know.' Powell's voice was an intense whisper, 'Where do the lights come from? Where does anything come from?'

'Well, how are we going to answer?' They had to speak in

the intervals between the loudly echoing, repeating message.

The walls were bare – as bare and as unbroken as smooth, curving metal can be. Powell said, 'Shout an answer.'

They did. They shouted, in turns, and together, 'Position unknown! Ship out of control! Condition desperate!'

Their voices rose and cracked. The short businesslike sentences became interlarded and adulterated with screaming and emphatic profanity, but the cold, calling voice repeated and repeated and repeated unwearingly.

'They don't hear us,' gasped Donovan. 'There's no sending mechanism. Just a receiver.' His eyes focused blindly at a random spot on the wall.

Slowly the din of the outside voice softened and receded. They called again when it was a whisper, and they called again, hoarsely, when there was silence.

Something like fifteen minutes later, Powell said lifelessly, 'Let's go through the ship again. There must be something to eat somewheres.' He did not sound hopeful. It was almost an admission of defeat.

They divided in the corridor to the right and left. They could follow one another by the hard footsteps resounding, and they met occasionally in the corridor, where they would glare at each other and pass on.

Powell's search ended suddenly and as it did, he heard Donovan's glad voice rise boomingly.

'Hey, Greg,' it howled, 'the ship *has* got plumbing. How did we miss it?'

It was some five minutes later that he found Powell by hit-and-miss. He was saying, 'Still no shower baths, though,' but it got choked off in the middle.

'Food,' he gasped.

The wall had dropped away, leaving a curved gap with two

shelves. The upper shelf was loaded with unlabeled cans of a bewildering variety of sizes and shapes. The enameled cans on the lower shelf were uniform and Donovan felt a cold draft about his ankles. The lower half was refrigerated.

'How . . . how—'

'It wasn't there, before,' said Powell, curtly. 'That wall section dropped out of sight as I came in the door.'

He was eating. The can was the pre-heating type with enclosed spoon and the warm odor of baked beans filled the room. 'Grab a can, Mike!'

Donovan hesitated, 'What's the menu?'

'How do I know! Are you finicky?'

'No, but all I eat on ships are beans. Something else would be first choice.' His hand hovered and selected a shining elliptical can whose flatness seemed reminiscent of salmon or similar delicacy. It opened at the proper pressure.

'Beans!' howled Donovan, and reached for another. Powell hauled at the slack of his pants. 'Better eat that, sonny boy. Supplies are limited and we may be here a long, long time.'

Donovan drew back sulkily, 'Is that all we have? Beans?'

'Could be.'

'What's on the lower shelf?'

'Milk.'

'Just milk?' Donovan cried in outrage.

'Looks it.'

The meal of beans and milk was carried through in silence, and as they left, the strip of hidden wall rose up and formed an unbroken surface once more.

Powell signed, 'Everything automatic. Everything just so. Never felt so helpless in my life. Where's your plumbing?'

'Right there. And that wasn't among those present when we first looked, either.'

Fifteen minutes later they were back in the glassed-in room, staring at each other from opposing seats.

Powell looked gloomily at the one gauge in the room. It still said 'parsecs', the figures still ended in '1,000,000' and the indicating needle was still pressed hard against the zero mark.

In the innermost offices of the US Robots and Mechanical Men Corp. Alfred Lanning was saying wearily, 'They won't answer. We've tried every wavelength, public, private, coded, straight, even this subether stuff they have now. And The Brain still won't say anything?' He shot this at Dr Calvin.

'It won't amplify on the matter, Alfred,' she said, emphatically. 'It says they can hear us . . . and when I try to press it, it becomes . . . well, it becomes sullen. And it's not supposed to— Whoever heard of a sullen robot?'

'Suppose you tell us what you have, Susan,' said Bogert.

'Here it is! It admits it controls the ship itself entirely. It is definitely optimistic about their safety, but without the details. I don't dare press it. However, the center of disturbance seems to be about the interstellar jump itself. The Brain definitely laughed when I brought up the subject. There are other indications, but that is the closest it's come to an open abnormality.'

She looked at the others, 'I refer to hysteria. I dropped the subject immediately, and I hope I did no harm, but it gave me a lead. I can handle hysteria. Give me twelve hours! If I can bring it back to normal, it will bring back the ship.'

Bogert seemed suddenly stricken. 'The interstellar jump!'

'What's the matter?' The cry was double from Calvin and Lanning.

'The figures for the engine The Brain gave us. Say . . . I just thought of something.'

He left hurriedly.

Lanning gazed after him. He said brusquely to Calvin, 'You take care of your end, Susan.'

Two hours later, Bogert was talking eagerly. 'I tell you, Lanning, that's it. The interstellar jump is not instantaneous – not as long as the speed of light is finite. Life can't exist . . . *matter and energy* as such can't exist in the space warp. I don't know what it would be like – but that's it. That's what killed Consolidated's robot.'

Donovan felt as haggard as he looked. 'Only five days?'

'Only five days. I'm sure of it.'

Donovan looked about him wretchedly. The stars through the glass were familiar but infinitely indifferent. The walls were cold to the touch; the lights, which had recently flared up again, were unfeelingly bright; the needle on the gauge pointed stubbornly to zero; and Donovan could not get rid of the taste of beans.

He said, morosely, 'I need a bath.'

Powell looked up briefly, and said, 'So do I. You needn't feel self-conscious. But unless you want to bathe in milk and do without drinking—'

'We'll do without drinking eventually, anyway. Greg, where does this interstellar travel come in?'

'You tell me. Maybe we just keep on going. We'd get there, eventually. At least the dust of our skeletons would – but isn't our death the whole point of The Brain's original break-down?'

Donovan spoke with his back to the other, 'Greg, I've been thinking. It's pretty bad. There's not much to do – except walk around or talk to yourself. You know those stories about guys marooned in space. They go nuts long before they starve. I don't know, Greg, but ever since the lights went on, I feel funny.'

There was a silence, then Powell's voice came thin and small. 'So do I. What's it like?'

The redheaded figure turned. 'Feel funny inside. There's a pounding in me with everything tense. It's hard to breathe. I can't stand still.'

'Um-m-m. Do you feel vibration?'

'How do you mean?'

'Sit down for a minute and listen. You don't hear it, but you feel it – as if something's throbbing somewheres and it's throbbing the whole ship, and you, too, along with it. Listen—'

'Yeah . . . yeah. What do you think it is, Greg? You don't suppose it's us?'

'It might be.' Powell stroked his mustache slowly. 'But it might be the ship's engines. It might be getting ready.'

'For what?'

'For the interstellar jump. It may be coming and the devil knows what it's like.'

Donovan pondered. Then he said, savagely, 'If it does, let it. But I wish we could fight. It's humiliating to have to wait for it.'

An hour later, perhaps, Powell looked at his hand on the metal chair-arm and said with frozen calm, 'Feel the wall, Mike.'

Donovan did, and said, 'You can feel it shake, Greg.'

Even the stars seemed blurred. From somewhere came the vague impression of a huge machine gathering power with the walls, storing up energy for a mighty leap, throbbing its way up the scales of strength.

It came with a suddenness and a stab of pain. Powell stiffened, and half-jerked from his chair. His sight caught Donovan and blanked out while Donovan's thin shout whimpered and died in his ears. Something writhed within him and struggled against a growing blanket of ice, that thickened.

Something broke loose and whirled in a blaze of flickering light and pain. It fell—

—and whirled

—and fell headlong

—into silence!

It was death!

It was a world of no motion and no sensation. A world of dim, unsensing consciousness; a consciousness of darkness and of silence and of formless struggle.

Most of all a consciousness of eternity.

. He was a tiny white threat of ego – cold and afraid.

Then the words came, unctuous and sonorous, thundering over him in a foam of sound:

'Does your coffin fit differently lately? Why not try Morbid M. Cadaver's extensible caskets? They are scientifically designed to fit the natural curves of the body, and are enriched with Vitamin B_1. Use Cadaver's caskets for comfort. Remember – you're – going – to – be – dead – a – long – long – time!'

It wasn't quite sound, but whatever it was, it died away in an oily rumbling whisper.

The white thread that might have been Powell heaved uselessly at the insubstantial eons of time that existed all about him – and collapsed upon itself as the piercing shriek of a hundred million ghosts of a hundred million soprano voices rose to a crescendo of melody:

> 'I'll be glad when you're dead, you rascal, you.
> 'I'll be glad when you're dead, you rascal, you.
> 'I'll be glad—'

It rose up a spiral stairway of violent sound into the keening supersonics that passed hearing, and then beyond—

The white thread quivered with a pulsating pang. It strained quietly—

The voices were ordinary – and many. It was a crowd speaking; a swirling mob that swept through and past and over him with a rapid, headlong motion, that left drifting tatters of words behind them.

'What did they getcha for, boy? Y'look banged up—'

'—a hot fire, I guess, but I got a case—'

'—I've made Paradise, but old St Pete—'

'Naah, I got a pull with the boy. Had dealings with him—'

'Hey, Sam, come this way—'

'Ja get a mouthpiece? Beelzebub says—'

'—going on, my good imp? My appointment is with Sa—'

And above it all the original stentorian roar, that plunged across all:

'HURRY! HURRY! HURRY! Stir your bones, and don't keep us waiting – there are many more in line. Have your certificates ready, and make sure Peter's release is stamped across it. See if you are at the proper entrance gate. There will be plenty of fire for all. Hey, you – YOU DOWN THERE. TAKE YOUR PLACE IN LINE OR—'

The white thread that was Powell groveled backward before the advancing shout, and felt the sharp stab of the pointing finger. It all exploded into a rainbow of sound that dripped its fragments on to an aching brain.

Powell was in the chair, again. He felt himself shaking.

Donovan's eyes were opening into two large popping bowls of glazed blue.

'Greg,' he whispered in what was almost a sob. 'Were you dead?'

'I . . . felt dead.' He did not recognize his own croak.

Donovan was obviously making a bad failure of his attempt to stand up. 'Are we alive now? Or is there more?'

'I . . . feel alive.' It was the same hoarseness. Powell said cautiously, 'Did you . . . hear anything, when . . . when you were dead?'

Donovan paused, and then very slowly nodded his head, 'Did you?'

'Yes. Did you hear about coffins . . . and females singing . . . and the lines forming to get into Hell? Did you?'

Donovan shook his head. 'Just one voice.'

'Loud?'

'No. Soft, but rough like a file over the fingertips. It was a sermon, you know. About hell-fire. He described the tortures of . . . well, *you know*. I once heard a sermon like that – almost.'

He was perspiring.

They were conscious of sunlight through the port. It was weak, but it was blue-white – and the gleaming pea that was the distant source of light was not Old Sol.

And Powell pointed a trembling finger at the single gauge. The needle stood stiff and proud at the hairline whose figure read 300,000 parsecs.

Powell said, 'Mike, if it's true, we must be out of the Galaxy altogether.'

Donovan said, 'Blazes! Greg! We'd be the first men out of the Solar System.'

'Yes! That's just it. We've escaped the sun. We've escaped the Galaxy. Mike, this ship is the answer. It means freedom for all humanity – freedom to spread through to every star that exists – millions and billions and trillions of them.'

And then he came down with a hard thud, 'But how do we get back, Mike?'

Donovan smiled shakily, 'Oh, that's all right. The ship brought us here. The ship will take us back. Me for more beans.'

'But Mike . . . hold on, Mike. If it takes us back the way it brought us here—'

Donovan stopped half-way up and sat back heavily into the chair.

Powell went on, 'We'll have to . . . die again, Mike.'

'Well,' sighed Donovan, 'if we have to, we have to. At least it isn't permanent, not *very* permanent.'

Susan Calvin was speaking slowly now. For six hours she had been slowly prodding The Brain – for six fruitless hours. She was weary of repetitions, weary of circumlocutions, weary of everything.

'Now, Brain, there's just one more thing. You must make a special effort to answer simply. Have you been entirely clear about the interstellar jump? I mean does it take them very far?'

'As far as they want to go, Miss Susan. Golly, it isn't any trick through the warp.'

'And on the other side, what will they see?'

'Stars and stuff. What do you suppose?'

The next question slipped out. 'They'll be alive, then?'

'Sure!'

'And the interstellar jump won't hurt them?'

She froze as The Brain maintained silence. That was it! She had touched the sore spot.

'Brain,' she supplicated faintly, 'Brain, do you hear me?'

The answer was weak, quivering. The Brain said, 'Do I have to answer? About the jump, I mean?'

'Not if you don't want to. But it would be interesting – I mean if you wanted to.' Susan Calvin tried to be bright about it.

'Aw-w-w. You spoil everything.'

And the psychologist jumped up suddenly, with a look of flaming insight on her face.

'Oh, my,' she gasped. 'Oh, my.'

And she felt the tension of hours and days released in a burst.

It was later that she told Lanning, 'I tell you it's all right. No, you must leave me alone, now. The ship will be back safely, *with* the men, and I want to rest. I *will* rest. Now go away.'

The ship returned to Earth as silently, as unjarringly as it had left. It dropped precisely into place and the main lock gaped open. The two men who walked out felt their way carefully and scratched their rough and scrubbily-stubbled chins.

And then, slowly and purposefully, the one with red hair knelt down and planted upon the concrete of the runway a firm, loud kiss.

They waved aside the crowd that was gathering and made gestures of denial at the eager couple that had piled out of the down-swooping ambulance with a stretcher between them.

Gregory Powell said, 'Where's the nearest shower?'

They were led away.

They were gathered, all of them, about a table. It was a full staff meeting of the brains of US Robots and Mechanical Men Corp.

Slowly and climactically, Powell and Donovan finished a graphic and resounding story.

Susan Calvin broke the silence that followed. In the few days that had elapsed she had recovered her icy, somewhat acid, calm – but still a trace of embarrassment broke through.

'Strictly speaking,' she said, 'this was my fault – all of it. When we first presented this problem to The Brain, as I hope some of you remember, I went to great lengths to impress upon it the importance of rejecting any item of information capable of creating a dilemma. In doing so I said something like "Don't get excited about the death of humans. We don't mind it at all. Just give the sheet back and forget it."'

'Hm-m-m,' said Lanning. 'What follows?'

'The obvious. When that item entered its calculations which yielded the equation controlling the length of minimum interval for the interstellar jump – it meant death for humans. That's where Consolidated's machine broke down completely. But I had depressed the importance of death to The Brain – not entirely, for the First Law can never be broken – but just sufficiently so that The Brain could take a second look at the equation. Sufficiently to give it time to realize that after the interval was passed through, the men would return to life – just as the matter and energy of the ship itself would return to being. This so-called "death", in other words, was a strictly temporary phenomenon. You see?'

She looked about her. They were all listening.

She went on, 'So he accepted the item, but not without a certain jar. Even with death temporary and its importance depressed, it was enough to unbalance him very gently.'

She brought it out calmly, 'He developed a sense of humor – it's escape, you see, a method of partial escape from reality. He became a practical joker.'

Powell and Donovan were on their feet.

'What?' cried Powell.

Donovan was considerably more colorful about it.

'It's so,' said Calvin. 'He took care of you, and kept you safe, but you couldn't handle any controls, because they weren't for you – just for the humorous Brain. We could reach you by radio, but you couldn't answer. You had plenty of food, but all of it beans and milk. Then you died, so to speak, and were reborn, but the period of your death was made . . . well . . . interesting. I wish I knew how he did it. It was The Brain's prize little joke, but he meant no harm.'

'No harm!' gasped Donovan. 'Oh, if that cute little tyke only had a neck.'

Lanning raised a quieting hand, 'All right, it's been a mess, but it's all over. What now?'

'Well,' said Bogert, quietly, 'obviously it's up to us to improve the space-warp engine. There must be some way of getting around that interval of jump. If there is, we're the only organization left with a grand-scale super-robot, so we're bound to find it if anyone. And then – US Robots has interstellar travel, and humanity has the opportunity for galactic empire.'

'What about Consolidated?' said Lanning.

'Hey,' interrupted Donovan suddenly, 'I want to make a suggestion there. They landed US Robots into quite a mess. It wasn't as bad a mess as they expected and it turned out well, but their intentions weren't pious. And Greg and I bore the most of it.

'Well, they wanted an answer, and they've got one. Send them that ship, guaranteed, and US Robots can collect their two hundred thou plus construction costs. And if they test it – then suppose we let The Brain have just a little more fun before it's brought back to normal.'

Lanning said gravely, 'It sounds just and proper to me.'

To which Bogert added absently, 'Strictly according to contract, too.'

8

Evidence

'But that wasn't it, either,' said Dr Calvin thoughtfully. 'Oh, eventually, the ship and others like it became government property; the Jump through hyperspace was perfected, and now we actually have human colonies on the planets of some of the nearer stars, but that wasn't it.'

I had finished eating and watched her through the smoke of my cigarette.

'It's what has happened to the people here on Earth in the last fifty years that really counts. When I was born, young man, we had just gone through the last World War. It was a low point in history – but it was the end of nationalism. Earth was too small for nations and they began grouping themselves into Regions. It took quite a while. When I was born the United States of America was still a nation and not merely a part of the Northern Region. In fact, the name of the corporation is still "United States Robots—". And the change from nations to Regions, which has stabilized our economy and brought about what amounts to a Golden Age, when this century is compared with the last, was also brought about by our robots.'

'You mean the Machines,' I said. 'The Brain you talked about was the first of the Machines, wasn't it?'

'Yes, it was, but it's not the Machines I was thinking of. Rather of

a man. He died last year.' Her voice was suddenly deeply sorrowful.
'Or at least he arranged to die, because he knew we needed him no
longer. —Stephen Byerley.'

　　'Yes, I guessed that was who you meant.'

　　'He first entered public office in 2032. You were only a boy then,
so you wouldn't remember the strangeness of it. His campaign for the
Mayoralty was certainly the queerest in history—'

Francis Quinn was a politician of the new school. That, of course,
is a meaningless expression, as are all expressions of the sort.
Most of the 'new schools' we have were duplicated in the social
life of ancient Greece, and perhaps, if we knew more about it,
in the social life of ancient Sumeria and in the lake dwellings
of prehistoric Switzerland as well.

　　But, to get out from under what promises to be a dull and
complicated beginning, it might be best to state hastily that
Quinn neither ran for office nor canvassed for votes, made no
speeches and stuffed no ballot boxes. Any more than Napoleon
pulled a trigger at Austerlitz.

　　And since politics makes strange bedfellows, Alfred Lanning
sat at the other side of the desk with his ferocious white eyebrows
bent far forward over eyes in which chronic impatience had
sharpened to acuity. He was not pleased.

　　The fact, if known to Quinn, would have annoyed him not
the least. His voice was friendly, perhaps professionally so.

　　'I assume you know Stephen Byerley, Dr Lanning.'

　　'I have heard of him. So have many people.'

　　'Yes, so have I. Perhaps you intend voting for him at the next
election.'

　　'I couldn't say.' There was an unmistakable trace of acidity
here. 'I have not followed the political currents, so I'm not aware
that he is running for office.'

'He may be our next mayor. Of course, he is only a lawyer now, but great oaks—'

'Yes,' interrupted Lanning, 'I have heard the phrase before. But I wonder if we can get to the business at hand.'

'We *are* at the business at hand, Dr Lanning.' Quinn's tone was very gentle. 'It is to my interest to keep Mr Byerley a district attorney at the very most, and it is to your interest to help me do so.'

'To *my* interest? Come!' Lanning's eyebrows hunched low.

'Well, say then to the interest of the US Robots and Mechanical Men Corporation. I come to you as Director-Emeritus of Research, because I know that your connection to them is that of, shall we say, "elder statesman". You are listened to with respect and yet your connection with them is no longer so tight but that you cannot possess considerable freedom of action; even if the action is somewhat unorthodox.'

Dr Lanning was silent a moment, chewing the cud of his thoughts. He said more softly, 'I don't follow you at all, Mr Quinn.'

'I am not surprised, Dr Lanning. But it's all rather simple. Do you mind?' Quinn lit a slender cigarette with a lighter of tasteful simplicity and his big-boned face settled into an expression of quiet amusement. 'We have spoken of Mr Byerley – a strange and colorful character. He was unknown three years ago. He is very well known now. He is a man of force and ability, and certainly the most capable and intelligent prosecutor I have ever known. Unfortunately he is not a friend of mine—'

'I understand,' said Lanning, mechanically. He stared at his fingernails.

'I have had occasion,' continued Quinn, evenly, 'in the past year to investigate Mr Byerley – quite exhaustively. It is always useful, you see, to subject the past life of reform politicians to

rather inquisitive research. If you knew how often it helped—'
He paused to smile humorlessly at the glowing tip of his cigarette. 'But Mr Byerley's past is unremarkable. A quiet life in a
small town, a college education, a wife who died young, an auto
accident with a slow recovery, law school, coming to the metropolis, an attorney.'

Francis Quinn shook his head slowly, then added, 'But his
present life. Ah, that is remarkable. Our district attorney never
eats!'

Lanning's head snapped up, old eyes surprisingly sharp,
'Pardon me?'

'Our district attorney never eats.' The repetition thumped by
syllables. 'I'll modify that slightly. He has never been seen to eat
or drink. Never! Do you understand the significance of the word?
Not rarely, but never!'

'I find that quite incredible. Can you trust your investigators?'

'I can trust my investigators, and I don't find it incredible at
all. Further, our district attorney has never been seen to drink
– in the aqueous sense as well as the alcoholic – nor to sleep.
There are other factors, but I should think I have made my point.'

Lanning leaned back in his seat, and there was the rapt silence
of challenge and response between them, and then the old roboticist shook his head. 'No. There is only one thing you can be
trying to imply, if I couple your statements with the fact that
you present them to me, and that is impossible.'

'But the man is quite inhuman, Dr Lanning.'

'If you told me he were Satan in masquerade, there would be
a faint chance that I might believe you.'

'I tell you he is a robot, Dr Lanning.'

'I tell you it is as impossible a conception as I have ever heard,
Mr Quinn.'

Again the combative silence.

'Nevertheless,' and Quinn stubbed out his cigarette with elaborate care, 'you will have to investigate this impossibility with all the resources of the Corporation.'

'I'm sure that I could undertake no such thing, Mr Quinn. You don't seriously suggest that the Corporation take part in local politics.'

'You have no choice. Supposing I were to make my facts public without proof. The evidence is circumstantial enough.'

'Suit yourself in that respect.'

'But it would not suit me. Proof would be much preferable. And it would not suit *you*, for the publicity would be very damaging to your company. You are perfectly well acquainted, I suppose, with the strict rules against the use of robots on inhabited worlds.'

'Certainly!' —brusquely.

'You know that the US Robots and Mechanical Men Corporation is the only manufacturer of positronic robots in the Solar System, and if Byerley is a robot, his is a *positronic* robot. You are also aware that all positronic robots are leased, and not sold; that the Corporation remains the owner and manager of each robot, and is therefore responsible for the actions of all.'

'It is an easy matter, Mr Quinn, to prove the Corporation has never manufactured a robot of a humanoid character.'

'It can be done? To discuss merely possibilities.'

'Yes. It can be done.'

'Secretly, I imagine, as well. Without entering it in your books.'

'Not the positronic brain, sir. Too many factors are involved in that, and there is the tightest possible government supervision.'

'Yes, but robots are worn out, break down, go out of order – and are dismantled.'

'And the positronic brains re-used or destroyed.'

'Really?' Francis Quinn allowed himself a trace of sarcasm. 'And if one were, accidentally, of course, not destroyed – and there happened to be a humanoid structure waiting for a brain.'

'Impossible!'

'You would have to prove that to the government and the public, so why not prove it to me now.'

'But what could our purpose be?' demanded Lanning in exasperation. 'Where is our motivation? Credit us with a minimum of sense.'

'My dear sir, please. The Corporation would be only too glad to have the various Regions permit the use of humanoid positronic robots on inhabited worlds. The profits would be enormous. But the prejudice of the public against such a practice is too great. Suppose you get them used to such robots first – see, we have a skillful lawyer, a good mayor – and he is a robot. Won't you buy our robot butlers?'

'Thoroughly fantastic. An almost humorous descent to the ridiculous.'

'I imagine so. Why not prove it? Or would you still rather try to prove it to the public?'

The light in the office was dimming, but it was not yet too dim to obscure the flush of frustration on Alfred Lanning's face. Slowly, the roboticist's finger touched a knob and the wall illuminators glowed to gentle life.

'Well, then,' he growled, 'let us see.'

The face of Stephen Byerley is not an easy one to describe. He was forty by birth certificate and forty by appearance – but it was a healthy, well-nourished good-natured appearance of forty; one that automatically drew the teeth of the bromide about 'looking one's age'.

This was particularly true when he laughed, and he was laughing now. It came loudly and continuously, died away for a bit, then began again—

And Alfred Lanning's face contracted into a rigidly bitter monument of disapproval. He made a half gesture to the woman who sat beside him, but her thin, bloodless lips merely pursed themselves a trifle.

Byerley gasped himself a state nearer normality.

'Really, Dr Lanning . . . really – I . . . I . . . a robot?'

Lanning bit his words off with a snap, 'It is no statement of mine, sir. I would be quite satisfied to have you a member of humanity. Since our corporation never manufactured you, I am quite certain that you are – in a legalistic sense, at any rate. But since the contention that you are a robot has been advanced to us seriously by a man of certain standing—'

'Don't mention his name, if it would knock a chip off your granite block of ethics, but let's pretend it was Frank Quinn, for the sake of argument, and continue.'

Lanning drew in a sharp, cutting snort at the interruption, and paused ferociously before continuing with added frigidity '—by a man of certain standing, with whose identity I am not interested in playing guessing games, I am bound to ask your co-operation in disproving it. The mere fact that such a contention could be advanced and publicized by the means at this man's disposal would be a bad blow to the company I represent – even if the charge were never proven. You understand me?'

'Oh, yes, your position is clear to me. The charge itself is ridiculous. The spot you find yourself in is not. I beg your pardon, if my laughter offended you. It was the first I laughed at, not the second. How can I help you?'

'It could be very simple. You have only to sit down to a meal at a restaurant in the presence of witnesses, have your picture taken, and eat.' Lanning sat back in his chair, the worst of the interview over. The woman beside him watched Byerley with an apparently absorbed expression but contributed nothing of her own.

Stephen Byerley met her eyes for an instant, was caught by them, then turned back to the roboticist. For a while his fingers were thoughtful over the bronze paper-weight that was the only ornament on his desk.

He said quietly, 'I don't think I can oblige you.'

He raised his hand, 'Now wait, Dr Lanning. I appreciate the fact that this whole matter is distasteful to you, that you have been forced into it against your will, that you feel you are playing an undignified and even ridiculous part. Still, the matter is even more intimately concerned with myself, so be tolerant.

'First, what makes you think that Quinn – this man of certain standing, you know – wasn't hoodwinking you, in order to get you to do exactly what you are doing?'

'Why, it seems scarcely likely that a reputable person would endanger himself in so ridiculous a fashion, if he weren't convinced he were on safe ground.'

There was little humor in Byerley's eyes. 'You don't know Quinn. He could manage to make safe ground out of a ledge a mountain sheep could not handle. I suppose he showed the particulars of the investigation he claims to have made of me?'

'Enough to convince me that it would be too troublesome to have our corporation attempt to disprove them when you could do so more easily.'

'Then you believe him when he says I never eat. You are a scientist, Dr Lanning. Think of the logic required. I have not been observed to eat, therefore, I never eat, QED. After all!'

'You are using prosecution tactics to confuse what is really a very simple situation.'

'On the contrary, I am trying to clarify what you and Quinn between you are making a very complicated one. You see, I don't sleep much, that's true, and I certainly don't sleep in public. I have never cared to eat with others – an idiosyncrasy which is unusual and probably neurotic in character, but which harms no one. Look, Dr Lanning, let me present you with a supposititious case. Supposing we had a politician who was interested in defeating a reform candidate at any cost and while investigating his private life came across oddities such as I have just mentioned.

'Suppose further that in order to smear the candidate effectively, he comes to your company as the ideal agent. Do you expect him to say to you, "So-and-so is a robot because he hardly ever eats with people, and I have never seen him fall asleep in the middle of a case; and once when I peeped into his window in the middle of the night, there he was, sitting up with a book; and I looked in his frigidaire and there was no food in it"?

'If he told you that, you would send for a straitjacket. But if he tells you, "He *never* sleeps; he *never* eats," then the shock of the statement blinds you to the fact that such statements are impossible to prove. You play into his hands by contributing to the to-do.'

'Regardless, sir,' began Lanning, with a threatening obstinacy, 'of whether you consider this matter serious or not, it will require only the meal I mentioned to end it.'

Again Byerley turned to the woman, who still regarded him expressionlessly. 'Pardon me. I've caught your name correctly, haven't I? Dr Susan Calvin?'

'Yes, Mr Byerley.'

'You're US Robots' psychologist, aren't you?'

'*Robo*psychologist, please.'

'Oh, are robots so different from men, mentally?'

'Worlds different.' She allowed herself a frosty smile, 'Robots are essentially decent.'

Humor tugged at the corners of the lawyer's mouth, 'Well, that's a hard blow. But what I wanted to say was this. Since you're a psycho – a robopsychologist, *and* a woman, I'll bet you've done something that Dr Lanning hasn't thought of.'

'And what is that?'

'You've got something to eat in your purse.'

Something caught in the schooled indifference of Susan Calvin's eyes. She said, 'You surprise me, Mr Byerley.'

And opening her purse, she produced an apple. Quietly, she handed it to him. Dr Lanning, after an initial start, followed the slow movement from one hand to the other with sharply alert eyes.

Calmly, Stephen Byerley bit into it, and calmly he swallowed it.

'You see, Dr Lanning?'

Dr Lanning smiled in a relief tangible enough to make even his eyebrows appear benevolent. A relief that survived for one fragile second.

Susan Calvin said, 'I was curious to see if you would eat it, but, of course, in the present case, it proves nothing.'

Byerley grinned. 'It doesn't?'

'Of course not. It is obvious, Dr Lanning, that if this man were a humanoid robot, he would be a perfect imitation. He is almost too human to be credible. After all, we have been seeing and observing human beings all our lives; it would be impossible to palm something merely nearly right off on us. It would have to be *all* right. Observe the texture of the skin, the quality of the irises, the bone formation of the hand. If he's a robot, I wish US Robots *had* made him, because he's a good job. Do you suppose then, that anyone capable of paying attention to such niceties would neglect a few gadgets to take care of such things as eating, sleeping, elimination? For emergency use only, perhaps; as, for instance, to prevent such situations as are arising here. So a meal won't prove anything.'

'Now wait,' snarled Lanning, 'I am not quite the fool both of you make me out to be. I am not interested in the problem of Mr Byerley's humanity or nonhumanity. I am interested in getting the corporation out of a hole. A public meal will end the matter and keep it ended no matter what Quinn does. We can leave the finer details to lawyers and robopsychologists.'

'But, Dr Lanning,' said Byerley, 'you forget the politics of the situation. I am as anxious to be elected, as Quinn is to stop me. By the way, did you notice that you used his name. It's a cheap shyster trick of mine; I knew you would, before you were through.'

Lanning flushed. 'What has the election to do with it?'

'Publicity works both ways, sir. If Quinn wants to call me a robot, and has the nerve to do so, I have the nerve to play the game his way.'

'You mean you—' Lanning was quite frankly appalled.

'Exactly. I mean that I'm going to let him go ahead, choose his rope, test its strength, cut off the right length, tie the noose, insert his head and grin. I can do what little else is required.'

'You are mighty confident.'

Susan Calvin rose to her feet, 'Come, Alfred, we won't change his mind for him.'

'You see.' Byerley smiled gently. 'You're a human psychologist, too.'

But perhaps not all the confidence that Dr Lanning had remarked upon was present that evening when Byerley's car parked on the automatic treads leading to the sunken garage, and Byerley himself crossed the path to the front door of his house.

The figure in the wheel chair looked up as he entered and smiled. Byerley's face lit with affection. He crossed over to it.

The cripple's voice was a hoarse, grating whisper that came out of a mouth forever twisted to one side, leering out of a face that was half scar tissue. 'You're late, Steve.'

'I know, John, I know. But I've been up against a peculiar and interesting trouble today.'

'So?' Neither the torn face nor the destroyed voice could carry expression but there was anxiety in the clear eyes. 'Nothing you can't handle?'

'I'm not exactly certain. I may need your help. *You're* the brilliant one in the family. Do you want me to take you out into the garden? It's a beautiful evening.'

Two strong arms lifted John from the wheel chair. Gently, almost caressingly, Byerley's arms went around the shoulders and under the swathed legs of the cripple. Carefully, and slowly, he walked through the rooms, down the gentle ramp that had been built with a wheel chair in mind, and out the back door into the walled and wired garden behind the house.

'Why don't you let me use the wheel chair, Steve? This is silly.'

'Because I'd rather carry you. Do you object? You know that you're as glad to get out of that motorized buggy for a while as I am to see you out. How do you feel today?' He deposited John with infinite care upon the cool grass.

'How should I feel? But tell me about your trouble.'

'Quinn's campaign will be based on the fact that he claims I'm a robot.'

John's eyes opened wide. 'How do you know? It's impossible. I won't believe it.'

'Oh, come, I tell you it's so. He had one of the big-shot scientists of US Robots and Mechanical Men Corporation over at the office to argue with me.'

Slowly John's hands tore at the grass. 'I see. I see.'

Byerley said, 'But we can let him choose his ground. I have an idea. Listen to me and tell me if we can do it—'

The scene as it appeared in Alfred Lanning's office that night was a tableau of stares. Francis Quinn stared meditatively at Alfred Lanning. Lanning's stare was savagely set upon Susan Calvin, who stared impassively in her turn at Quinn.

Francis Quinn broke it with a heavy attempt at lightness, 'Bluff. He's making it up as he goes along.'

'Are you going to gamble on that, Mr Quinn?' asked Dr Calvin, indifferently.

'Well, it's your gamble, really.'

'Look here,' Lanning covered definite pessimism with bluster, 'we've done what you asked. We witnessed the man eat. It's ridiculous to presume him a robot.'

'Do *you* think so?' Quinn shot toward Calvin. 'Lanning said you were the expert.'

Lanning was almost threatening, 'Now, Susan—'

Quinn interrupted smoothly, 'Why not let her talk, man? She's been sitting there imitating a gatepost for half an hour.'

Lanning felt definitely harassed. From what he experienced then to incipient paranoia was but a step. He said, 'Very well. Have your say, Susan. We won't interrupt you.'

Susan Calvin glanced at him humorlessly, then fixed cold eyes on Mr Quinn. 'There are only two ways of definitely proving Byerley to be a robot, sir. So far you are presenting circumstantial evidence, with which you can accuse, but not prove – and I think Mr Byerley is sufficiently clever to counter that sort of material. You probably think so yourself, or you wouldn't have come here.

'The two methods of *proof* are the physical and the

psychological. Physically, you can dissect him or use an X-ray. How to do that would be *your* problem. Psychologically, his behavior can be studied, for if he *is* a positronic robot, he must conform to the three Rules of Robotics. A positronic brain cannot be constructed without them. You know the Rules, Mr Quinn?'

She spoke them carefully, clearly, quoting word for word the famous bold print on page one of the 'Handbook of Robotics'.

'I've heard of them,' said Quinn, carelessly.

'Then the matter is easy to follow,' responded the psychologist, dryly. 'If Mr Byerley breaks any of those three rules, he is not a robot. Unfortunately, this procedure works in only one direction. If he lives up to the rules, it proves nothing one way or the other.'

Quinn raised polite eyebrows, 'Why not, doctor?'

'Because, if you stop to think of it, the three Rules of Robotics are the essential guiding principles of a good many of the world's ethical systems. Of course, every human being is supposed to have the instinct of self-preservation. That's Rule Three to a robot. Also every "good" human being, with a social conscience and a sense of responsibility, is supposed to defer to proper authority; to listen to his doctor, his boss, his government, his psychiatrist, his fellow man; to obey laws, to follow rules, to conform to custom – even when they interfere with his comfort or his safety. That's Rule Two to a robot. Also, every "good" human being is supposed to love others as himself, protect his fellow man, risk his life to save another. That's Rule One to a robot. To put it simply – if Byerley follows all the Rules of Robotics, he may be a robot, and may simply be a very good man.'

'But,' said Quinn, 'you're telling me that you can never prove him a robot.'

'I may be able to prove him *not* a robot.'

'That's not the proof I want.'

'You'll have such proof as exists. You are the only one responsible for your own wants.'

Here Lanning's mind leaped suddenly to the sting of an idea. 'Has it occurred to anyone,' he ground out, 'that district attorney is a rather strange occupation for a robot? The prosecution of human beings – sentencing them to death – bringing about their infinite harm—'

Quinn grew suddenly keen, 'No, you can't get out of it that way. Being district attorney doesn't make him human. Don't you know his record? Don't you know that he boasts that he has never prosecuted an innocent man; that there are scores of people left untried because the evidence against them didn't satisfy him, even though he could probably have argued a jury into atomizing them? That happens to be so.'

Lanning's thin cheeks quivered, 'No, Quinn, no. There is nothing in the Rules of Robotics that makes any allowance for human guilt. A robot may not judge whether a human being deserves death. It is not for him to decide. *He may not harm a human* – variety skunk, or variety angel.'

Susan Calvin sounded tired. 'Alfred,' she said, 'don't talk foolishly. What if a robot came upon a madman about to set fire to a house with people in it. He would stop the madman, wouldn't he?'

'Of course.'

'And if the only way he could stop him was to kill him—'

There was a faint sound in Lanning's throat. Nothing more.

'The answer to that, Alfred, is that he would require psychotherapy because he might easily go mad at the conflict presented him – of having broken Rule One to adhere to Rule One in a higher sense. But a man would be dead and a robot would have killed him.'

'Well, *is* Byerley mad?' demanded Lanning, with all the sarcasm he could muster.

'No, but he has killed no man himself. He has exposed facts which might represent a particular human being to be dangerous to the large mass of other human beings we call society. He protects the greater number and thus adheres to Rule One at maximum potential. That is as far as he goes. It is the judge who then condemns the criminal to death or imprisonment, after the jury decides on his guilt or innocence. It is the jailer who imprisons him, the executioner who kills him. And Mr Byerley has done nothing but determine truth and aid society.

'As a matter of fact, Mr Quinn, I have looked into Mr Byerley's career since you first brought this matter to our attention. I find that he has never demanded the death sentence in his closing speeches to the jury. I also find that he has spoken on behalf of the abolition of capital punishment and contributed generously to research institutions engaged in criminal neurophysiology. He apparently believes in the cure, rather than the punishment of crime. I find that significant.'

'You do? Quinn smiled. 'Significant of a certain odor of roboticity, perhaps?'

'Perhaps. Why deny it? Actions such as his could come only from a robot, or from a very honorable and decent human being. But you see, you just can't differentiate between a robot and the very best of humans.'

Quinn sat back in his chair. His voice quivered with impatience. 'Dr Lanning, it's perfectly possible to create a humanoid robot that would perfectly duplicate a human in appearance, isn't it?'

Lanning harrumphed and considered, 'It's been done experimentally by US Robots,' he said reluctantly, 'without the addition of a positronic brain, of course. By using human ova and hormone control, one can grow human flesh and skin over a skeleton of porous silicone plastics that would defy external examination. The eyes, the hair, the skin would be really human, not humanoid. And if you put a positronic brain and such other gadgets as you might desire inside, you have a humanoid robot.'

Quinn said shortly, 'How long would it take to make one?'

Lanning considered, 'If you had all your equipment – the brain, the skeleton, the ovum, the proper hormones and radiations – say, two months.'

The politician straightened out of his chair. 'Then we shall see what the insides of Mr Byerley look like. It will mean publicity for US Robots – but I gave you your chance.'

Lanning turned impatiently to Susan Calvin, when they were alone. 'Why do you insist—'

And with real feeling, she responded sharply and instantly, 'Which do you want – the truth or my resignation? I won't lie for you. US Robots can take care of itself. Don't turn coward.'

'What,' said Lanning, 'if he opens up Byerley, and wheels and gears fall out. What then?'

'He won't open Byerley,' said Calvin, disdainfully. 'Byerley is as clever as Quinn, at the very least.'

The news broke upon the city a week before Byerley was to have been nominated. But 'broke' is the wrong word. It staggered upon the city, shambled, crawled. Laughter began, and wit was free. And as the far-off hand of Quinn tightened its pressure in easy stages, the laughter grew forced, an element of hollow uncertainty entered, and people broke off to wonder.

The convention itself had the air of a restive stallion. There had been no contest planned. Only Byerley could possibly have been nominated a week earlier. There was no substitute even now. They had to nominate him, but there was complete confusion about it.

It would not have been so bad if the average individual were not torn between the enormity of the charge, if true, and its sensational folly, if false.

The day after Byerley was nominated perfunctorily, hollowly – a newspaper finally published the gist of a long interview with Dr Susan Calvin, 'world famous expert on robopsychology and positronics'.

What broke loose is popularly and succinctly described as hell.

It was what the Fundamentalists were waiting for. They were not a political party; they made pretense to no formal religion. Essentially they were those who had not adapted themselves to what had once been called the Atomic Age, in the days when atoms were a novelty. Actually, they were the Simple-Lifers, hungering after a life, which to those who had lived it had probably appeared not so Simple, and who had been, therefore, Simple-Lifers themselves.

The Fundamentalists required no new reason to detest robots and robot manufacturers; but a new reason such as the Quinn accusation and the Calvin analysis was sufficient to make such detestation audible.

The huge plants of the US Robots and Mechanical Men Corporation was a hive that spawned armed guards. It prepared for war.

Within the city the house of Stephen Byerley bristled with police.

The political campaign, of course, lost all other issues, and resembled a campaign only in that it was something filling the hiatus between nomination and election.

Stephen Byerley did not allow the fussy little man to distract him. He remained comfortably unperturbed by the uniforms in the background. Outside the house, past the line of grim guards, reporters and photographers waited according to the tradition of the caste. One enterprising 'visor station even had a scanner focused on the blank entrance to the prosecutor's unpretentious home, while a synthetically excited announcer filled in with inflated commentary.

The fussy little man advanced. He held forward a rich, complicated sheet. 'This, Mr Byerley, is a court order authorizing me to search these premises for the presence of illegal . . . uh . . . mechanical men or robots of any description.'

Byerley half rose, and took the paper. He glanced at it indifferently, and smiled as he handed it back. 'All in order. Go ahead. Do your job. Mrs Hoppen' – to his housekeeper, who appeared reluctantly from the next room – 'please go with them, and help out if you can.'

The little man, whose name was Harroway, hesitated, produced an unmistakable blush, failed completely to catch Byerley's eyes, and muttered, 'Come on,' to the two policemen.

He was back in ten minutes.

'Through?' questioned Byerley, in just the tone of a person who is not particularly interested in the question, or its answer.

Harroway cleared his throat, made a bad start in falsetto, and began again, angrily, 'Look here, Mr Byerley, our special instructions were to search the house very thoroughly.'

'And haven't you?'

'We were told exactly what to look for.'

'Yes?'

'In short, Mr Byerley, and not to put too fine a point on it, we were told to search you.'

'Me?' said the prosecutor with a broadening smile. 'And how do you intend to do that?'

'We have a Penet-radiation unit—'

'Then I'm to have my X-ray photograph taken, hey? You have the authority?'

'You saw my warrant.'

'May I see it again?'

Harroway, his forehead shining with considerably more than mere enthusiasm, passed it over a second time. Byerley said evenly, 'I read here as the description of what you are to search; I quote: "the dwelling place belonging to Stephen Allen Byerley, located at 355 Willow Grove, Evanstron, together with any garage, storehouse or other structures or buildings thereto appertaining, together with all grounds thereto appertaining" . . . um . . . and so on. Quite in order. But, my good man, it doesn't say anything about searching my interior. I am not part of the premises. You may search my clothes if you think I've got a robot hidden in my pocket.'

Harroway had no doubt on the point of to whom he owed his job. He did not propose to be backward, given a chance to earn a much better – i.e., more highly paid – job.

He said, in a faint echo of bluster, 'Look here. I'm allowed to search the furniture in your house, and anything else I find in it. You are in it, aren't you?'

'A remarkable observation. I *am* in it. But I'm not a piece of furniture. As a citizen of adult responsibility – I have the psychiatric certificate proving that – I have certain rights under the Regional Articles. Searching me would come under the heading of violating my Right of Privacy. That paper isn't sufficient.'

'Sure, but if you're a robot, you don't have Right of Privacy.'

'True enough – but that paper still isn't sufficient. It recognizes me implicitly as a human being.'

'Where?' Harroway snatched at it.'

'Where it says "dwelling place belonging to" and so on. A robot cannot own property. And you may tell your employer,

Mr Harroway, that if he tries to issue a similar paper which does *not* implicitly recognize me as a human being, he will be immediately faced with a restraining injunction and a civil suit which will make it necessary for him to *prove* me a robot by means of information *now* in his possession, or else to pay a whopping penalty for an attempt to deprive me unduly of my Rights under the Regional Articles. You'll tell him that, won't you?'

Harroway marched to the door. He turned. 'You're a slick lawyer—' His hand was in his pocket. For a short moment, he stood there. Then he left, smiled in the direction of the 'visor scanner, still playing away – waved to the reporters, and shouted, 'We'll have something for you tomorrow, boys. No kidding.'

In his ground car, he settled back, removed the tiny mechanism from his pocket and carefully inspected it. It was the first time he had ever taken a photograph by X-ray reflection. He hoped he had done it correctly.

Quinn and Byerley had never met face-to-face alone. But visorphone was pretty close to it. In fact, accepted litterally, perhaps the phrase was accurate, even if to each, the other were merely the light and dark pattern of a bank of photocells.

It was Quinn who had initiated the call. It was Quinn who spoke first, and without particular ceremony. 'Thought you would like to know, Byerley, that I intend to make public the fact that you're wearing a protective shield against Penet-radiation.'

'That so? In that case, you've probably already made it public. I have a notion our enterprising press representatives have been tapping my various communication lines for quite a while. I know they have my office lines full of holes; which is why I've dug in at my home these last weeks.' Byerley was friendly, almost chatty.

Quinn's lips tightened slightly, 'This call is shielded – thoroughly. I'm making it at a certain personal risk.'

'So I should imagine. Nobody knows you're behind this campaign. At least, nobody knows it officially. Nobody doesn't know it unofficially. I wouldn't worry. So I wear a protective shield? I suppose you found that out when your puppy dog's Penet-radiation photograph, the other day, turned out to be over-exposed.'

'You realize, Beverley, that it would be pretty obvious to everyone that you don't dare face X-ray analysis.'

'Also that you, or your men, attempted illegal invasion of my Right of Privacy.'

'The devil they'll care for that.'

'They might. It's rather symbolic of our two campaigns, isn't it? You have little concern with the rights of the individual citizen. I have great concern. I will not submit to X-ray analysis, because I wish to maintain my rights on principle. Just as I'll maintain the rights of others when elected.'

'That will no doubt make a very interesting speech, but no one will believe you. A little too high-sounding to be true. Another thing,' a sudden, crisp change, 'the personnel in your home was not complete the other night.'

'In what way?'

'According to the report,' he shuffled papers before him that were just within the range of vision of the visiplate, 'there was one person missing – a cripple.'

'As you say,' said Byerley, tonelessly, 'a cripple. My old teacher, who lives with me and who is now in the country – and has been for two months. A "much-needed rest" is the usual expression applied in the case. He has your permission?'

'Your teacher? A scientist of sorts?'

'A lawyer once – before he was a cripple. He has a government license as a research biophysicist, with a laboratory of his own, and a complete description of the work he's doing filed with the proper authorities, to whom I can refer you. The work is minor, but is a harmless and engaging hobby for a – poor cripple. I am being as helpful as I can, you see.'

'I see. And what does this . . . teacher . . . know about robot manufacture?'

'I couldn't judge the extent of his knowledge in a field with which I am unacquainted.'

'He wouldn't have access to positronic brains?'

'Ask your friends at US Robots. They'd be the ones to know.'

'I'll put it shortly, Byerley. Your crippled teacher is the real Stephen Byerley. You are his robot creation. We can prove it. It was he who was in the automobile accident, not you. There will be ways of checking the records.'

'Really? Do so, then. My best wishes.'

'And we can search your so-called teacher's "country place", and see what we can find there.'

'Well, not quite, Quinn.' Byerley smiled broadly. 'Unfortunately for you, my so-called teacher is a sick man. His country place is his place of rest. His Rights of Privacy as a citizen of adult responsibility are naturally even stronger, under the circumstances. You won't be able to obtain a warrant to enter his grounds without showing just cause. However, I'd be the last to prevent you from trying.'

There was a pause of moderate length, and then Quinn leaned forward, so that his imaged-face expanded and the fine lines on his forehead were visible, 'Byerley, why do you carry on? You can't be elected.'

'Can't I?'

'Do you think you can? Do you suppose that your failure to make any attempt to disprove the robot charge – when you could easily, by breaking one of the Three Laws – does anything but convince the people that you *are* a robot?'

'All I see so far is that from being a rather vaguely known, but still largely obscure metropolitan lawyer, I have now become a world figure. You're a good publicist.'

'But you *are* a robot.'

'So it's been said, but not proven.'

'It's been proven sufficiently for the electorate.'

'Then relax – you've won.'

'Good-bye,' said Quinn, with his first touch of viciousness, and the visorphone slammed off.

'Good-bye,' said Byerley imperturbably, to the blank plate.

Byerley brought his 'teacher' back the week before election. The air car dropped quickly in an obscure part of the city.

'You'll stay here till after election,' Byerley told him. 'It would be better to have you out of the way if things take a bad turn.'

The hoarse voice that twisted painfully out of John's crooked mouth might have had accents of concern in it. 'There's danger of violence?'

'The Fundamentalists threaten it, so I suppose there is in a theoretical sense. But I really don't expect it. The Fundies have no real power. They're just the continuous irritant factor that might stir up a riot after a while. You don't mind staying here? Please. I won't be myself if I have to worry about you.'

'Oh, I'll stay. You still think it will go well?'

'I'm sure of it. No one bothered you at the place?'

'No one. I'm certain.'

'And your part went well?'

'Well enough. There'll be no trouble there.'

'Then take care of yourself, and watch the televisor tomorrow, John.' Byerley pressed the gnarled hand that rested on his.

Lenton's forehead was a furrowed study in suspense. He had the completely unenviable job of being Byerley's campaign manager in a campaign that wasn't a campaign, for a person that refused to reveal his strategy, and refused to accept his manager's.

'You can't!' It was his favorite phrase. It had become his only phrase. 'I tell you, Steve, you can't!'

He threw himself in front of the prosecutor, who was spending his time leafing through the typed pages of his speech.

'Put that down, Steve. Look, that mob has been organized by the Fundies. You won't get a hearing. You'll be stoned more likely. Why do you have to make a speech before an audience? What's wrong with a recording, a visual recording?'

'You want me to win the election, don't you?' asked Byerley, mildly.

'Win the election! You're not going to win, Steve. I'm trying to save your life.'

'Oh, I'm not in danger.'

'He's not in danger. He is not in danger.' Lenton made a queer, rasping sound in his throat. 'You mean you're getting out on that balcony in front of fifty thousand crazy crack-pots and try to talk sense to them – on a balcony like a medieval dictator?'

Byerley consulted his watch. 'In about five minutes – as soon as the television lines are free.'

Lenton's answering remark was not quite transliterable.

The crowd filled a roped-off area of the city. Trees and houses seemed to grow out of a mass-human foundation. And by ultra-wave, the rest of the world watched. It was a purely local election, but it had a world audience just the same. Byerley thought of that and smiled.

But there was nothing to smile at in the crowd itself. There were banners and streamers, ringing every possible change on his supposed robotcy. The hostile attitude rose thickly and tangibly into the atmosphere.

From the start the speech was not successful. It competed against the inchoate mob howl and the rhythmic cries of the Fundie claques that formed mob-islands within the mob. Byerley spoke on, slowly, unemotionally—

Inside, Lenton clutched his hair and groaned – and waited for the blood.

There was a writhing in the front ranks. An angular citizen with popping eyes, and clothes too short for the lank length of his limbs, was pulling to the fore. A policeman dived after him, making slow, struggling passage. Byerley waved the latter off, angrily.

The thin man was directly under the balcony. His words tore unheard against the roar.

Byerley leaned forward. 'What do you say? If you have a legitimate question, I'll answer it.' He turned to a flanking guard. 'Bring that man up here.'

There was a tensing in the crowd. Cries of 'Quiet' started in various parts of the mob, and rose to a bedlam, then toned down raggedly. The thin man, red-faced and panting, faced Byerley.

Byerley said, 'Have you a question?'

The thin man stared, and said in a cracked voice, 'Hit me!'

With sudden energy, he thrust out his chin at an angle. 'Hit me! You say you're not a robot. Prove it. You can't hit a human, you monster.'

There was a queer, flat, dead silence. Byerley's voice punctured it. 'I have no reason to hit you.'

The thin man was laughing wildly. 'You *can't* hit me. You *won't* hit me. You're not a human. You're a monster, a make-believe man.'

And Stephen Byerley, tight-lipped, in the face of thousands, who watched in person and the millions who watched by screen, drew back his fist and caught the man crackingly upon the chin. The challenger went over backwards in sudden collapse, with nothing on his face, but blank, blank surprise.

Byerley said, 'I'm sorry. Take him in and see that he's comfortable. I want to speak to him when I'm through.'

And when Dr Calvin, from her reserved space, turned her automobile and drove off, only one reporter recovered sufficiently from the shock to race after her, and shout an unheard question.

Susan Calvin called over her shoulder, 'He's human.'

That was enough. The reporter raced away in his own direction.

The rest of the speech might be described as 'Spoken but not heard'.

Dr Calvin and Stephen Byerley met once again – a week before he took the oath of office as mayor. It was late – past midnight.

Dr Calvin said, 'You don't look tired.'

The mayor-elect smiled. 'I may stay up for a while. Don't tell Quinn.'

'I shan't. But that was an interesting story of Quinn's, since you mention him. It's a shame to have spoiled it. I suppose you knew his theory?'

'Parts of it.'

'It was highly dramatic. Stephen Byerley was a young lawyer, a powerful speaker, a great idealist – and with a certain flair for biophysics. Are you interested in robotics, Mr Byerley?

'Only in the legal aspects.'

'*This* Stephen Byerley was. But there was an accident. Byerley's wife died; he himself, worse. His legs were gone; his face was gone; his voice was gone. Part of his mind was – bent. He would not submit to plastic surgery. He retired from the world, legal career gone – only his intelligence, and his hands left. Somehow he could obtain positronic brains, even a complex one, one which had the greatest capacity for forming judgments in ethical problems – which is the highest robotic function so far developed.

'He grew a body about it. Trained it to be everything he would have been and was no longer. He sent it out into the world as Stephen Byerley, remaining behind himself as the old, crippled teacher that no one ever saw—'

'Unfortunately,' said the mayor-elect, 'I ruined all that by hitting a man. The papers say it was your official verdict on the occasion that I was human.'

'How did that happen? Do you mind telling me? It couldn't have been accidental.'

'It wasn't entirely. Quinn did most of the work. My men started quietly spreading the fact that I had never hit a man; that I was unable to hit a man; that to fail to do so under provocation would be sure proof that I was a robot. So I arranged for a silly speech in public, with all sorts of publicity overtones, and almost inevitably, some fool fell for it. In its essence, it was what I call a shyster trick. One in which the artificial atmosphere which has been created does all the work. Of course, the emotional effects made my election certain, as intended.'

The robopsychologist nodded. 'I see you intrude on my field – as every politician must, I suppose. But I'm very sorry it turned out this way. I like robots. I like them considerably better than I do human beings. If a robot can be created capable of being a civil executive, I think he'd make the best one possible. By the laws of Robotics, he'd be incapable of harming humans, incapable of tyranny, of corruption, of stupidity, of prejudice. And after he had served a decent term, he would leave, even though he were immortal, because it would be impossible for him to hurt humans by letting them know that a robot had ruled them. It would be most ideal.'

'Except that a robot might fail due to the inherent inadequacies of his brain. The positronic brain has never equalled the complexities of the human brain.'

'He would have advisers. Not even a human brain is capable of governing without assistance.'

Byerley considered Susan Calvin with grave interest. 'Why do you smile, Dr Calvin?'

'I smiled because Mr Quinn didn't think of everything.'

'You mean there could be more to that story of his.'

'Only a little. For the three months before election, this Stephen Byerley that Mr Quinn spoke about, this broken man, was in the country for some mysterious reason. He returned in time for that famous speech of yours. And after all, what the old cripple did once, he could do a second time, particularly where the second job is very simple in comparison to the first.'

'I don't quite understand.'

Dr Calvin rose and smoothed her dress. She was obviously ready to leave. 'I mean there is one time when a robot may strike a human being without breaking the First Law. Just one time.'

'And when is that?'

Dr Calvin was at the door. She said quietly, 'When the human to be struck is merely another robot.'

She smiled broadly, her thin face glowing. 'Good-bye, Mr Byerley. I hope to vote for you five years from now – for co-ordinator.'

Stephen Byerley chuckled. 'I must reply that that is a somewhat farfetched idea.'

The door closed behind her.

I stared at her with a sort of horror, 'Is that true?'

'All of it,' she said.

'And the great Byerley was simply a robot.'

'Oh, there's no way of ever finding out. I think he was. But when he decided to die, he had himself atomized, so that there will never be any legal proof. —Besides, what difference would it make?'

'Well—'

'You share a prejudice against robots which is quite unreasoning. He was a very good Mayor; five years later he did *become Regional Co-ordinator. And when the Regions of Earth formed their Federation in 2044, he became the first World Co-ordinator. By that time it was the Machines that were running the world anyway.'*

'Yes, but—'

'No buts! The Machines are robots, and they are running the world. It was five years ago that I found out all the truth. It was 2052; Byerley was completing his second term as World Co-ordinator—'

The Evitable Conflict

The Co-ordinator, in his private study, had that medieval curiosity, a fireplace. To be sure, the medieval man might not have recognized it as such, since it had no functional significance. The quiet, licking flame lay in an insulated recess behind clear quartz.

The logs were ignited at long distance through a trifling diversion of the energy beam that fed the public buildings of the city. The same button that controlled the ignition first dumped the ashes of the previous fire, and allowed for the entrance of fresh wood. —It was a thoroughly domesticated fireplace, you see.

But the fire itself was real. It was wired for sound, so that you could hear the crackle and, of course, you could watch it leap in the air stream that fed it.

The Co-ordinator's ruddy glass reflected, in miniature, the discreet gamboling of the flame, and, in even further miniature, it was reflected in each of his brooding pupils.

And in the frosty pupils of his guest, Dr Susan Calvin of US Robots and Mechanical Men Corporation.

The Co-ordinator said, 'I did not ask you here entirely for social purposes, Susan.'

'I did not think you did, Stephen,' she replied.

'—And yet I don't quite know how to phrase my problem. On the one hand, it can be nothing at all. On the other, it can mean the end of humanity.'

'I have come across so many problems, Stephen, that presented the same alternative. I think all problems do.'

'Really? Then judge this— World Steel reports an overproduction of twenty thousand long tons. The Mexican Canal is two months behind schedule. The mercury mines at Almaden have experienced a production deficiency since last spring, while the Hydroponics plant at Tientsin has been laying men off. These items happen to come to mind at the moment. There is more of the same sort.'

'Are these things serious? I'm not economist enough to trace the fearful consequences of such things.'

'In themselves, they are not serious. Mining experts can be sent to Almaden, if the situation were to get worse. Hydroponics engineers can be used in Java or in Ceylon, if there are too many at Tientsin. Twenty thousand long tons of steel won't fill more than a few days of world demand, and the opening of the Mexican Canal two months later than the planned date is of little moment. It's the Machines that worry me; – I've spoken to your Director of Research about them already.'

'To Vincent Silver? —He hasn't mentioned anything about it to me.'

'I asked him to speak to no one. Apparently, he hasn't.'

'And what did he tell you?'

'Let me put that item in its proper place. I want to talk about the Machines first. And I want to talk about them to you, because you're the only one in the world who understands robots well enough to help me now. —May I grow philosophical?'

'For this evening, Stephen, you may talk how you please and

of what you please, provided you tell me first what you intend to prove.'

'That such small unbalances in the perfection of our system of supply and demand, as I have mentioned, may be the first step towards the final war.'

'Hmp. Proceed.'

Susan Calvin did not allow herself to relax, despite the designed comfort of the chair she sat in. Her cold, thin-lipped face and her flat, even voice were becoming accentuated with the years. And although Stephen Byerley was one man she could like and trust, she was almost seventy and the cultivated habits of a lifetime are not easily broken.

'Every period of human development, Susan,' said the Co-ordinator, 'has had its own particular type of human conflict – its own variety of problem that, apparently, could be settled only by force. And each time, frustratingly enough, force never really settled the problem. Instead, it persisted through a series of conflicts, then vanished to itself – what's the expression, – ah, yes "not with a bang, but a whimper", as the economic and social environment changed. And then, new problems, and a new series of wars. —Apparently endlessly cyclic.

'Consider relatively modern times. There were the series of dynastic wars in the sixteenth to eighteenth centuries, when the most important question in Europe was whether the houses of Hapsburg or Valois-Bourbon were to rule the continent. It was one of those "inevitable conflicts", since Europe could obviously not exist half one and half the other.

'Except that it did, and no war ever wiped out the one and established the other, until the rise of a new social atmosphere in France in 1789 crumbled first the Bourbons and, eventually, the Hapsburgs down the dusty chute to history's incinerator.

'And in those same centuries there were the more barbarous

religious wars, which revolved about the important question of whether Europe was to be Catholic or Protestant. Half and half she could not be. It was "inevitable" that the sword decide. —Except that it didn't. In England, a new industrialism was growing, and on the continent, a new nationalism. Half and half Europe remains to this day and no one cares much.

'In the nineteenth and twentieth centuries, there was a cycle of nationalist-imperialist wars, when the most important question in the World was which portions of Europe would control the economic resources and consuming capacity of which portions of non-Europe. All non-Europe obviously could not exist part English and part French and part German and so on. —Until the forces of nationalism spread sufficiently, so that non-Europe ended what all the wars could not, and decided it could exist quite comfortably *all* non-European.

'And so we have a pattern—'

'Yes, Stephen, you make it plain,' said Susan Calvin. 'These are not very profound observations.'

'No. —But then, it is the obvious which is so difficult to see most of the time. People say "It's as plain as the nose on your face." But how much of the nose on your face can you see, unless someone holds a mirror up to you? In the twentieth century, Susan, we started a new cycle of wars – what shall I call them? Ideological wars? The emotions of religion applied to economic systems, rather than to extra-natural ones? Again the wars were "inevitable" and this time there were atomic weapons, so that mankind could no longer live through its torment to the inevitable wasting away of inevitability. —And positronic robots came.

'They came in time, and, with it and alongside it, interplanetary travel. —So that it no longer seemed so important whether the world was Adam Smith or Karl Marx. Neither made very much sense under the new circumstances. Both had to adapt and they ended in almost the same place.'

'A deus ex machina, then, in a double sense,' said Dr Calvin, dryly.

The Co-ordinator smiled gently. 'I have never heard you pun before, Susan, but you are correct. And yet there was another danger. The ending of every other problem had merely given birth to another. Our new world-wide robot economy may develop its own problems, and for that reason we have the Machines. The Earth's economy is stable, and will *remain* stable, because it is based upon the decisions of calculating machines that have the good of humanity at heart through the overwhelming force of the First Law of Robotics.'

Stephen Byerley continued, 'And although the Machines are nothing but the vastest conglomeration of calculating circuits ever invented, they are still robots within the meaning of the First Law, and so our Earth-wide economy is in accord with the best interests of Man. The population of Earth knows that there will be no unemployment, no overproduction or shortages. Waste and famine are words in history books. And so the question of ownership of the means of production becomes obsolescent. Whoever owned them (if such a phrase has meaning), a man, a group, a nation, or all mankind, they could be utilized only as the Machines directed. —Not because men were forced to but because it was the wisest course and men knew it.

'It puts an end to war – not only to the last cycle of wars, but to the next and all of them. Unless—'

A long pause, and Dr Calvin encouraged him by repetition. 'Unless—'

The fire crouched and skittered along a log, then popped up.

'Unless,' said the Co-ordinator, 'the Machines don't fulfill their function.'

'I see. And that is where those trifling maladjustments come in which you mentioned a while ago – steel, hydroponics and so on.'

'Exactly. Those errors should not be. Dr Silver tells me they *cannot* be.'

'Does he deny the facts? How unusual!'

'No, he admits the facts, of course. I do him an injustice. What he denies is that any error in the machine is responsible for the so-called (his phrase) errors in the answers. He claims that the Machines are self-correcting and that it would violate the fundamental laws of nature for an error to exist in the circuits of relays. And so I said—'

'And you said, "Have your boys check them and make sure, anyway."'

'Susan, you read my mind. It was what I said, and he said he couldn't.'

'Too busy?'

'No, he said that no human could. He was frank about it. He told me, and I hope I understand him properly, that the Machines are a gigantic extrapolation. Thus— A team of mathematicians work several years calculating a positronic brain equipped to do certain similar acts of calculation. Using this brain they make further calculations to create a still more complicated brain, which they use again to make one still more complicated and so on. According to Silver, what we call the Machines are the result of ten such steps.'

'Ye-es, that sounds familiar. Fortunately, I'm not a mathematician. —Poor Vincent. He is a young man. The Directors before him, Alfred Lanning and Peter Bogert, are dead, and they had no such problems. Nor had I. Perhaps roboticists as a whole should now die, since we can no longer understand our own creations.'

'Apparently not. The Machines are not super-brains in Sunday supplement sense – although they are so pictured in the Sunday supplements. It is merely that in their own particular province of collecting and analyzing a nearly infinite number of data and relationships thereof, in nearly infinitesimal time, they have progressed beyond the possibility of detailed human control.

'And then I tried something else. I actually asked the Machine. In the strictest secrecy, we fed it the original data involved in the steel decision, its own answer, and the actual developments since – the overproduction, that is – and asked for an explanation of the discrepancy.'

'Good, and what was its answer?'

'I can quote you that word for word: "The matter admits of no explanation."'

'And how did Vincent interpret that?'

'In two ways. Either we had not given the Machine enough data to allow a definite answer, which was unlikely. Dr Silver admitted that. —Or else, it was impossible for the Machine to admit that it could give any answer to data which implied that it could harm a human being. This, naturally, is implied by the First Law. And then Dr Silver recommended that I see you.'

Susan Calvin looked very tired. 'I'm old, Stephen. When Peter Bogert died, they wanted to make me Director of Research and I refused. I wasn't young then, either, and I did not wish the responsibility. They let young Silver have it and that satisfied me; but what good is it, if I am dragged into such messes.

'Stephen, let me state my position. My researches do indeed involve the interpretation of robot behavior in the light of the Three Laws of Robotics. Here, now, we have these incredible calculating machines. They are positronic robots and therefore obey the Laws of Robotics. But they lack personality; that is, their functions are extremely limited. —Must be, since they are so specialized. Therefore, there is very little room for the interplay of the Laws, and my one method of attack is virtually useless. In short, I don't know that I can help you, Stephen.'

The Co-ordinator laughed shortly, 'Nevertheless, let me tell you the rest. Let me give you *my* theories, and perhaps you will then be able to tell me whether they are possible in the light of robopsychology.'

'By all means. Go ahead.'

'Well, since the Machines are giving the wrong answers, then, assuming that they cannot be in error, there is only one possibility. *They are being given the wrong data!* In other words, the trouble is human, and not robotic. So I took my recent planetary inspection tour—'

'From which you have just returned to New York.'

'Yes. It was necessary, you see, since there are four Machines, one handling each of the Planetary Regions. And *all four are yielding imperfect results.*'

'Oh, but that follows, Stephen. If any one of the Machines is imperfect, that will automatically reflect in the results of the other three, since each of the others will assume as part of the data on which they base their own decisions, the perfection of the imperfect fourth. With a false assumption, they will yield false answers.'

'Uh-huh. So it seemed to me. Now, I have here the records of my interviews, with each of the Regional Vice-Co-ordinators. Would you look through them with me? —Oh, and first, have you heard of the "Society for Humanity"?'

'Umm, yes. They are an outgrowth of the Fundamentalists who have kept US Robots from ever employing positronic robots on the grounds of unfair labor competition and so on. The "Society for Humanity" itself is anti-Machine, is it not?'

'Yes, yes, but— Well, you will see. Shall we begin? We'll start with the Eastern Region.'

'As you say—'

The Eastern Region
  a—Area: 7,500,000 square miles
  b—Population: 1,700,000,000
  c—Capital: Shanghai

Ching Hso-lin's great-grandfather had been killed in the Japanese invasion of the old Chinese Republic, and there had been no one beside his dutiful children to mourn his loss or even to know he was lost. Ching Hso-lin's grandfather had survived the civil war of the late forties, but there had been no one beside *his* dutiful children to know or care of that.

And yet Ching Hso-lin was a Regional Vice-Co-ordinator, with the economic welfare of half the people of Earth in his care.

Perhaps it was with the thought of all that in mind, that Ching had two maps as the only ornaments on the wall of his office. One was an old hand-drawn affair tracing out an acre or two of land, and marked with the now outmoded pictographs of old China. A little creek trickled aslant the faded markings and there were the delicate pictorial indications of lowly huts, in one of which Ching's grandfather had been born.

The other map was a huge one, sharply delineated, with all markings in neat Cyrillic characters. The red boundary that marked the Eastern Region swept within its grand confines all that had once been China, India, Burma, Indo-China, and Indonesia. On it, within the old province of Szechuan, so light and gentle that none could see it, was the little mark placed there by Ching which indicated the location of his ancestral farm.

Ching stood before these maps as he spoke to Stephen Byerley in precise English. 'No one knows better than you, Mr Co-ordinator, that my job, to a large extent, is a sinecure. It carries with it a certain social standing, and I represent a convenient focal point for administration, but otherwise it is the Machine! —The Machine does all the work. What did you think, for instance, of the Tientsin Hydroponics works?'

'Tremendous!' said Byerley.

'It is but one of dozens, and not the largest. Shanghai, Calcutta, Batavia, Bangkok— They are widely spread and they are the answer to feeding the billion and three quarters of the East.'

'And yet,' said Byerley, 'you have an unemployment problem there at Tientsin. Can you be over-producing? It is incongruous to think of Asia as suffering from too much food.'

Ching's dark eyes crinkled at the edges. 'No. It has not come to that yet. It is true that over the last few months, several vats at Tientsin have been shut down, but it is nothing serious. The men have been released only temporarily and those who do not care to work in other fields have been shipped to Colombo in Ceylon, where a new plant is being put into operation.'

'But why should the vats be closed down?'

Ching smiled gently, 'You do not know much of hydroponics, I see. Well, that is not surprising. You are a Northerner, and there soil farming is still profitable. It is fashionable in the North to think of hydroponics, when it is thought of at all, as a device for growing turnips in a chemical solution, and so it is – in an infinitely complicated way.

'In the first place, by far the largest crop we deal with (and the percentage is growing) is yeast. We have upward of two thousand strains of yeast in production and new strains are added monthly. The basic food-chemicals of the various yeasts are nitrates and phosphates among the inorganics together with proper amounts of the trace metals needed, down to the fractional parts per million of boron and molybdenum which are required. The organic matter is mostly sugar mixtures derived from the hydrolysis of cellulose, but, in addition, there are various food factors which must be added.

'For a successful hydroponics industry – one which can feed seventeen hundred million people – we must engage in an immense reforestation program throughout the East; we must have huge wood-conversion plants to deal with our southern jungles; we must have power, and steel, and chemical synthetics above all.'

'Why the last, sir?'

'Because, Mr Byerley, these strains of yeast have each their peculiar properties. We have developed, as I said, two thousand strains. The beef steak you thought you ate today was yeast. The frozen fruit confection you had for dessert was iced yeast. We have filtered yeast juice with the taste, appearance, and all the food value of milk.

'It is flavor, more than anything else, you see, that makes yeast feeding popular and for the sake of flavor we have developed artificial, domesticated strains that can no longer support themselves on a basic diet of salts and sugar. One needs biotin; another needs pteroylglutamic acid; still others need seventeen different amino acids supplied them as well as all the Vitamins B, but one (and yet it is popular and we cannot, with economic sense, abandon it) —'

Byerley stirred in his seat, 'To what purpose do you tell me all this?'

'You asked me, sir, why men are out of work in Tientsin. I have a little more to explain. It is only that we must have these various and varying foods for our yeast; but there remains the complicating factor of popular fads with passing time; and of the possibility of the development of new strains with the new requirements and new popularity. All this must be foreseen, and the Machine does the job—'

'But not perfectly.'

'Not very *imperfectly*, in view of the complications I have mentioned. Well, then, a few thousand workers in Tientsin are temporarily out of a job. But, consider this, the amount of waste in this past year (waste that is, in terms of either defective supply or defective demand) amounts to not one-tenth of one percent of our total productive turnover. I consider that—'

'Yet in the first year of the Machine, the figure was nearer one-thousandth of one percent.'

'Ah, but in the decade since the Machine began its operations in real earnest, we have made use of it to increase our old pre-Machine yeast industry twenty-fold. You expect imperfections to increase with complications, though—'

'Though?'

'There *was* the curious instance of Rama Vrasayana.'

'What happened to him?'

'Vrasayana was in charge of a brine-evaporation plant for the production of iodine, with which yeast can do without, but human beings not. His plant was forced into receivership.'

'Really? And through what agency?'

'Competition, believe it or not. In general, one of the chiefest functions of the Machine's analyses is to indicate the most efficient distribution of our producing units. It is obviously faulty to have areas insufficiently serviced, so that the transportation costs account for too great a percentage of the overhead. Similarly, it is faulty to have an area too well serviced, so that factories must be run at lowered capacities, or else compete harmfully with one another. In the case of Vrasayana, another plant was established in the same city, and with a more efficient extracting system.'

'The Machine permitted it?'

'Oh, certainly. That is not surprising. The new system is becoming widespread. The surprise is that the Machine failed to warn Vrasayana to renovate or combine. —Still, no matter. Vrasayana accepted a job as engineer in the new plant, and if his responsibility and pay are now less, he is not actually suffering. The workers found employment easily; the old plant has been converted to – something or other. Something useful. We left it all to the Machine.'

'And otherwise you have no complaints.'

'None!'

The Tropic Region:
    a—Area: 22,000,000 square miles
    b—Population: 500,000,000
    c—Capital: Capital City

The map in Lincoln Ngoma's office was far from the model of neat precision of the one in Ching's Shanghai dominion. The boundaries of Ngoma's Tropic Region were stenciled in dark, wide brown and swept about a gorgeous interior labeled 'jungle' and 'desert' and 'here be Elephants and All Manner of Strange Beasts'.

It had much to sweep, for in land area the Tropic Region enclosed most of two continents: all of South America north of Argentina and all of Africa south of the Atlas. It included North America south of the Rio Grande as well, and even Arabia and Iran in Asia. It was the reverse of the Eastern Region. Where the ant hives of the Orient crowded half of humanity into 15 percent of the land mass, the Tropics stretched its 15 percent of Humanity over nearly half of all the land in the world.

But it was growing. It was the one Region whose population

increase through immigration exceeded that through births. —And for all who came it had use.

To Ngoma, Stephen Byerley seemed like one of these immigrants, a pale searcher for the creative work of carving a harsh environment into the softness necessary for man, and he felt some of that automatic contempt of the strong man born to the strong Tropics for the unfortunate pallards of the colder suns.

The Tropics had the newest capital city on Earth, and it was called simply that! 'Capital City', in the sublime confidence of youth. It spread brightly over the fertile uplands of Nigeria and outside Ngoma's windows, far below, was life and color; the bright, bright sun and the quick, drenching showers. Even the squawking of the rainbowed birds was brisk and the stars were hard pinpoints in the sharp night.

Ngoma laughed. He was a big, dark man, strong-faced and handsome.

'Sure,' he said, and his English was colloquial and mouthfilling, 'the Mexican Canal is overdue. What the hell? It will get finished just the same, old boy.'

'It was doing well up to the last half year.'

Ngoma looked at Byerley and slowly crunched his teeth over the end of a big cigar, spitting out one end and lighting the other. 'Is this an official investigation, Byerley? What's going on?'

'Nothing. Nothing at all. It's just my function as Co-ordinator to be curious.'

'Well, if it's just that you are filling in a dull moment, the truth is that we're always short on labor. There's lots going on in the Tropics. The Canal is only one of them—'

'But doesn't your Machine predict the amount of labor available for the Canal – allowing for all the competing projects?'

Ngoma placed one hand behind his neck and blew smoke rings at the ceiling. 'It was a little off.'

'Is it often a little off?'

'Not oftener than you would expect. —We don't expect too much of it, Byerley. We feed it data. We take its results. We do what it says. —But it's just a convenience; just a labor-saving device. We could do without it, if we had to. Maybe not as well. Maybe not as quickly. But we'd get there.

'We've got confidence out here, Byerley, and that's the secret. Confidence! We've got new land that's been waiting for us for thousands of years, while the rest of the world was being ripped apart in the lousy fumblings of pre-atomic time. We don't have to eat yeast like the Eastern boys, and we don't have to worry about the stale dregs of the last century like you Northerners.

'We've wiped out the tsetse fly and the Anopheles mosquito, and people find they can live in the sun and like it, now. We've thinned down the jungles and found soil; we've watered the deserts and found gardens. We've got coal and oil in untouched fields, and minerals out of count.

'Just step back. That's all we ask the rest of the world to do. —Step back, and let us work.'

Byerley said, prosaically, 'But the Canal – it was on schedule six months ago. What happened?'

Ngoma spread his hands, 'Labor troubles.' He felt through a pile of papers skeltered about his desk and gave it up.

'Had something on the matter here,' he muttered, 'but never mind. There was a work shortage somewhere in Mexico once on the question of women. There weren't enough women in the neighborhood. It seemed no one had thought of feeding sexual data to the Machine.'

He stopped to laugh, delightedly, then sobered, 'Wait a while. I think I've got it. —Villafranca!'

'Villafranca?'

'Francisco Villafranca. —He was the engineer in charge. Now let me straighten it out. Something happened and there was a cave-in. Right. Right. That was it. Nobody died, as I remember, but it made a hell of a mess. —Quite a scandal.'

'Oh?'

'There was some mistake in his calculations. —Or at least, the Machine said so. They fed through Villafranca's data, assumptions, and so on. The stuff he had started with. The answers came out differently. It seems the answers Villafranca had used didn't take account of the effect of a heavy rainfall on the contours of the cut. —Or something like that. I'm not an engineer, you understand.

'Anyway, Villafranca put up a devil of a squawk. He claimed the Machine's answer had been different the first time. That he had followed the Machine faithfully. Then he quit! We offered to hold him on – reasonable doubt, previous work satisfactory, and all that – in a subordinate position, of course – had to do that much – mistakes can't go unnoticed – bad for discipline— Where was I?'

'You offered to hold him.'

'Oh yes. He refused. —Well, take all in all, we're two months behind. Hell, that's nothing.'

Byerley stretched out his hand and let the fingers tap lightly on the desk. 'Villafranca blamed the Machine, did he?'

'Well, he wasn't going to blame himself, was he? Let's face it; human nature is an old friend of ours. Besides, I remember something else now— Why the hell can't I find documents when I want them? My filing system isn't worth a damn— This Villafranca was a member of one of your Northern organizations. Mexico is too close to the North, that's part of the trouble.'

'Which organization are you speaking of?'

'The Society for Humanity, they call it. He used to attend the annual conferences in New York, Villafranca did. Bunch of crackpots, but harmless. —They don't like the Machines; claim they're destroying human initiative. So naturally Villafranca would blame the Machine. —Don't understand that group myself. Does Capital City looks as if the human race were running out of initiative?'

And Capital City stretched out in golden glory under a golden sun – the newest and youngest creation of *Homo metropolis*.

The European Region
    a—Area: 4,000,000 square miles
    b—Population: 300,000,000
    c—Capital: Geneva

The European Region was an anomaly in several ways. In area, it was far the smallest; not one fifth the size of the Tropic Region in area, and not one fifth the size of the Eastern Region in population. Geographically, it was only somewhat similar to pre-Atomic Europe, since it excluded what had once been European Russia and what had once been the British Isles, while it included the Mediterranean coasts of Africa and Asia, and, in a queer jump across the Atlantic, Argentina, Chile, and Uruguay as well.

Nor was it likely to improve its relative status *vis-à-vis* the other regions of Earth, except for what vigor the South American provinces lent it. Of all the Regions, it alone showed a positive population decline over the past half century. It alone had not seriously expanded its productive facilities, or offered anything radically new to human culture.

'Europe,' said Madame Szegeczowska, in her soft French, 'is essentially an economic appendage of the Northern Region. We know it, and it doesn't matter.'

And as though in resigned acceptance of a lack of individuality, there was no map of Europe on the wall of the Madame Co-ordinator's office.

'And yet,' pointed out Byerley, 'you have a Machine of your own, and you are certainly under no economic pressure from across the ocean.'

'A Machine! Bah!' She shrugged her delicate shoulders, and allowed a thin smile to cross her little face as she tamped out a cigarette with long fingers. 'Europe is a sleepy place. And such of our men as do not manage to emigrate to the Tropics are tired and sleepy along with it. You see for yourself that it is myself, a poor woman, to whom falls the task of being Vice-Co-ordinator. Well, fortunately, it is not a difficult job, and not much is expected of me.

'As for the Machine— What can it say but "Do this and it will be best for you." But what is best for us? Why, to be an economic appendage of the Northern Region.

'And is it so terrible? No wars! We live in peace – and it is pleasant after seven thousand years of war. We are old, monsieur. In our borders, we have the regions where Occidental civilization was cradled. We have Egypt and Mesopotamia; Crete and Syria; Asia Minor and Greece. —But old age is not necessarily an unhappy time. It can be a fruition—'

'Perhaps you are right,' said Byerley, affably. 'At least the tempo of life is not as intense as in the other Regions. It is a pleasant atmosphere.'

'Is it not? —Tea is being brought, monsieur. If you will indicate your cream and sugar preferences, please. —Thank you.'

She sipped gently, then continued. 'It *is* pleasant. The rest of Earth is welcome to the continuing struggle. I find a parallel here; a very interesting one. There was a time when Rome was master of the world. It had adopted the culture and civilization of Greece; a Greece which had never been united, which had ruined itself with war, and which was ending in a state of decadent squalor. Rome united it, brought it peace and let it live a life of secure non-glory. It occupied itself with its philosophies and its art, far from the clash of growth and war. It was a sort of death, but it was restful, and it lasted with minor breaks for some four hundred years.'

'And yet,' said Byerley, 'Rome fell eventually, and the opium dream was over.'

'There are no longer barbarians to overthrow civilization.'

'We can be our own barbarians, Madame Szegeczowska. — Oh, I meant to ask you. The Almaden mercury mines have fallen off quite badly in production. Surely the ores are not declining more rapidly than anticipated?'

The little woman's gray eyes fastened shrewdly on Byerley, 'Barbarians – the fall of civilization – possible failure of the Machine. Your thought processes are very transparent, monsieur.'

'Are they?' Byerley smiled. 'I see that I should have had men to deal with as hitherto. —You consider the Almaden affair to be the fault of the Machine?'

'Not at all, but I think you do. You, yourself, are a native of the Northern Region. The Central Co-ordination Office is at New York.—And I have noticed for quite a while that you Northerners lack somewhat of faith in the Machine.'

'We do?'

'There is your "Society for Humanity" which is strong in the North, but naturally fails to find many recruits in tired, old Europe, which is quite willing to let feeble Humanity alone for a while. Surely, you are one of the confident North and not one of the cynical old continent.'

'This has a connection with Almaden?'

'Oh yes, I think so. The mines are in the control of Consolidated

Cinnabar, which is certainly a Northern company, with headquarters at Nikolaev. Personally, I wonder if the Board of Directors have been consulting the Machine at all. They said they had in our conference last month, and, of course, we have no evidence that they did not, but I wouldn't take the word of a Northerner in this matter – no offense intended – under any circumstances. — Nevertheless, I think it will have a fortunate ending.'

'In what way, my dear madame?'

'You must understand that the economic irregularities of the last few months, which, although small as compared with the great storms of the past, are quite disturbing to our peace-drenched spirits, have caused considerable restiveness in the Spanish province. I understand that Consolidated Cinnabar is selling out to a group of native Spaniards. It is consoling. If we are economic vassals of the North, it is humiliating to have the fact advertised too blatantly. —And our people can be better trusted to follow the Machine.'

'Then you think there will be no more trouble?'

'I am sure there will not be— In Almaden, at least.'

The Northern region
a—Area: 18,000,000 square miles
b—Population: 800,000,000
c—Capital: Ottawa

The Northern Region, in more ways than one, was at the top. This was exemplified quite well by the map in the Ottawa office of Vice-Co-ordinator Hiram Mackenzie, in which the North Pole was centered. Except for the enclave of Europe with its Scandinavian and Icelandic regions, all the Arctic area was within the Northern Region.

Roughly, it could be divided into two major areas. To the left on the map was all of North America above the Rio Grande. To the right was included all of what had once been the Soviet Union. Together these areas represented the centered power of the planet in the first years of the Atomic Age. Between the two was Great Britain, a tongue of the Region licking at Europe. Up at the top of the map, distorted into odd, huge shapes, were Australia and New Zealand, also member provinces of the Region.

Not all the changes of the past decades had yet altered the fact that the North was the economic ruler of the planet.

There was almost an ostentatious symbolism thereof in the fact that of the official Regional maps Byerley had seen, Mackenzie's alone showed all the Earth, as though the North feared no competition and needed no favoritism to point up its pre-eminence.

'Impossible,' said Mackenzie, dourly, over the whiskey. 'Mr Byerley, you have had no training as a robot technician, I believe.'

'No, I have not.'

'Hmp. Well, it is, in my opinion, a sad thing that Ching, Ngoma and Szegeczowska haven't either. There is too prevalent an opinion among the peoples of Earth that a Co-ordinator need only be a capable organizer, a broad generalizer, and an amiable person. These days he should know his robotics as well – no offense intended.'

'None taken. I agree with you.'

'I take it, for instance, from what you have said already, that you worry about the recent trifling dislocations in world economy. I don't know what you suspect, but it has happened in the past that people – who should have known better – wondered what would happen if false data were fed into the Machine.'

'And what would happen, Mr Mackenzie?'

'Well,' the Scotsman shifted his weight and sighed, 'all collected data goes through a complicated screening system which involves both human and mechanical checking, so that the problem is not likely to arise. —But let us ignore that. Humans are fallible, also corruptible, and ordinary mechanical devices are liable to mechanical failure.

'The real point of the matter is that what we call a "wrong datum" is one which is inconsistent with all other known data. It is our only criterion of right and wrong. It is the Machine's as well. Order it, for instance, to direct agricultural activity on the basis of an average July temperature in Iowa of 57 degrees Fahrenheit. It won't accept that. It will not give an answer. —Not that it has any prejudice against that particular temperature, or that an answer is impossible; but because, in the light of all the other data fed it over a period of years, it knows that the probability of an average July temperature of 57 is virtually nil. It rejects that datum.

'The only way a "wrong datum" can be forced on the Machine is to include it as part of a self-consistent whole, all of which is subtly wrong in a manner either too delicate for the Machine to detect or outside the Machine's experience. The former is beyond human capacity, and the latter is almost so, and is becoming more nearly so as the Machine's experience increases by the second.'

Stephen Byerley placed two fingers to the bridge of his nose. 'Then the Machine cannot be tampered with— And how do you account for recent errors, then?'

'My dear Byerley, I see that you instinctively follow that great error – that the Machine knows all. Let me cite you a case from my personal experience. The cotton industry engages experienced buyers who purchase cotton. Their procedure is to pull a tuft of cotton out of a random bale of a lot. They will look at that tuft and feel it, tease it out, listen to the crackling perhaps as they do so, touch it with their tongue – and through this procedure they will determine the class of cotton the bales represent. As a result of their decisions, purchases are made at certain prices, blends are made in certain proportions. —Now these buyers cannot yet be replaced by the Machine.'

'Why not? Surely the data involved is not too complicated for it?'

'Probably not. But what data is this you refer to? No textile chemist knows exactly what it is that the buyer tests when he feels a tuft of cotton. Presumably there's the average length of the threads, their feel, the extent and nature of their slickness, the way they hang together and so on. —Several dozen items, subconsciously weighed, out of years of experience. But the *quantitative* nature of these tests is not known; maybe even the very nature of some of them is not known. So we have nothing to feed the Machine. Nor can the buyers explain their own judgment. They can only say, "Well, look at it. Can't you *tell* it's class-such-and-such?"'

'I see.'

'There are innumerable cases like that. The Machine is only a tool after all, which can help humanity progress faster by taking some of the burdens of calculations and interpretations off his back. The task of the human brain remains what it has always been; that of discovering new data to be analyzed, and of devising new concepts to be tested. A pity the Society for Humanity won't understand that.'

'They are against the Machine?'

'They would be against mathematics or against the art of writing if they had lived at the appropriate time. These reactionaries of the Society claim the Machine robs man of his soul. I notice that capable men are still at a premium in our society;

we still need the man who is intelligent enough to think of the proper questions to ask. Perhaps if we could find enough of such, these dislocations you worry about, Co-ordinator, wouldn't occur.'

Earth (Including the uninhabited continent, Antarctica)
  a—Area: 54,000,000 square miles (land surface)
  b—Population: 3,300,000,000
  c—Capital: New York

The fire behind the quartz was weary now, and sputtered its reluctant way to death.

The Co-ordinator was somber, his mood matching the sinking flame.

'They all minimize the state of affairs.' His voice was low. 'Is it not easy to imagine that they laugh at me? And yet – Vincent Silver said the Machines cannot be out of order, and I must believe him. Hiram Mackenzie says they cannot be fed false data, and I must believe him. But the Machines are going wrong, somehow, and I must believe that, too, – and so there is *still* an alternative left.'

He glanced sidewise at Susan Calvin, who, with closed eyes, for a moment seemed asleep.

'What is that?' she asked, prompt to her cue, nevertheless.

'Why, that correct data is indeed given, and correct answers are indeed received, but that they are then ignored. There is no way the Machine can enforce obedience to its dictates.'

'Madame Szegeczowska hinted as much, with reference to Northerners in general, it seems to me.'

'So she did.'

'And what purpose is served by disobeying the Machine? Let's consider motivations.'

'It's obvious to me, and should be to you. It is a matter of rocking the boat, deliberately. There can be no serious conflicts on Earth, in which one group or another can seize more power than it has for what it thinks is its own good despite the harm to Mankind as a whole, while the Machines rule. If popular faith in the Machines can be destroyed to the point where they are abandoned, it will be the law of the jungle again. —And not one of the four Regions can be freed of the suspicion of wanting just that.

'The East has half of humanity within its borders, and the Tropics more than half of Earth's resources. Each can feel itself the natural ruler of all Earth, and each has a history of humiliation by the North, for which it can be human enough to wish a senseless revenge. Europe has a tradition of greatness, on the other hand. It once *did* rule the Earth, and there is nothing so eternally adhesive as the memory of power.

'Yet, in another way, it's hard to believe. Both the East and the Tropics are in a state of enormous expansion within their own borders. Both are climbing incredibly. They cannot have the spare energy for military adventures. And Europe can have nothing but its dreams. It is a cipher, militarily.'

'So, Stephen,' said Susan, 'you leave the North.'

'Yes,' said Byerley, energetically, 'I do. The North is now the strongest, and has been for nearly a century, or its component parts have been. But it is losing relatively, now. The Tropic Regions may take their place in the forefront of civilization for the first time since the Pharaohs, and there are Northerners who fear that.

'The "Society for Humanity" is a Northern organization primarily, you know, and they make no secret of not wanting the Machines. —Susan, they are few in numbers, but it is an association of powerful men. Heads of factories; directors of industries and agricultural combines who hate to be what they call "the Machine's office-boy" belong to it. Men with ambition belong to it. Men who feel themselves strong enough to decide for themselves what is best for themselves, and not just to be told what is best for others.

'In short, just those men who, by together refusing to accept the decisions of the Machine, can, in a short time, turn the world topsy-turvy; – just those belong to the Society.

'Susan, it hangs together. Five of the Directors of World Steel are members, and World Steel suffers from overproduction. Consolidated Cinnabar, which mined mercury at Almaden, was a Northern concern. Its books are still being investigated, but one, at least, of the men concerned was a member. Francisco Villafranca, who, singlehanded, delayed the Mexican Canal for two months, was a member, we know already – and so was Rama Vrasayana, I was not at all surprised to find out.'

Susan said quietly, 'These men, I might point out, have all done badly—'

'But naturally,' interjected Byerley. 'To disobey the Machine's analyses is to follow a non-optimal path. Results are poorer than they might be. It's the price they pay. They will have it rough now but in the confusion that will eventually follow—'

'Just what do you plan doing, Stephen?'

'There is obviously no time to lose. I am going to have the Society outlawed, every member removed from any responsible post. And all executive and technical positions, henceforward, can be filled only by applicants signing a non-Society oath. It will mean a certain surrender of basic civil liberties, but I am sure the Congress—'

'It won't work!'

'What!—Why not?'

'I will make a prediction. If you try any such thing, you will find yourself hampered at every turn. You will find it impossible to carry out. You will find your every move in that direction will result in trouble.'

Byerley was taken aback. 'Why do you say that?— I was rather hoping for your approval in this matter.'

'You can't have it as long as your actions are based on a false premise. You admit the Machine can't be wrong, and can't be fed wrong data. I will now show you that it cannot be disobeyed, either, as you think is being done by the Society.'

'*That* I don't see at all.'

'Then listen. Every action by any executive which does not follow the exact directions of the Machine he is working with becomes part of the data for the next problem. The Machine, therefore, knows that the executive has a certain tendency to disobey. He can incorporate that tendency into that data – even quantitatively; that is, judging exactly how much and in what direction disobedience would occur. Its next answers would be just sufficiently biased so that after the executive concerned disobeyed, he would have automatically corrected those answers to optimal directions. The Machine knows, Stephen!'

'You can't be sure of all this. You are guessing.'

'It is a guess based on a lifetime's experience with robots. You had better rely on such a guess, Stephen.'

'But then what is left? The Machines themselves are correct and the premises they work on are correct. That we have agreed upon. Now you say that it cannot be disobeyed. Then what is wrong?'

'You have answered yourself. *Nothing is wrong!* Think about the Machines for a while, Stephen. They are robots, and they follow the First Law. But the Machines work not for any single human being, but for all humanity, so that the First Law becomes:

"No machines may harm humanity; or, through inaction, allow humanity to come to harm."

'Very well, then Stephen, what harms humanity? Economic dislocations most of all, from whatever cause. Wouldn't you say so?'

'I would.'

'And what is most likely in the future to cause economic dislocations? Answer that, Stephen.'

'I should say,' replied Byerley, unwillingly, 'the destruction of the Machines.'

'And so should I say, and so should the Machines say. Their first care, therefore, is to preserve themselves, for us. And so they are quietly taking care of the only elements left that threaten them. It is not the "Society for Humanity" which is shaking the boat so that the Machines may be destroyed. You have been looking at the reverse of the picture. Say rather that the Machine is shaking the boat – *very* slightly – just enough to shake loose those few which cling to the side for purposes the Machines consider harmful to Humanity.

'So Vrasayana loses his factory and gets another job where he can do no harm – he is not badly hurt, he is not rendered incapable of earning a living, for the Machine cannot harm a human being more than minimally, and that only to save a greater number. Consolidated Cinnabar loses control at Almaden. Villafranca is no longer a civil engineer in charge of an important project. And the directors of World Steel are losing their grip on the industry – or will.'

'But you don't really know all this,' insisted Byerley, distractedly. 'How can we possibly take a chance on your being right?'

'You must. Do you remember the Machine's own statement when you presented the problem to it? It was: "The matter admits of no explanation." The Machine did not say there was no explanation, or that it could determine no explanation. It simply was not going to *admit* any explanation. In other words, it would be harmful to humanity to have the explanation known, and that's why we can only guess – and keep on guessing.'

'But how can the explanation do us harm? Assume that you are right, Susan.'

'Why, Stephen, if I am right, it means that the Machine is conducting our future for us not simply in direct answer to our direct questions, but in general answer to the world situation and to human psychology as a whole. And to know that may make us unhappy and may hurt our pride. The Machine cannot, *must* not, make us unhappy.

'Stephen, how do we know what the ultimate good of Humanity will entail? We haven't at *our* disposal the infinite factors that the Machine has at *its*! Perhaps, to give you a not unfamiliar example, our entire technical civilization has created more unhappiness and misery than it has removed. Perhaps an agrarian or pastoral civilization, with less culture and less people, would be better. If so, the Machines must move in that direction, preferably without telling us, since in our ignorant prejudices we only know that what we are used to is good – and we would then fight change. Or perhaps a complete urbanization, or a completely caste-ridden society, or complete anarchy, is the answer. We don't know. Only the Machines know, and they are going there and taking us with them.'

'But you are telling me, Susan, that the "Society for Humanity" is right; and that Mankind *has* lost its own say in its future.'

'It never had any, really. It was always at the mercy of economic and sociological forces it did not understand – at the whims of climate, and the fortunes of war. Now the Machines understand them; and no one can stop them, since the Machines will deal with them as they are dealing with the Society – having, as they do, the greatest of weapons at their disposal, the absolute control of our economy.'

'How horrible!'

'Perhaps how wonderful! Think, that for all time, all conflicts are finally evitable. Only the Machines, from now on, are inevitable!'

And the fire behind the quartz went out and only a curl of smoke was left to indicate its place.

'And that is all,' said Dr Calvin, rising. 'I saw it from the beginning, when the poor robots couldn't speak, to the end, when they stand between mankind and destruction. I will see no more. My life is over. You will see what comes next.'

I never saw Susan Calvin again. She died last month at the age of eighty-two.